THE TRIP

PHOEBE MORGAN

ONE PLACE. MANY STORIES

HQ
An imprint of HarperCollins*Publishers* Ltd
1 London Bridge Street
London SE1 9GF

www.harpercollins.co.uk

HarperCollins*Publishers*
Macken House, 39/40 Mayor Street Upper,
Dublin 1, D01 C9W8, Ireland

This edition 2024

2

First published in Great Britain by
HQ, an imprint of HarperCollins*Publishers* Ltd 2024

Copyright © Phoebe Morgan 2024

Phoebe Morgan asserts the moral right to be
identified as the author of this work.
A catalogue record for this book is
available from the British Library.

ISBN: 9780008406998

This book is set in 10.7/15 pt. Sabon by Type-it AS, Norway

Printed and Bound in the UK using 100% Renewable Electricity at
CPI Group (UK) Ltd, Croydon, CR0 4YY

Praise for Phoebe Morgan

'An exhilarating, read-in-one-sitting ride'
Louise Candlish

'A deadly cocktail of lies, secrets, obsession and revenge'
T.M. Logan

'Morgan has a particular skill for creating a vivid sense of place'
Daily Mail

'Combines a beautiful, exotic location with
a slithering, unsettling sense of suspense.
A page-turner, full of secrets and reveals'
Adele Parks, *Platinum*

'A delightfully sinister tale'
Crime Monthly

'A heart-stopping rollercoaster of a read with a dark
sense of menace and hugely relatable characters'
B.A. Paris

'This chilling thriller is packed with tension and twists!'
My Weekly

'Dark, twisty plotting, compelling characterisation
and an ending I didn't see coming at all'
Harriet Tyce

'Superb . . . toxic, sinister and mysterious – this
nail-biter is sure to keep you guessing'
Woman's Own

'A hugely entertaining thriller that turns
a dream holiday into a nightmare'
Jane Casey

Phoebe Morgan is a bestselling author and award-winning editor. She studied English at the University of Leeds after growing up in the Suffolk countryside. She edits commercial fiction for a publishing house during the day, and writes her own novels in the evenings. She was shortlisted for Editor of the Year at the British Book Awards in 2022, and has won both a Trailblazer Award in association with the London Book Fair in 2018 and the Bookseller Shooting Star Award in 2021. She lives in London and you can follow her on X @Phoebe_A_Morgan, Instagram @phoebeannmorgan, and Facebook @PhoebeMorganAuthor. You can find her blog about writing and publishing at www.phoebemorganauthor.com.

Her books have sold over 250,000 copies worldwide, and have been translated into ten languages including French, Italian, Polish and Croatian. They are also on sale in the US, Canada and Australia. Phoebe has also contributed short stories to the award-winning charity anthologies *Afraid of the Light*, *Afraid of the Shadows*, and *Afraid of the Christmas Lights*. Her short story *Sleep Time* is being adapted into a short film.

Also by Phoebe Morgan

The Doll House
The Girl Next Door
The Babysitter
The Wild Girls

For my beautiful Grandmother, Margaret Joan Parkinson

Prologue

You'd have to be looking carefully to see it. The body, carried by the waves, a flash of white in a beautiful turquoise sea. At first, you might think it was a trick of the light, or something innocent – a piece of rubbish, maybe, floating on the breeze. Disrupting the paradise. You'd dismiss it as nothing.

You'd have to be standing there on the golden sand to see it for what it really is – a person, or what remains of one. You'd need to be right up close to see the blood staining the skin, the clothes heavy with water, the dead eyes staring up at the sky, the light extinguished from them forever. You'd need to be paying attention.

Luckily – or unluckily, depending on whose side you are on – that day, somebody was.

Chapter One

Saskia

'We're going to be late!'

Theo, my boyfriend – sorry, *husband*, I've got to get used to saying that – is calling me from the bedroom. My suitcase is on our bed, and my clothes are scattered everywhere; I can't decide among three swimming costumes. There's the one with the high-cut legs, the one with the scallop neckline and the red one Theo likes, but my case is crammed full, and I can't fit them all in.

'Come on, Sask,' he says, appearing in the doorway. He's been packed for ages – he's always like that – and he's right, we are going to be late if we don't leave for the airport in the next ten minutes.

'Got your passport?' he asks me, and I nod, point to my handbag. 'Right there. Can you help me shut this case? You might need to sit on it.'

I close my eyes and grab one of the costumes at random, shoving it into the side of the case, the material slippery between my fingers. Theo grins.

'Good choice. You look great in the red.'

He dutifully sits on top of the suitcase and I just about manage to zip it up, wincing at the effort. Anyone would think we were going for a month, not a week, but I've never been a particularly light packer.

'Have you heard from the others?' I ask him, and he nods.

'Yep, they're already on their way. We're meeting them at Terminal 5. So – you ready?'

I take a final glance around the room, checking I haven't forgotten anything. Swimming costume – check. Sun cream – check. Sunglasses – check. Silk shawl for when we go to the temple, like it said in the guidebook – check. Phone charger and adaptor – check. I've also got some sleeping pills and an eye mask for the plane, in case I need to relax, and a couple of books so that I can maybe try to do a bit of reading while I'm out there, when we get to the beach.

'OK,' I say, grabbing my handbag as Theo picks up my case and pretends to drop it because it's so heavy. 'You're hilarious. Now let's go.'

*

The cab drops us off outside Terminal 5. It's a grey January day in London, overcast and cold, and I feel a shiver of excitement run through me when I think about the sunshine waiting for us on the other side of the plane journey. England in the winter is miserable – it feels like ages since I've felt the warmth of the sun on my face. I can't wait. This morning when we got out of bed, there was ice on the roads outside, dead Christmas trees dotting the pavements like discarded clothes, their trunks split, pine needles scattering the tarmac. The whole city has a gloomy air, and it feels great to be escaping it, to be flying towards sun and sand and sea.

'Thanks,' I say to Theo as he heaves my case out of the boot, and he loops an arm round my shoulders as the taxi drives off. I inhale the smell of him – clean, calm, familiar. Sometimes, I can't believe he's real, and that he's mine. If you'd told me five years ago that I'd be married to a man like him, I wouldn't have believed it. I wouldn't have thought I deserved it.

My breath mists the air as we walk into the airport, a little grey ghost forming in front of my mouth, but Theo's arm is nice and warm around my shoulders. I like the way my head tucks neatly beneath his arm; he's a fair bit taller than me, but it's always felt safe rather than intimidating. The double doors slide open automatically for us and we head inside, immediately met with a cacophony of noise.

Inside the terminal, it's packed. I scan the huge room for our friends, Lucas and Holly, but there are so many people that it's hard to make anyone out. A bunch of teenagers push past us, heading in the direction of the Wetherspoons in the corner, and Theo raises his eyebrows at me.

'Fancy it?'

I shove him on the arm. 'No way!'

The last time I set foot in a Wetherspoons was a long time ago; in another life.

'There they are,' Theo says and then I see them – Lucas and Holly – coming towards us, each pulling a suitcase.

'You're here!' I say, opening my arms to them, and I wrap Holly in a big hug, her long brown hair tickling my cheek as we embrace. She looks great; she's wearing a strappy black top with a loose white cardi over it, and black jeans with pink trainers.

'Comfy clothes for the plane,' she says, gesturing downwards, 'it was hard to dress this morning, wasn't it? Being so cold here and knowing we'll be going somewhere hot.'

I nod, smile. 'You look lovely though. Nice shoes.'

'Saskia, how are we?' Lucas says, pulling me in for a bear hug, and I kiss him on the cheek, feel the scratch of his beard against my skin.

'You going for the unkempt traveller look already?' Theo teases him, slapping him on the back, and Lucas grins good-naturedly. He's taller than Theo, by about a head, with dark swept-back hair and brown, almost black eyes.

'I'm so excited,' Holly says, clapping her hands together. 'A whole week in Thailand. It's going to be incredible. And just what I need after the Christmas I had at my mother's house.' She rolls her eyes and Lucas rubs her arm sympathetically. I know Holly's family can be a bit of a nightmare, she's mentioned it before. Something to do with her mum's drinking. I had Christmas with Theo's family this year – or *my* family, I should say, now that we're actually married. It was lovely – their house is huge, a big, Victorian build in west London. Three storeys. His dad had bought a crazily expensive bottle of champagne which we had first thing, even though he'd already given us so much for the wedding. It was actually one of the best Christmases I've ever had, though I don't say that to Holly right this second. I don't want to be insensitive.

'You've got all the bookings, right?' Lucas asks Theo, and he nods, waves his iPhone in the air.

'All on here, don't worry about a thing. I'll send you your boarding passes now.' He taps the screen and our phones ping in unison as the images come through to our WhatsApp group, inventively named Thailand 2024.

'Perfect,' I say. 'Now, I could do with a coffee. Have we got time to stop at Pret?'

'I'll come with you, you guys figure out where we're heading,' Holly says, and she links her arm through mine.

'Back in a minute,' we tell the boys, then head off towards the café.

'So how *are* you?' she asks me. 'How are things, how was Christmas?'

'All good,' I say, 'we were almost late because I couldn't decide which swimming costume to bring but hey, that's the worst of my problems at the moment, so I'm doing pretty well. And Christmas was lovely, thanks. Theo's family are great.'

'What did you go for, swimwear-wise?'

'Red,' I say, 'a classic look.'

'Can't go wrong with red,' she says, and I grin at her, relaxing into the familiarity of our relationship. It's so wonderful to be part of a friendship group like this. I count myself lucky every single day.

'Let's get an airport selfie, just us two,' I say to Holly, and before she can protest, I pull out my phone. We push our heads together, grinning, and I take three – I'll check them later, work out which one looks best. Maybe put a filter on them too. I check how many likes the pic I put up of Theo and me in front of the Christmas tree has got – forty-four so far – and quickly tap the heart sign under a couple of other pics that pop up on my Instagram feed before shoving my phone back into my pocket. I get a rush of adrenaline every time I see the number of likes go up.

'Two cappuccinos please,' Holly says to the girl behind the counter in Pret. 'Did the boys want anything?'

'We forgot to ask,' I say. 'Let's just get them a coffee too. I'll drink extra if they don't want it.'

'You'll be bouncing off the walls,' Holly says, but she

changes the order to four and we wait for our hot drinks over to one side.

'What are you most looking forward to?' she asks me, her head tilted to one side so that her hair falls down across one shoulder. She's got lovely hair, thick and glossy, and she's one of those women who doesn't need much make-up – naturally clear skin, that English rose complexion. We're polar opposites in terms of our looks; I'm blonde with blue eyes, and I tend to wear quite a bit of make-up, painting it on religiously every day. I think of it as my armour, I suppose. Theo's mum got me a nice new lipstick for Christmas, I've brought it with me to wear out for dinner in Bangkok.

'Lying on the beach, to be honest,' I tell her, picturing it – it feels like so long since I really relaxed and did nothing, and the thought of stretching out on the golden sand, digging my toes in and closing my eyes against the hot sun is glorious. 'You?'

'Oh, I want to explore,' she says, picking up our coffees when the waitress calls our order, 'the food markets are meant to be incredible in Bangkok. I love Thai food.'

'Let me help you,' I say, taking two of the coffees, and we make our way back through the busy airport to where the boys are standing, under the departure boards, talking. As I watch, Lucas laughs at something Theo has said, throwing his head back. It's lovely seeing them so happy together. This trip is going to be amazing. I know it.

'All set?' Theo asks and I hand out the drinks, wincing slightly as one of them spills and burns my fingers.

'Let's go,' Lucas says, pointing towards the escalators over on the right. 'Check-in is up here, I think. Time to get rid of your knife stash, Hol.'

'Ha ha,' she says, rolling her eyes at me, and I smile at her.

7

'Only another week to put up with!' I say. 'Just grin and think of the cocktails.'

Holly

We're sat right at the back of the plane, Lucas and me on one row, and Saskia and Theo behind us. I've got the window seat, which is good because Lucas is a bit of an anxious flyer whereas I like to look out. I wriggle in my seat a bit, trying to get comfy, as the air hostess talks us through the safety procedures, pointing out the emergency exits, her arms moving up and down robotically.

'Why do they bother with this?' Lucas whispers in my ear, 'if anything happens, we're basically toast.'

'Don't be silly!' I say, 'that's not true at all. Stop worrying. Nothing's going to happen, and if it does, you'll get to go on one of those fun-looking air slides.' I grin at him, then reach out and ruffle his hair. 'We'll be there in a few hours. And it'll be worth it, I promise.'

'You commencing your usual in-flight anxiety?' Theo says, his head popping up from between the seats, and Lucas looks sheepish.

'I'm fine.'

I squeeze his hand. 'Of course you are.'

Lucas and I have been together for three years now, and I know the things that bother him – flying is one of them, me leaving toothpaste trails in the sink after brushing my teeth is another. You could say one is more of a problem than the other. Though we're saving for a flat together, working towards a deposit, so soon enough the toothpaste trails might become more of an issue. I've already found our dream place online, but we can't afford it. Doesn't stop me constantly looking at the Rightmove page, though. One day, our luck might change.

'We haven't been away for ages, have we?' I say, dreamily. 'It's going to be so brilliant.'

'Cabin crew, prepare for take-off,' comes the voice over the loudspeaker, and Lucas clutches his seatbelt, as though checking it's still fastened.

'You're all good,' I tell him, and he nods, swallows. He'll be fine once we get up there; he's always like this at the start. Though it has been a long time since we went abroad – I forgot how nervous he can get.

The plane begins to move forward, and I wipe my hand across the small rounded window, watch as the grey walls of Heathrow begin to fade into the distance. There are tiny ice crystals glittering on the glass, fracturing the light. Glancing across the aisle, I see there is a man with his head bowed and his hands clasped together, his lips moving soundlessly, as though he's praying. Lucas clocks him too and I roll my eyes to reassure him. Honestly, it's a bit unnerving, but people have their own rituals, don't they? Whatever makes him feel safe.

'Bye bye, London,' I say, then settle into my seat, tip my head back against the headrest. I love this part of flying – the feeling of ascending into the air, the drop in your stomach as the plane leaves the ground. It's exhilarating. It makes you feel like anything could happen. Anything at all.

*

I don't remember falling asleep, but the next thing I know, Lucas is shaking me awake, his hand on my shoulder. The plane is dark, shadowy; we must have been flying for a few hours already. My eyes feel gritty with sleep. There's a sudden, sharp pain in my legs as the woman in front of me pushes her seat back and I wince in annoyance.

'You OK, Luke?' I say, keeping my voice low.

'The plane's swaying a bit,' he says, and I sigh.

'It's just a bit of turbulence. Nothing to worry about. I promise.' It feels like I'm talking to a child, but I know this is what he needs – a bit of reassurance, that's all. It *does* feel a bit bumpy, and when I switch on the little overhead light, I can see that he looks very pale. He's playing with the seat tray, fiddling with the little latch and I gently put a hand out to cover his, stopping the repetitive anxious movement.

'Have you tried to sleep?' I ask him, thinking that might help, but he shakes his head, looking nauseous.

'I don't think I can.'

'Psst.' Saskia is leaning around the seats, holding something out in her hand.

'Sleeping tablets,' she says, 'try one, Lucas. It'll help you get through. They work really well.'

She presses them into his hand and I watch as he takes two, swallows them with water. The plane jolts as he does so and some of the water spills out onto his leg, making a dark patch on his jeans.

'Shit.'

'It's fine,' I say, 'it's only water. You'll feel better soon.'

He sits back and I see him close his eyes, can almost feel him trying to unknot the anxiety. Poor Luke. Still, we'll be there eventually, and then he'll feel better. There's a little screen on the back of the seat tracking the plane, marking our progress on a white dotted line across the globe; I touch it briefly. Around me, most people are plugged in, watching

TV, headphones on, screens flickering in front of them, casting eerie lights across their faces. We're all so disconnected from each other, I think briefly. All lost in our own worlds.

A few rows in front of us, a man stands to get something from the overhead lockers, the strap of his bag dangling down towards the floor. He must catch me looking at him, because he turns towards me slightly and I could swear that he winks. Quickly, I look away, feeling a flush across my cheeks. I don't look back up until I am sure he's sat down, but the creepy, crawling feeling stays with me for a few minutes. I'm glad Lucas didn't see. Perhaps I imagined it, maybe it was a trick of the light in the semi-darkness of the plane.

I take a deep breath, push the creepy guy out of my head, and focus on where we're going. I've never been to Thailand before. It feels almost surreal to be going – to be away from work, my out-of-office on, knowing we're hours away from Bangkok. We don't exactly go on many holidays, not compared to Saskia and Theo – but then, they've got a lot more money than we do, and every penny we've got is being saved up so that we can get a flat together. It's not like we're desperately short of money, not exactly, but Lucas is a teacher and I work in publishing so it's not like we're rolling in it either, and certainly not when you think about the others. We've never let it become an issue between us – money, that is – and God knows they're both generous with it. I've budgeted carefully for this trip – working it all out on an Excel spreadsheet that even Lucas laughed at – and I think we should be fine, provided nothing goes wrong. We did go back and forth about it, when Theo first came up with the idea of going away – we wondered if perhaps we shouldn't, if maybe we ought to forgo all holidays until we've bought a place together, but it seemed so dull, and neither of us could bear the thought of missing out. Hence the spreadsheet, the tight budget – and I think we can make it work.

We're booked into a fancy hotel for the first few nights, a place called the Omni Tower Hotel. Theo's idea, and way pricier than I'd usually think to pick, but to be fair, it does look gorgeous – and then we're taking the ferry over to Koh Samet island, and staying on the beach in a villa, complete with a private pool. I can't wait – the photos look beautiful. I've spent the last couple of weeks googling it when I'm supposed to be working, gazing at the pictures of the perfect turquoise sea, the golden sand, the beautiful blue skies. I had to minimise my browser window quickly when my boss walked past the other day. Last year felt like a long one, and we've both been a bit stressed since Christmas – so this trip really couldn't have come at a better time.

The plane jolts again, and I feel my stomach lurch. Thankfully, Lucas has his eyes closed now, and I turn backwards towards Saskia, give her a thumbs-up. She winks back at me.

'Quiet as a baby. Told you.'

The seatbelt sign pings on above us, and the announcement over the Tannoy tells us that we're experiencing turbulence, as if we didn't know already. I take a deep breath, my hands on the cold metal of the seatbelt clasp. I know it's nothing, and I'd never let on to Lucas, but I don't exactly relish the bumps and lurches any more than he does. I can be a bit of a nervous traveller, I worry about things going wrong, though I don't want him to know that. Across the aisle from us, the man is praying again, his eyes tightly closed, his lips moving rapidly, although I can't work out what he's saying. The woman beside him sees me looking and meets my eye, but her expression is blank, unreadable. I can't work out if they're together or not, but I look away quickly, embarrassed that she's caught me staring. I can still feel her gaze on me though, even as the plane shifts and jolts, and the overhead lights briefly flicker. My stomach twists, slightly, and I force myself to take a slow, deep breath. There's nothing to worry about. Nothing at all.

*

'Wow. Look at that,' Saskia breathes, her blonde head popping up between the seats from behind us. With a start, I realise that we're almost there; she's pointing out of the window, at the dark sparkling blue ocean below, and I gaze down at it in awe as the plane glides towards the ground. The lights of the plane bounce against the water, like tiny diamonds glittering before us.

Beside me, Lucas is somehow still sleeping, his mouth slightly open, and I pull out my phone, snap a photo of him, just to wind him up later. The turbulence is over, and the last hour or so has been smooth, but the sleeping tablets have obviously done a pretty good job.

'I can't wait to see the hotel,' Saskia says, 'it's going to be so great. God, this is a million times better than being at work, isn't it? I've taken everything off my phone – emails, Microsoft Teams, the lot. Out-of-office is ON! We're going off-grid!'

'You, off-grid?' Theo teases her. 'You do know that means you can't use Instagram?'

'Instagram doesn't count,' she says, rolling her eyes, and I smile, catching Theo doing the same.

'If it isn't on Saskia's Instagram, did it really happen?' he asks, and she pretends to punch him in the arm. 'You love it as much as I do, Theo.'

I don't really use social media much, but Saskia loves it – she's already posted that pic of us at the airport, tagging us at Heathrow. I wish she wouldn't add the geotags, I don't like the idea of everyone knowing where I am all the time, I suppose. I know that's silly, so I've never said anything.

'Cabin crew, prepare for landing,' comes the pilot's voice over the loudspeaker, and I face forwards in my seat, put my hands on the headrest in front to steady myself as the plane jolts slightly. I had my nails done especially for the trip – coral shellac that Saskia predicted is going to be the 'in' colour this summer – and I focus on them now to distract myself from the odd sensation of descending through the clouds.

'The "in" colour?' Lucas had asked, laughing. 'What on earth does that mean?'

'You wouldn't understand!' Saskia and I had said in unison, rolling our eyes.

The plane sways, and Lucas opens his eyes.

'Don't worry, we're landing now,' I tell him quickly, and he blinks and yawns like a cat, peers over me to check out the view from the window. I put my hand on his thigh and squeeze it. *Here we go.*

The plane bumps down to landing, and there's a cheer from behind us, the passengers clapping and whooping as the pilot announces our safe arrival. We join in; Saskia wolf-whistles.

'Made it,' Theo says, exhaling. 'Thailand, are you ready for us?!'

'Are we ready for Thailand, more like,' I say. 'Come on, Lucas, up you get, sleepyhead. Can you grab my bag down please? Thank you!' I kiss him on the cheek. He looks immensely relieved to be back on solid ground, and I make a note to get some of those sleeping tablets for the next time we go away. As we file off the plane, I catch sight of the man who winked at me up ahead, holding hands with a blonde woman who looks much younger than him. Ugh.

As we disembark from the plane, the heat of Bangkok hits us straight away, and the whole place just seems to have so much energy; it feels a million miles away from home in London, from my tiny little flat, from the remnants of Christmas that hung in the cold January air. Adrenaline pumps through me as we walk across the tarmac to the waiting shuttle bus at the airport – Lucas is carrying my little bag for me, so I feel suddenly light, carefree, like I could virtually skip inside to immigration control. A whole glorious week off work, in the sunshine – with Luke by my side.

I think about the photos of the villa on Koh Samet that Theo sent to our WhatsApp group – it looks *amazing*. Four-poster beds, our own private pool, a view of the beach – a million miles away from rainy old London.

I've been picturing it every night for weeks, before I go to sleep – the four of us sitting on the beach having cocktails, the sand between our toes; wandering the streets of Bangkok together, laughing at everything and nothing; soaking up the heat in a rooftop bar, the glittering lights of the city dancing below us. Waking up beside Lucas every day, his body curved against mine under hotel sheets. A little preview of when we live together, when I can wake up next to him every single morning.

'Wait for me, Hol.'

Saskia bounces up beside me; she slides her arm through mine easily, pulls me close to her even though we're both way too hot already – I can feel sweat slicking the back of my neck and the undersides of my arms. Saskia's bleached-blonde hair is tied up into a stylish knot on the top of her head, and her skin looks dewy, somehow, whereas mine feels tight and dry from the plane. I keep meaning to ask her what skincare she uses. Something pricy, probably, but maybe I could get a sample or something from a department store, couldn't I?

'I can't believe we're finally here – it's boiling, isn't it? God, I love the heat. Bring on global warming, I say.'

I laugh. 'You can't say that, Sask. But yes, it's amazing, good to be off the plane. Though I actually do like flying really, except for the turbulence. Being up above the clouds, it's beautiful, isn't it?'

We go through the airport doors, immediately greeted by a waft of air-con.

'Yeah, I agree,' Saskia says. 'There's nothing to be nervous about, is there? Poor old Lucas, worrying like that. Is he always so anxious on planes? Also, did you see that weirdo praying?' She carries on without waiting for an answer. 'Where are the boys, anyway? Lagging behind as ever. Let's just keep going, they're bound to catch up.' We round the corner towards immigration control, and she squeezes my arm. 'I'm so excited! What shall we do tonight?'

'Food and cocktails?!' I say. 'Can't go wrong with that, can we?'

'Perfect. This is going to be such a great trip, Holly, I know it,' Saskia says, squeezing my arm tightly with pink manicured fingers.

'Gotcha!'

We both scream as the boys run up behind us and grab our waists, lifting us into the air. The queue to get through passport control doesn't take long, and then we're almost out, waiting for our luggage. With a start, the baggage carousel in front of us grinds and cranks into life and suitcases start to spill out. Ours come quickly and the boys pull them off for us, waving away our feeble attempts to take them.

'Come on,' says Theo. 'Let's get this party started! I for one could do with a cold beer. Or five.'

'Woop woop,' Saskia shouts, and we laugh when an elderly couple give us a disapproving look. 'Bangkok, baby, bring it on. But first, selfie time.'

She sticks her arm out in front of us and we all gather together, the four of us, our heads pressed up against each other.

'Smile!' she says and we do, the big grins splitting our faces as the camera flashes, the bright white light making me blink.

'Perfect,' she says. 'Let's go.'

Chapter Two

Lucas

Lucas feels a bit sick from the plane, not that he wants to admit it – it was embarrassing enough having to take sleeping tablets. It's nearing nine o'clock at night by the time they've got their luggage from the carousel, and he knows that means there is plenty of time for the night to get started. Theo and Saskia won't want to go to bed – no way. They're both full of energy; he needs to get up to speed. He doesn't want to be left behind; tonight is going to be fun. He still feels a bit bad about the fact that he hasn't paid Theo back for the flights, but he will. As soon as he can. He mustn't forget.

The airport is rammed – just past baggage claim, tourists are gathering around a huge colourful statue of a golden serpent being pulled in two directions by Hindu gods, a tug of war, and Lucas's eyes come to rest on the snake's head, its open mouth, the jewelled fangs. Around him, camera phones snap. He sees a group of teenagers stuffing thin Burger King chips into their mouths, hears their laughter carrying on the air. He swallows. They look so much younger, as if there's a whole lifetime between them. He wishes he didn't feel so old these days. But perhaps a holiday will sort him out, perhaps it is just what he needs.

'You OK?' Holly is next to him, slipping an arm around his waist, and immediately he rearranges his face into a reassuring smile. She looks up at him, and he bends down to kiss her quickly, pulling her close. They haven't been away together for ages, and they've never been away with Theo and Saskia before – well, apart from that weekend in the UK last summer, but that doesn't count. It had rained the whole time and they'd been stuck in the pub playing card games for hours on end. He grins, remembering Theo getting competitive and Holly being particularly good at keeping a poker face. He's so glad they all get on so well, that he and Theo have managed to stay close for all this time, and that the girls complete their little group. Who cares if they're a bit older than the average traveller? Thailand is amazing, the things Theo has booked look great, and it's so nice not to be at school, hunched over his marking or trying to control the classroom. He smiles, picturing the four of them lying on sunloungers, a cold beer in his hand. Bliss. He and Holly need this.

'Absolutely,' he says to Holly, 'I'm fine, I'm great. Excited! Come on, let's go.'

The four of them – Saskia, Theo, Holly and Lucas – group together as they make their way out of Bangkok airport, past the hordes of people queuing for food, hot drinks, taxis, information.

'Wow, it's beautiful, isn't it?' Holly says, her face turned upwards towards the ceiling, taking it all in, and Lucas nods.

'An architectural feat.'

It is an incredible building – almost futuristic, with huge glass curved walls and at least four floors, crammed with restaurants and shopping outlets. Rows of tall plants line the gaps between the escalators, and light bounces off the tiled floor. Theo shepherds them forward, and the three of them follow him blindly.

'We don't need to bother with the information desk,' he shouts back to them – 'just come with me, follow your leader, leader, leader!' He does a little dance, waggling his backside at them all and raising his hands in the air and Saskia giggles.

'Stop embarrassing yourself!'

He says he knows exactly where they're going, and how to get there. Holly points at a train map on the wall and Saskia says something about a shuttle bus, but Theo waves a hand airily.

'I've booked the car in advance,' he tells them, and Lucas grins, slaps him on the back as a thank you. It's better than navigating the Bangkok metro, with its brightly coloured lines dissecting the city like confusing veins. Hopefully a car won't take long – they're only about twenty-five kilometres away from the city centre. Mentally, he tots up the cost of it – he must keep track, not let Theo get carried away and then have to pay back a big sum. He doesn't want to owe Theo money again – he's helped him out a few times in the past, and Lucas knows he doesn't mind, but he'd rather not have to, really. He needs to find a way to stand on his own two feet – but he still hasn't admitted to Holly what happened at the school three months ago. He hasn't told her that his salary isn't what it was – that the numbers she's working with when it comes to buying the flat are wrong. *Christ.* Lucas pushes the thought out of his head – he just wants a week of not thinking about it, just one week, that's all he's asking for.

'Do you think they have bag thieves here?' Holly is asking, clutching her handbag to her chest rather too tightly, and Theo smiles, a flash of perfect white teeth.

'Oh, you don't need to worry about things like that, Hol,' he says, 'chill out, you guys! We're on holiday. This trip is going to be' – he raises his hands into the air, mimes a chef's kiss – '*a-mazing*. Trust me.'

Saskia giggles, kisses Theo on the cheek. Lucas reaches for Holly's hand, squeezes it three times, their own version of Morse code, *dot dot dot*. His way of telling her he loves her.

Everything is going to be fine. More than fine. It's going to be great – the trip of their lives. Everything else, he can sort out when they're back in the UK.

Chapter Three

Saskia

The driver is waiting for us outside the airport, holding up a sign with our names on it: Mr and Mrs Sanderson. It gives me a little thrill to see our names together, I'm Saskia Sanderson now, and it feels great. I finger my wedding ring, twist it round, the new yet familiar comfort of it. We had such a wonderful day, we really did. We're still waiting for the official photos to come through, it's taking longer than expected, but I can't wait to see them.

'Please,' the driver says, 'come with me, OK?' His buddies beside him jostle him slightly, call something out in Thai that I can't understand. We follow him obediently, to where a waiting black car sits, and there's a clunk as he unlocks it for us, deftly takes our luggage and loads it into the boot.

'Mr and Mrs Sanderson, is there room for two more?' Holly says, and Theo opens the car door for her, grinning.

'But of course.'

We pile into the backseat and Theo goes in the front, next to the driver, who is tapping away at his phone, saying something into a little earpiece in his left ear.

'Omni Tower Hotel please, mate,' Theo says, and the driver nods discreetly, starting the engine with a quiet purr. We pull away from the car park of the airport, out onto the main road, where the streetlights are already on, little white orbs in the darkening sky.

'Your first time in Thailand?' he asks us, after a moment or two of silence, and we nod, scrambling to put our seatbelts on in the dark of the back of the car.

'Welcome. You will love it here,' he says, and he smiles at me in the rear-view mirror, catching my eye. I smile back, then tip my head against the seat, enjoying the softness of the leather headrest after the uncomfortable feeling of the plane. We're on a motorway, by the looks of it, and there's a steady hum of traffic alongside us, mostly cabs ferrying people to and from the airport.

It takes longer than I'd thought it would to get to the hotel, and I start to feel a tiny bit sick in the back of the car. I open the window, letting the warm air hit my face, and close my eyes briefly.

'You must be careful in Bangkok,' the taxi driver is saying to Theo in the front, their voices drifting back to us. 'Beautiful city, but not always safe. Especially for tourists. You know?'

Theo laughs. 'We know what we're doing.' He does, I think, he always does – it was part of what made me fall for him in the first place. His easy confidence, his self-assurance. He made me feel safe, safer than I've ever felt before in my life.

'What's not safe about it?' Holly says, leaning forward in her seat – she's in the middle, between me and Lucas – and I hear a spike of anxiety in her tone.

We round a corner, the car jolting slightly to the right, and the driver presses his horn as another car gets too close, mutters something unintelligible under his breath. As we near the city, the traffic seems to be increasing, becoming more chaotic – motorbikes have joined the throng, and the driver swears as one cuts out in front of us, the rider's face obscured under a big black helmet, a plume of smoke chugging out of the exhaust.

'Thieves,' he says eventually, 'the pickpockets, you know. You must stay together, watch your things. Not be too trusting.'

'Oh, we'll be fine,' Theo says confidently, 'but thanks for the tip.'

The driver raises his eyebrows, and I see a flicker of something flash across his face.

'The guidebook said to avoid the red-light areas,' whispers Holly, leaning towards Lucas, who puts a hand on her knee.

'Let's not start worrying even before we're at the hotel.'

The car is illuminated suddenly by bright, white light, and the driver exclaims, raises a hand to his rear-view mirror to protect his eyes. I twist in my seat and see that there is another car, driving far too close to us, its headlights beaming into the backseat. My heart gives a little jolt – why is it so close?

Our driver leans on the horn again, and this time there is an eruption of angry beeps in return, like wild animals howling to each other in the night.

'What's wrong?' I say, nervously, but the driver doesn't answer, just swears again, and we accelerate, the light in the backseat dimming as we pull away from the other car. My seatbelt digs into my shoulder as I strain to see what's going on, but it's too dark to make anything out.

'Probably just some moron,' Lucas says, seeing my expression. 'The traffic's notorious in Bangkok.'

'Right.' I nod, put my head back against the seat and take a deep breath, trying to quell the flash of anxiety in my stomach, the old butterflies rising. It's just the Bangkok traffic, that's all. Nothing to worry about.

But still, I check behind us a few more times, just to make sure that the other car has gone. The driver, clearly annoyed, turns the radio on and the car fills with the sound of tinny pop music, in a language I don't understand. We're on the edges of the city now – huge advertising billboards dangle above our heads, bright lights burn into my retinas. The roads feel like an obstacle course, with cars pulling out from all directions, horns blaring and brakes screeching, although nobody seems particularly bothered. A woman's laughter peals through the still-open window, carrying on the breeze, and more music coming from outside mixes with the beat of the radio, creating a cacophony of noise.

'We must be almost there,' Lucas mutters, and as if on cue, the car spins to the left and comes to rather an abrupt stop, the engine dying as quickly as it started.

'Here we are, sir,' the taxi driver addresses Theo as we finally arrive at the hotel. It's huge – tall and imposing, with the words 'Omni Tower Hotel' scripted on the front in gold lettering. It's quite dark outside now, but sparkling lights flash on either side of the revolving doors. Fronds of greenery frame the door, the leaves stretching upwards to the sky. Ornate iron framework curls around the entrance, and Lucas whistles.

'Nice digs, Theo. Good shout.'

'It looks amazing,' Holly says.

We clamber out of the car, and the heat of the evening washes over me; it's balmy, almost overwhelmingly warm. The driver comes round to the back of the car and opens the boot; it rises with a sleek, electric whirr and we pull our bags from within it.

'Let me help you,' Theo says to me, taking my case, and he grabs my hand with his other one, his skin warm and dry against my palm.

'Thank you,' I say to the taxi driver, and he nods silently, raises a hand to us.

'Have a good trip. Be careful. Look out for each other.' He winds the window up, and the engine roars back into life. There is a tiny silence between us as we stand on the roadside, and I know the driver's warnings are ringing in our heads.

'He was a bit serious,' Holly says, lightly, 'wasn't he?'

We watch as the tail-lights of the car pull away and it immediately gets lost in the rush of Bangkok traffic, the red and yellow flashes of the other cars, the smoke rising from the engines. For some reason, I have a sudden flash of anxiety, a longing to be back inside the safety and comfort of the car. I shake the feeling off as quickly as it came – the old fears, not to be indulged any more.

'Let's go inside,' Theo says, 'I could do with a drink. Come on, you.' He puts his arm around me, and we push open the revolving doors and are hit by a wave of cool air-con. Inside, it's beautiful – the marble floor shines, bouncing white light from the ceiling back upwards, and the walls are red wood embossed with swirly carvings. Dark blue velvet chairs line the sides, a deep, sumptuous shade, and in the middle of the room, a large spiral staircase draws my eye. Two women stand on either side of it, dressed in neat, tailored black-and-white uniforms, their mouths slashes of red lipstick. I smile at them and one of them extends her hand, gestures to the left, where the reception desk stands, a long black marble table framed by two tall white vases, filled with pink flowers, tilting their heads together.

'God, it's so nice, isn't it,' Holly whispers, pointing at the ceiling, where two glittering chandeliers drip down, their crystals sparkling in the light. She sounds almost a bit intimidated, and I know what she means. The place has a hushed feel, a complete contrast from the noise outside, and it feels like a haven, like we're cut off temporarily from the world.

'Welcome to the Omni.'

A smartly dressed Thai man gets to his feet abruptly as we approach the reception desk. His shirt is a crisp white, slightly open at the top, and his hair is slicked back neatly. Everything about him is polished and I find myself running a hand through my own hair, wishing I didn't look so scruffy.

'Hi, yeah, we've got a booking. Theo Sanderson,' he says, and I feel that thrill again standing next to him, the rings on our fingers, a married couple at last.

'Very good, sir,' he says, smoothly; 'Praew', his name badge says. Holly is whispering something to Lucas behind us and I turn to grin at them. I'm desperate to get to see the bedrooms – they must be beautiful, if the lobby is anything to go by. There's a soft, sweet scent to the air too, and I dip my head towards the vase of huge pink flowers.

'Lovely, aren't they?' Holly murmurs, and I nod.

'Gorgeous.'

'The name again please, sir?' Praew asks and this time I step forward.

'Sanderson, it's two double rooms.' I put my hand on Theo's arm, smile at Praew. 'We just got married, actually. I'm Mrs Sanderson. Saskia.'

It sounds alien in my mouth, but delicious at the same time.

He inclines his head slightly, smiles at us. 'Then I offer you my congratulations.'

I beam back. 'Thank you. We had such a wonderful day. Didn't we?'

Theo nods. 'We certainly did. Any luck with finding the booking, my man?' His tone is jovial but I can hear the slight strain in it; he's tired, I think, from the journey, from having to make small talk with the weird driver the whole way.

'I am having some difficulty finding it,' Praew says. He's frowning, not looking at us any more, his head bent towards the computer screen in front of him.

'It must be there,' Theo says, 'look, I've got a screenshot of the email reference, if that helps?'

But Praew is shaking his head. 'Nothing for tonight, sir. Are you sure it isn't under a different name?'

Theo frowns. 'Nope, definitely mine.' He pauses. 'Can you have another look?'

I turn around while he's sorting it out – he will sort it out, he always does. It's so nice having such absolute faith in someone. It hasn't always been that way for me, but that's why I love him so much.

'Look at this,' Holly is saying to Lucas; I wander over to join them. She's pointing at the restaurant menu, framed in a silver stand at the end of the desks. 'We ought to eat here one night, see what it's like. Sounds delicious.'

'How much is it though?' Lucas says, his voice low, and I feel a pang – are they worrying about money? I know they don't have as much as Theo and I, it's always been a bit of a thing between us, but I want them to be able to relax and enjoy the trip. Theo's always been so generous – perhaps I'll tell him to cover them a bit; he won't mind. Just so we can all have a good time.

'Sask.' Theo's calling me over, and I return to his side. 'There's been some sort of mix-up, I'm sorry. They're saying they have no record of the booking for tonight.'

I blink at him. 'No record? What do you mean?'

'I'm very sorry, madam.' Praew looks it, too, and I glance at Theo, confused.

'How can that be?'

He throws his hands in the air. 'I've no idea. I'm sorry – it's so weird – I thought I had the email confirmation but I can't get it to work here, the reception's dodgy or something, and they're saying they can't fit us in. My emails won't load properly and I can't get on the Wi-Fi.' He pauses, frowning. 'Maybe I made some sort of mistake.'

'But we've come all the way from London!' I say, stupidly, and Praew bows his head.

'So sorry, madam. We would be very happy to accommodate you on another occasion, in fact we have space later this week, as soon as tomorrow. Just not for tonight. January is a busy time in Thailand. Good weather. We are very sorry.'

I pause. 'But we just got married!' I feel tears prick my eyes – frustration, that's all it is. I just wanted everything to be perfect, and I know how hard Theo has worked to organise it all. It must be a mistake on their booking system. Maybe they'll take pity on us. It can't be his fault.

'Everything OK?' Lucas and Holly are back, looking at us expectantly.

'No, there's been some sort of mix-up,' Theo says. 'Doesn't look like we can stay here tonight after all. And the bloody internet isn't working for me to check.'

'Oh,' Holly says, and she and Lucas exchange glances. Is it me, or do they look slightly relieved?

'Well, look, never mind,' Lucas says, 'let's just go find somewhere else for the night, shall we? I'm knackered and we need to dump our bags.'

'But I booked *this* place,' Theo says, refreshing his phone screen repeatedly, and I put my hand on his arm.

'Don't worry,' I say, 'we'll come back. Promise.'

He shakes his head and I can see how disappointed he is with himself, that he'll blame himself for the mix-up even though it's really not that big a deal. Anxiety twinges in my gut – I don't want him to get annoyed tonight, I want us all to have a nice evening.

'There'll be somewhere else nearby,' Lucas says, pulling out his phone. 'I'll have a quick look. My signal seems OK.'

We trail away from the desk, back to the revolving doors, and stand outside on the street with our bags. I take a quick snap of the hotel, the ornate carvings above the door, and quickly upload it to my Instagram story, adding the heart-eyes emoji. We'll come back here, anyway, so it's not a total lie.

Lucas says he can see somewhere marked on the map a few streets over and suggests we try that, and so we hoist our suitcases back up and reluctantly leave the Omni, the heat encasing us again. My feet already look dirty – grey dust is coating the tops of them, and somehow, it feels like we're second-class citizens, not good enough for the swanky hotel. I vow to come back – they said they had space tomorrow, didn't they?

At the last moment, I look back through the glowing doors to see that the two women have gone to join Praew at the reception desk, and that all three are watching us leave, their eyes tracking our movements. I smile at them weakly, but I'm too far away to tell if they smile back. I follow the others down the street, away from the hotel, but I can't shake the odd feeling of someone watching me, the prickle at the back of my neck that I can't quite explain.

Chapter Four

Holly

There's a bit of a mix-up with the booking when we got to the hotel in Bangkok. The cab from the airport took us straight there, after what felt like a roller-coaster ride through the city with a slightly sinister driver, but when we arrived, they told us they had no record of it at all. Theo being Theo, of course, rested both hands on the reception desk and demanded to see the manager, but in the end, there was nothing they could do – it was fully booked. Even Theo didn't manage to charm our way in.

'Are you *sure* there's nothing you can do? We've come *such* a long way,' he'd wheedled, 'all the way from London town!' Saskia and I had exchanged a glance, trying not to laugh as he'd smiled at the guy behind the desk.

'Who could resist that megawatt smile?' she'd whispered, and then, to Theo, 'Oh come on, you know I love it really.'

'You can come back soon,' the man at the reception desk had told us firmly, 'but I can't fit you in tonight. I'm sorry.' It was Saskia who eventually pulled Theo away, and Lucas who said we ought to just try to find the nearest hostel, at least for this evening. I don't think any of us could face walking around any longer, not after the plane journey – we were all desperate to dump our bags and unwind. Secretly, I felt a bit relieved that we might be able to save some money – the hotel was even more extravagant in real life than it had looked in the pictures.

Anyway, we found this place, a couple of streets over. Pho Hostel. Cheap and cheerful, a backpackers' place really, but it'll do for tonight. It's a different vibe to the Omni, that's for sure, but it has a certain charm to it. It's set back from the road slightly, down a little alleyway, and when we get inside, the check-in process doesn't take long at all. Admittedly, the alleyway isn't the most attractive – it's dark and there are loose stones underfoot, one of which flies up and scrapes across my ankle, plus there's a bit of a strange smell, and I don't think I'd want to walk down here alone at night – but the hostel itself is bright and it's here and it'll do for now.

'We don't actually have a booking,' Theo says, but the woman behind the desk doesn't seem fussed – she simply shrugs.

'No worries, I should be able to fit you in, mate, if it's just the one night.' Her accent is Australian, and she looks about twenty – probably here on a gap year, I think, and the thought makes me feel old.

'Can I get a copy of one of your passports?' She stretches out a hand and I see that her nails are short and stubby, painted in chipped black polish, and her wrist is swarming with festival bands and full-moon party straps, mixed in with colourful cotton friendship bracelets that look like they're about to disintegrate. Definitely on a gap year, then.

'Sure,' Theo says easily, and he swings his backpack round and rummages in the front pocket for his passport. It's well over an hour since we got off the plane now, and I can feel tiredness starting to creep in, blurring my edges, but I give myself a little shake – I want to stay awake, have a good night on our first evening in Bangkok.

'Shit,' Theo says, 'I can't – I thought it was in here.' His rummaging takes on a more urgent air, his fingers scrabbling through his bag, unzipping the main pocket as well as the sides.

'Have you lost your passport?' Saskia asks him, a twinge of anxiety in her voice, and he shakes his head impatiently.

'I can't have. It was right 'ere.'

'It'll be in there,' Saskia says, 'let me have a look.' She takes his bag and feels around in the pockets, a frown on her face.

'I can give you mine,' Lucas says to the receptionist, pulling it out of his pocket, and she takes it with a disinterested smile, flips to the photo page and stands up to photocopy it. Theo and Saskia look a bit panicked, and I'm about to suggest that we retrace our steps or maybe call the cab company, when Saskia crows, 'Got it!' and then they're both grinning with relief and Theo's passport is found, the flash of burgundy leather a sudden comfort to us all.

'Thank God for that,' Saskia says, 'imagine if we got stuck out here!'

'Oh, it wouldn't be all bad,' Theo says, but I can tell he's relieved too.

The receptionist scans Lucas's passport in anyway and then hands us a room key, along with a card that has the Wi-Fi details on.

'Only thing available tonight is the six-person dorm,' she says, 'but it's the cheapest option, too. Plus you can check out a bit later, long as you're out by tomorrow afternoon you should be fine. The next party missed their flight, aren't arriving 'til tomorrow evening. So lucky you.'

'A dorm?' Theo repeats, as though he's never heard the word before, and she nods, raising her eyebrows with a slightly bored expression.

'It'll be fine,' I say, quickly, after a swift glance at Lucas – I know we both picked up on the word 'cheapest'. Any opportunity to save money out here can only be a bonus – and besides, how bad can a dorm be?

It turns out, quite bad. We troop up the stairs to the room and it really is pretty basic – three bunk beds pushed up against the wall, with bog-standard, thin blue duvets and flat white pillows that don't exactly look inspiring. There's a fan in the centre of the room, the blades spinning round with a slight rattling sound, and someone else's suitcase is lying half open next to one of the bunk beds, a messy array of clothes spilling out – T-shirts and jeans, a pair of swimming trunks. One small window is on the right, slightly cracked open, but the air feels still and stale.

There's a brief silence.

'Hmm,' Lucas says, 'not *quite* what we were picturing.'

'God, it's a bit grim,' Theo says, but I decide I'm going to be the one to cheer the group up so I paste on a smile and throw my bag onto one of the top bunks.

'Bagsy top bunk! Come on, let's dump our things and go get a drink.'

'It's only for a night, I suppose,' Theo says begrudgingly, and I nod.

'Exactly.'

'I wonder who else is in the room with us,' Saskia says, looking at the anonymous suitcase uncertainly. 'I don't really like the idea of sharing with someone we don't know. Looks like a man's things, doesn't it?'

'It'll be fine,' Theo says, a bit dismissively I think, 'we'll try to get back to the hotel as soon as we can though. I'll give them a call in the morning.'

'OK . . .' she says, but she still looks a bit anxious and I see her gaze flickering over the suitcase, and the slightly unmade bed beside it. There's a phone charger plugged in behind the bed on the wall, the white cord snaking out from beneath the duvet, and an empty water bottle sits discarded beside the pile of clothing. I suppose it is a bit weird sharing with a stranger, but more and more, I can't help thinking of the money we're saving. Besides, isn't this what travelling is all about – meeting strangers, embracing the unknown?

'Let's go down to the bar, get a drink,' Theo says, decisively, and the rest of them each choose a bed, then we place our bags down and get ready to go downstairs.

'I just want to wash my face quickly,' Saskia says, and she disappears into the bathroom – I poke my head in quickly behind her, and see a side room that's as basic as the dorm – just one shower with someone else's rusty blue BIC razor resting on the side, half a bottle of dodgy-looking shower gel that's doubtless seen better days, and a small silver mirror with a crack down one edge. It's not exactly somewhere you'd want to spend tons of time in.

'Ugh, this is grim,' Theo says, 'there's hair everywhere!'

'We won't be here long,' I say to him reassuringly. 'We'll just kip here tonight then get something proper sorted in the morning, shall we? We probably are too old to stay here!'

It makes me *feel* old, when I say that – I almost wish I hadn't. Lucas is thirty-two next month, the rest of us are all thirty, thirty-one. I'm the youngest, Saskia and Theo are almost exactly the same age.

While Saskia's in the loo, I gather everyone's passports and put them in one of the six red lockers standing in the corner, fumbling slightly with the padlock. I give it a wiggle to make sure it's closed, thinking of what our taxi driver said, then put the little gold key in my pocket. I mustn't lose it.

'D'you think we need to put our bags in the lockers too?' I ask Lucas. 'They don't really fit.'

'Nah,' he says, 'it'll be fine, just shove them under the bed, take out your valuables. Who's going to want my towel and T-shirts?'

'No one, mate,' Theo says, jokingly, 'not unless they're blind.'

I hesitate, but eventually do as Lucas says and push my suitcase underneath the bed, along with my little brown rucksack that I've brought for carrying around during the days. There's nothing of value in there, really – my phone is in my pocket, and my money's tucked into the back of my phone case, along with my credit card in case of emergencies.

'All right, let's go,' Theo says, when Saskia re-emerges. She's put on a slash of red lipstick, too, and her face looks brighter, clearer. She takes a selfie, pouting for the camera, and I watch over her shoulder as she uploads it to Instagram, tagging the hotel, the caption: 'change of plan! Party at Pho Hostel instead, who said the fun stops when you're 30?!' She tries to take a picture of me but I duck out of the way, feeling sweaty and self-conscious.

'Cool,' Lucas says, 'after you, ladies.' He gestures ahead of him and Saskia and I head out of the dorm, the boys following behind.

'We should lock the door! Who's got the key?' I say, at the last minute, but we're already halfway down the stairs and nobody seems to hear me. I think about going back up, but there's the thump of music coming from the bar and I figure that it will be fine – we've locked up our valuables, after all, and nobody's going to want to steal anything else. Maybe it locks automatically? Theo probably has the key.

Despite the pulse of the music, it's actually relatively quiet in the bar area, apart from a couple of girls in one corner, and a guy behind the counter pouring drinks. There's a semi-circular bar stretching along one wall, and stools dotted around, with bright neon-pink legs. A disco ball hangs from the ceiling towards the back of the room – clearly, that's where the dancefloor is – and there's a strange, slightly synthetic smell in the air, a bit like you'd get in a nightclub back at home.

'Right, I need a drink,' Lucas says, and we head over to the bar, which, when I lean on it, is sticky to the touch.

'Tequila?' Theo says, grinning, pointing at us all and nodding.

'Yes, mate,' Lucas laughs, 'why the hell not, eh?'

'Oh God, really?' I say, but the others are instantly outraged.

'Four tequilas please,' Theo says to the man behind the bar. It's dark so I can barely see his face, but I notice the flash of his hands as he pulls the bottle down from the shelf, lines the four shot glasses up quickly on the bar.

'I haven't had tequila for ages,' I say – the thought of it makes me feel a bit sick, bringing back flashbacks of university at Bristol – but the others insist, and we end up ordering rounds. It hits me quickly, the first shot – and then the second, and the third. I flag a bit on the third one, tell them it's going to make me ill, but Theo is adamant, putting a strong tanned arm around my neck, pulling me towards him.

'Come on, Holly, you love tequila really! Get it down you. Shots, shots, shots!'

Theo is buying, he's got thick wads of cash that looks like Monopoly money, and he keeps calling to the guy behind the bar to pour us another set of drinks, joking with him as he brings them across, winning him over in the way that only Theo can. Lucas is more relaxed now, which I'm glad to see after the plane journey – he's leaning over and shouting something in Theo's ear, the pair of them grinning like schoolboys. Saskia smiles at me, and I know she's thinking the same. It's sweet how Lucas and Theo look out for each other. He was so excited about being best man at their wedding, he practised his speech for weeks in advance. I could hear him reciting it in the bathroom sometimes when he got out of the shower if I was staying at his; I can even quote sections of it myself even now it's over, and he did a terrific job on the day. *I first met Theo back when we were both much better looking, if you can believe that . . . don't all laugh at once . . .*

It's later, now, probably about half past ten, and although the mix-up with the booking is a shame, I actually don't really mind. The hostel is fun – it feels real, like we're in the heart of things. There's music playing, a sort of heady, thumping beat in the background, and although the bar was quiet when we came in, now it's getting busy. The doors at the front are thrown wide open onto the street and the air is still hot, hot, hot. It's just so good to be away, to feel free.

There's a pool table over in the corner, and a group of guys are crowded round it – they look younger than us, in their early twenties maybe, and as I watch, they all start laughing, big, wide, open laughs, nudging and jostling, ruffling one another's hair. Maybe we can have a game of pool later – I'm rubbish but Lucas is quite good, and Theo always likes a bit of competition.

Now that it's busier, the guy behind the bar clearly can't keep up with the orders. He's pouring the drinks freestyle, which you'd never see back home – in my local in London it's all little silver measuring cups, not a drop too much, mind how you go. Here, it's a free for all – I watch as amber liquid hits freezing-cold ice, as vodka slips over little shards of lemon, as the people around me reach out and shove brightly coloured straws into their mouths.

There are neon lights on the walls that I don't think were switched on when we arrived – hot-pink outlines of flamingos, lime-green palm trees, electric-blue love hearts with fluorescent arrows piercing their sides. They flicker over people's faces, casting strange shadows over the room, and when I close my eyes briefly, I can still see the imprint of them on the back of my eyelids. Saskia turns in a circle on the spot, filming on her phone for Instagram stories.

'Come on then, Hol,' she says, putting her phone back in her pocket, 'let's have a dance, shall we?' My stomach drops. Saskia's a good dancer – sexy, confident – but I'm not. The thought of it makes me cringe.

'Nooo!' I say. 'God, Saskia, I haven't had enough drinks yet for that! You know what I'm like, I'm a crap dancer.'

She pulls a face at me, pouting. 'You are not! You're fabulous.'

'Kind but untrue,' I reply, and she laughs, pulls me towards her affectionately.

Her lips are still bright red, glossy – we didn't have long in the room to get ready, so I still feel like a sweaty mess, but she manages to look gorgeous, as usual.

'Come on, you need to let off some steam, Hol!' Saskia says. 'You're a great dancer, really, I've seen you! At Jamie's thirtieth, remember? You were on fire!'

I laugh, remembering. Our friend had a big party, and I might have overindulged. Still, that was a fun night. 'Oh God, don't remind me. I was drunk!'

'Well, there's an easy answer to that, isn't there?! The bar's right there . . .'

She puts her arms around my waist, shimmies a little, wiggles her eyebrows suggestively. She's wearing a silver top threaded with little rows of sequins, and pink high-waisted trousers that I couldn't pull off in a million years. Her eyes are rimmed with dark kohl – I didn't notice them before, but she must have done it in the bathroom, while I was fiddling with the padlock for the locker with our passports.

I look around for Lucas and Theo; they're by the bar, talking, looking at something on Lucas's phone. You can just about see the sweat forming on Lucas's back and under his arms; it *is* really hot in here. Theo gestures at the barman, again, and I catch sight of the Rolex watch glinting on his wrist – the expensive one his family bought him for his thirtieth. He went all out for that, booked a restaurant in Mayfair. We all went; it was a lot of fun, though I felt a bit out of place among the rest of their friends – most of which I think are originally Theo's. Lucas kept telling me that it was all fine, but to be honest, he was out of place too. Not that they made us feel that way – they never would. The two of them have always tried really hard not to notice that Luke and I don't come from the same kind of backgrounds as they do, I think. Tried hard to make us feel comfortable, which I appreciate.

'I really can't dance,' I protest again, but Saskia shushes me, guides me over to where there are already a group of people writhing to the music, tossing back their heads, raising their hands in the air to some imaginary force.

'This is an old one,' Saskia shouts in my ear; they're playing Shakira's 'Hips Don't Lie' and she duly grabs my hips, moves them side to side, making me laugh in spite of myself. 'Come on, Holly, we're on holiday!'

Saskia is so close to me that I can smell her lip balm, a sweet, strawberry scent, and when I look into her eyes, I can see all the tiny black dots in her irises; miniscule imperfections. She's laughing and I can't help but join her, her enthusiasm is always so infectious.

I try to relax, letting her guide me a bit, telling myself that nobody is watching me anyway, that nobody cares if I look too old or too fat or too ridiculous to be dancing in a Bangkok bar with a load of people who are probably ten years younger than me. Someone comes round with a tray of sambuca shots lit up in flames, and Saskia grabs us both one, screaming excitedly as she does so. 'Here you go, this will sort you out!' Her voice is so high-pitched, it rises above the music, it feels like it's directly in my ear.

We tip the drinks down our throats; I feel the alcohol burning a line down towards my stomach, the distinctive aniseed taste of it making me wince.

My head is beginning to feel a bit fuzzy, and I have a sudden vision of waking up in our crowded hostel room in the morning, in a top bunk without any water. Oh God, I do want to feel fresh tomorrow – we'd planned to spend the first day going round the food markets, sampling everything, getting our bearings, maybe visiting one of the temples. I don't want to drink too much, or feel too hungover the next day. Does that make me boring?

'I just need some water,' I say to Saskia, leaning closer to her, pushing aside strands of blonde hair that have escaped from her bun. She nods, her eyes closed, still dancing. She looks beautiful; I can see a couple of guys watching her from the side of the makeshift dancefloor, their eyes narrowed, their mouths like slits. They remind me of crocodiles, circling the water, waiting to pounce. Maybe I shouldn't leave her on her own . . .

I catch sight of Lucas and Theo, over in the corner now – they're watching us too, and I smile at Lucas, give him a little wave with my fingers.

'I'll be back in one minute, Sask, stay here, OK?' I say to Saskia. She nods, giving me a thumbs-up, and then I slip away, back to the bar area.

'Can I get a glass of water, please?' I shout to the barman, leaning forward across the bar so that he can hear me. I worry about my top falling too far down, yank it up quickly with slightly sweaty fingers. God, my mouth feels dry. The music is still pumping and I realise I'm tapping my foot to the beat of it – I'm getting into it, now.

'Here you go.' The barman hands me a glass of cloudy water and catches my eye as he does so. There's something in his expression that makes me feel slightly unnerved – his gaze flickers to where my top has slipped down again and I turn abruptly, wanting to get away from him, wishing I wasn't so exposed. But it's so hot in here, far too hot to put a jacket or anything on. I feel his eyes on me as I walk away, hear him saying something that I can't quite make out.

'The guy behind the bar is a bit of a creep I think,' I shout in Saskia's ear when I get back to the dancefloor, but she frowns at me and mouths that she can't hear me. I lean in closer to her, say it again, but she rolls her eyes, grabs my hand and drags me from the dancefloor, over towards the open door of the bar.

'Needed a breather anyway. What did you say?'

'Oh, just the barman,' I say, relieved to be away from the loud thump of the music. There's the gentlest of breezes coming in through the door, fluttering the hair off my sticky forehead, and I blow my cheeks out, fan my face with one hand.

'What about him?'

'He was staring at me weirdly when I went to get water. Just a bit gross.'

Saskia looks dismayed, and I wish I hadn't told her.

'Don't worry, it's not a big deal,' I say, reassuringly, but I see her glance nervously over at the bar, and unfortunately, he's watching us, a small smile curving across his lips.

'Ugh.' I turn away with a shudder. 'What is wrong with people?'

'Didn't do that when the boys were with us,' Saskia says wryly, then scans the dancefloor, looking for them. 'Where have they got to, anyway?'

'I don't know actually,' I say, 'shall we do a scout round to find them?'

We link hands again, like we're teenagers, and push our way back into the throng of people. More are dancing, now, the room is a whirlwind of colours and movement, and the waitresses with the flaming sambuca are still circulating the floor, the flames casting strange orange shadows across people's faces. I catch sight of a girl with large gold hoop earrings crying in one corner, her friend rubbing her back consolingly, and I wonder fleetingly what it is she's crying about, all the way over here in paradise.

An old Abba song comes on and I turn back to tell Saskia

how much I love it, then suddenly realise her hand is no longer in mine.

'Saskia?' I say, but she's disappeared.

A guy barges into me slightly, spilling sticky liquid onto my hand, then immediately apologises, slurring the word.

'Shit, shit, sorry darling.'

I grit my teeth. 'No problem.' I hate being called 'darling', but he's so out of it that there's no point making a fuss. I wipe my wet hand on my skirt and look around for Saskia – she can't have gone far, she was with me a second ago.

I catch sight of her, the flash of blonde hair, and am about to call out when I see the odd expression on her face. She is standing stock-still, her body rigid, and her face, eerily illuminated by the neon lights, is white as a sheet. She looks as though she's seen a ghost.

Chapter Five

Saskia

I'm holding Holly's hand when it happens. Just a flicker in the corner of my vision, and at first I almost don't notice. But then my brain seems to catch slightly, as though it's a thread caught on a loop, and I turn my head properly to the left, just to check.

I can see only the side of his face, and then just as quickly as I think I saw him, he's gone. It can only be a second or two, but my whole body freezes in shock, ice cascading through my limbs. A coldness washes over me, despite the heady heat of the room, and for a moment the pulse of the dancefloor fades away and it's just me, alone, trying to process what I thought I saw.

It cannot be him, not here, not after all this time. My mind is playing tricks on me – I've had too much tequila, not enough sleep. Imagining things. My heart feels like it's beating outside my body, the blood pumping through my veins with alarming intensity, and it's as though the world has gone silent, like I'm wrapped in cotton wool, a thick Perspex screen between me and everybody else. Memories threaten to crowd the sides of my vision – his grin, directed at me in the darkness; the chime of my phone, the phone that only he used; the figure following a pound sign, scrawled onto a piece of paper; the sense of intense desperation. All of it pushed into the deepest, darkest corner of my mind, the part I no longer access – the part I no longer *want* to access.

At some point, I realise I've let go of Holly's hand, our sweaty fingers have disconnected, and I am alone, my feet rooted to the spot, my head twisted in the direction in which I think I saw him. But then Holly is there, in front of me, saying my name, and gradually, the sounds of the music come back – they're playing something by Abba, an old one that I used to love, and the lights flicker slightly and I am back in the present, back in my body, back with my friend, back in the room.

'Sorry,' I say, though my throat feels dry, sticky, as though it's an effort to get the words out. 'I thought— I just thought I saw someone I used to know.'

She looks blank. 'Oh really? Who?'

I hesitate, briefly close my eyes. I replay what I saw in my mind's eye – just the turn of a head, the outline of a jaw, the familiar stature. Something about the way he turned. But no. Loads of men look like that. It was nothing. It had to be.

'No one,' I say at last, 'long story. Just a guy I once knew, that's all.'

She looks at me quizzically, and for a moment, I think about what a relief it might be to tell her, for the whole story to spill out of my mouth like lava, fiery and dangerous, destroying everything in its path, destroying the life I have worked so hard to build. I imagine us going to the bar, sitting in the corner, talking it all over for hours and hours. Would it help? Would she understand?

But no. I've never been able to tell anyone about him. I can't.

The risk is too high. And so I just paste on my largest smile, and start singing along to Abba.

The boys find us a few minutes later, collapsed on the fake leather seating that surrounds the room – I can tell Theo is drunk, even more than I am. He kisses me sloppily on the mouth, rests his head on my shoulder, and I feel the familiar warmth of him seeping through my bones, relaxing me. My heart still feels like it is going a bit too quickly, and there's a sort of metallic taste in my mouth, panic and fear and alcohol all rolled into one. I stretch my lips into a smile, push the feelings away. It wasn't him. It can't have been.

'Come on, you,' I say, 'I think it's probably time for bed.'

He groans. 'But we're having so much fun.'

'There's more fun available tomorrow,' Holly says, rolling her eyes – Lucas is out of it too, and for a fleeting moment, I wonder if they might have taken something. I know they used to do cocaine together when they were younger, before we met and for the first year or so that we were together, but I'd been pretty sure they'd grown out of it by now. Theo knows I never liked it – had always been scared of drugs, of the feeling of losing control.

'One more dance,' Theo pleads, slurring the words a little, and I laugh in spite of myself, allow him to drag me to my feet. He puts his arms around my waist, nuzzles into my neck, and I remember our wedding dance, how wonderful it felt to have him steer me around the big white marquee we'd rented, watched by all our family and friends. It felt like I was being reborn. The memory of it plays on a loop in my head, calming me, reminding me how far I've come.

Holly and Lucas join us, and the four of us form a happy little circle. My hair whips across my face as I turn my head to the music, and at the climax of the song our sweaty bodies come together, the four of us screaming the lyrics in each other's faces, our breath mingling, alcohol fumes dissipating into the hazy air.

'Love you guys,' Holly says, sentimentally, and she's met with a chorus of 'we love you too'. I allow myself one last glance around the room, but it's emptied out a lot now – it must be getting late – and there is absolutely no sign of him, nothing untoward at all.

When my head hits the pillow in our dorm room at about 2am, I've managed to convince myself that it was just an illusion, that I imagined the whole thing. I fall asleep easily, quickly – Theo is in the bunk above me, there's not room for us both in one bed – but I clasp my hands together, reassured by the feel of my wedding ring, warm and tight against my finger, locking me into this perfect new life, keeping me safe from the secrets of the past.

Chapter Six

Holly

For a second when I open my eyes, I forget where I am. Then it all comes back to me – the plane journey, the hostel, dancing, the tequila shots. Ugh, my mouth feels dry. I'm in urgent need of some water.

I've woken up early, before the others – I didn't sleep very well. I thought I heard a noise in the night – voices in the corridor outside our dorm. It sounded like people arguing, maybe, but it was hard to tell because of the noise of the fan, whirring above us, trying rather unsuccessfully to keep us all cool. Then there was a banging, and someone opened our door a crack, letting a shaft of bright yellow light into the room. I thought I saw the outline of a figure on the other side of the door, heard the sound of someone breathing shallowly, but then it disappeared and I must have drifted back to sleep.

It might have been the other person we're sharing the room with, I suppose, but as far as I know, nobody actually came in, so perhaps whoever it was chose to sleep somewhere else. I looked over at the empty bed first thing, but it was the same as yesterday – rumpled duvet, empty water bottle, phone charger snaking out from the wall.

I'm on one of the top bunks, and I lean down to see that

while Lucas and Theo are still in bed, Saskia's bed below Theo is empty. The receptionist told us that they were serving breakfast, such as it is, up on the roof, and so I think perhaps she's already up there. Quietly I slip out of bed, wincing as my bare feet connect with the metal rungs of the ladder that leads down from my bunk. My bag is on the floor, shoved under Lucas's bunk, and I quietly pull it out and zip it open, trying not to wake him. He looks so peaceful in his sleep, his mouth slightly open, his forehead uncreased. He spends so much time these days looking a bit worried, I think – I've become accustomed to the little frown lines in his face. I know he's worried about the money side of the trip, and I resolve to make things as easy as I can – we don't need to spend lots, and we can keep a careful eye on everything. I've got a guidebook that I bought online last week, and it has lots of helpful hints about making savings, finding the cheap spots. The only problem is convincing Saskia and Theo to go with us.

I change quietly into a pair of shorts and a T-shirt, twisting my hair up into a knot on the top of my head. The window in our dorm room is half open, sunlight filtering across the beds, and I feel a shiver of excitement run through me. I can't wait to get out and explore.

I climb the stairwell outside our hostel room up towards a bright blue patch of sky, pressing a hand to my stomach as it rumbles with hunger. Sure enough, Saskia is up there, sitting on a deck chair with her back to me, looking out over the city.

'Saskia?' I go up to her and she jumps slightly, then smiles as I put a hand on her shoulder. She still looks gorgeous in purple harem pants and a black cropped T-shirt. Last night's make-up is gathered in the corners of her eyes.

'How're you feeling?' I say. 'Have you had some brekky?'

'Not yet,' she says, 'shall we get some? I wasn't feeling that hungry.'

'You should eat!' I say. 'You'll feel better. You hungover?'

She waves a hand airily. 'Not too bad. You?'

'Also better than expected.' I smile at her. 'Come on, let's see what Pho Hostel has to offer in the way of breakfast. Might be worth not raising our hopes *too* high . . . though I'm happy to be proven wrong.'

In the corner of the roof, there's a sort of DIY kitchen, with a little cupboard containing bread, juice, fruit. I pour us both a glass of juice and actually it tastes delicious, fresher than back at home. Sweeter. The sun is out – I can imagine it getting really white hot up here, it's so exposed – but they've put up umbrellas and hammocks that provide a bit of shade.

In the kitchen, there's a silver stainless-steel kettle, a row of plastic beakers and plates in rainbow colours, all a bit grubby-looking, and a sink with a note taped above it telling guests to wash up their own crockery. The fridge is quite small, and full of other people's stuff – tourists, I guess, who move on quickly.

'Why don't you try some fruit?' I say to Saskia. 'I'm going to have some. I can be your guinea pig, see what it's like before you try it.' I spoon some into a bowl; though the fruit looks a bit slimy, too bright in the sunlight. I eat a piece of mangosteen, feel the peachy tang of it on my tongue. 'Try some rambutan,' I urge Saskia, but she shakes her head. The rambutan are a bit like lychees, with bumpy, pinkish-red skin that stains my fingers.

'I'm fine. Thank you though, Hol. Sorry – I just don't feel great actually, but I'm fine, really.'

'You sure? You don't *seem* fine. What's up? Come on, you

can tell Aunty Holly.' I smile at her, trying to make her laugh, but her face doesn't budge.

'I just drank too much, that's all. Didn't sleep well.' She pauses. 'And I— I had this horrible, weird dream, this sensation that someone was standing over me in the night. As though somebody else was in the room. Like a presence, over the bed.' She glances up at me. 'That probably sounds mad, doesn't it? But I think we ought to go to the hotel tonight; I don't want to stay here any longer than necessary. It doesn't feel that safe. I mean, I don't think that door to our dorm even locks.'

I hesitate, thinking back to the sounds I heard in the night, the crack of light peeping through the door. The muffled voices. But I don't want to unnerve her any more than she already is, so I decide to say nothing. Hostels are full of random people, aren't they. It could have been anything – kids messing about, someone getting the wrong room by mistake.

'Jet lag can give you weird dreams sometimes, I think,' I say, trying to reassure her. 'I'm sure there was nobody else in the room. Poor you, though. Why don't you have some paracetamol, I've got some downstairs. You'll feel better once we get out and about! And I think Theo is going to sort us out the proper hotel today. You're right, we can't really stay in this place at our age, can we? Though it is nice up here. Such a great view, you can see half the city.'

I stretch my arms skywards, luxuriously. I picture the hotel we were planning to go to: quilted sunloungers around a sparkling blue pool, waiters serving us chilled glasses of champagne. I'd love a swim. But then I picture the money.

'Morning!'

Theo and Lucas appear on the roof. Theo immediately

circles his arms around Saskia, nuzzling his face into her neck, kissing her throat. She laughs, looking momentarily pleased, and I see her rearrange her face into more of a smile.

'You're up!' she says, turning to face him, kissing him quickly.

I grin at Lucas, reach out for his hand. 'Hope I didn't wake you when I got up?'

'Didn't wake me,' Theo says cheerfully, 'I was dead to the world.'

'Probably on account of the tequila,' Saskia says, and he holds his hands up in an innocent, *don't shoot me* gesture.

'Least none of us were sick,' Lucas says. 'Time was, five years ago there'd have been a cheeky chunder situation going on, I reckon.'

'We're older and wiser now,' I say, framing my face with my hands, pretending to be an angel, 'didn't you know?'

'I don't feel very wise,' Lucas groans, 'has anyone got any paracetamol?'

'In the room,' I say, 'I'll get you some in a minute; you're not the only one who needs some. Why don't you have some water? And I think there's coffee. That usually sorts you out.'

'God, I need a coffee too,' Theo says, rubbing a hand through his hair, then clapping his palms together. 'So, the street food market this morning? It's meant to be amazing. Then Wat Pho temple this afternoon? Also, the barman last night told me about this great restaurant near the Grand Palace, we could take a trip over there later, or maybe tomorrow? I'm keen for a swim at some point, too. If we can find a place with a pool. It's so fucking hot.'

'Sure,' Lucas agrees, 'that all sounds good. Though we don't have to fit everything into one day.'

'Also keen to swim,' I say, putting my hand in the air like a schoolgirl, 'one vote for a pool, please. Though I don't think we should be taking recommendations from that barman. He was a creep, kept staring at my boobs.'

'Really? You didn't say,' Lucas says, and I shrug.

'Well, it happens. Used to it. But I don't exactly think he's the gold standard for recommendations.'

'You should tell me if stuff like that happens,' Lucas says, and I look at him, surprised he's taking it so seriously.

'Nothing actually happened,' I say, 'really, it's fine. I was fine.'

He drops it, but I catch sight of the perturbed expression on his face. I'm glad I didn't tell him about the guy winking at me on the plane. The world is full of creeps – and men don't even realise.

'And the hotel?' Saskia adds quickly. 'What about getting back to the hotel, the original place?'

Lucas turns to look at her in surprise. 'You said last night that you wanted to stay here, Sask. More *authentic experience*. Remember? Or was that just the tequila talking?'

She looks a bit sheepish. 'Oh, did I? I've, er, I've changed my mind. Sorry, is that OK?'

'OK, sure,' Theo says easily, 'well look, I'll call the hotel this morning, we can figure out a plan from there and hopefully they can take us from tonight. We've only a couple of days here in the city until we go south to the beach villa, anyway.'

'Thanks, baby,' Saskia says, putting her hand on the back of Theo's neck. She's smiling suddenly, laughing, talking more loudly now about the beach villa in Koh Samet and something about going to a full-moon party, the usual tourist stuff we want to do. She seems to have perked up a lot, actually, but

I resolve to keep an eye on her, make sure she's OK as the day goes on.

We all want to head to the food market today and so after a couple of minutes sitting on the hammock with Lucas, making our travelling plans, I place my hands either side of his thighs and push myself upwards to standing.

'Right, I'm going to make myself look a bit more presentable – we ought to make a move if we're going to fit everything in.'

'You already look presentable. More than presentable,' Lucas says, grinning at me, and I roll my eyes.

'You're very sweet, but you're lying. I've barely brushed my hair.'

'That's part of the hostel vibe,' he says, and I smile, do a pretend catwalk twirl.

'Hostel chic, the new thing. Deodorant optional.'

'You can pull it off!' He winks at me.

'You coming with, Saskia?' I ask her, and she nods. Theo is still sitting over by the breakfast counter, chatting to a couple of other guys – I recognise them as the ones playing pool last night – his arms slung over the back of a chair, and I see her eyes dart over to them quickly.

'Want to grab Theo?' I say, but she just shakes her head.

'No, he'll come. Let's just get out of here.'

We walk down the short flight of stairs back to the corridor where our dorm room is. Saskia is silent, the only noise is the *slap slap slap* of my sandals on the stone. It's shady and cooler in here and the fan in the corridor is spinning, big whirring loops, the blades slicing through the air.

'You all right?' I ask her, and she nods, flashes me a smile.

'Fine, I'm fine. Just a bit tired.'

'You'll perk up once we get going.'

'I want to get changed,' Saskia says abruptly as we get to the dorm room, and I head into the bathroom, stare at myself in the mirror, wishing I'd thought to bring some dry shampoo with me. I probably ought to try to wash my hair, but when I turned on the shower earlier, a cold dribble came out and the thought of forcing myself under it is a bit much. I pull my hair down and then twist it back up into a kind of beachy topknot, find a yellow flowery headband from my bag and pull it over my forehead, teasing out a few wisps of hair so that they frame my face. Lucas always says he likes me with my hair up, and besides, this ought to help with the sweat and the heat. I fish out a red lipstick and swipe some on, smile at my reflection. I look all right, I think. Not twenty-two, but not bad either.

'Holly?'

It's Saskia, framed in the doorway, her head tilted to one side. She's biting her lip, jiggling from one foot to the other.

'You ready to go?'

I twist the lid of the lipstick on tightly and drop it into my make-up bag. 'Ready! What d'you think of this lippy?'

'Love it, you look fab.'

The door to the dorm bangs open and the boys barrel in, loud and talkative, a mini-hurricane.

'Let's go!' Theo says, grabbing his backpack from the foot of the bed and swinging it on. Lucas moves past me to get to the sink, his hands skimming my waist as he does so, then fills up his water bottle from the bathroom, grimacing as he forces it with difficulty under the too-low tap.

'Can you actually drink the water here?' Saskia asks, and Theo rolls his eyes.

'Course you can. Don't be such a worrier!'

She looks hurt, momentarily, but the expression vanishes

as quickly as it came. I give her a reassuring smile – I feel a bit sorry for her, she seems a bit off – and she smiles back, but something about it doesn't quite reach her eyes. Perhaps they had a row last night or something, I think, resolving to ask her later if everything's all right between the two of them.

Before we leave, I check our locker, where I put the passports. To my dismay, I see that the padlock's broken – the metal loop has been disconnected from the plastic roundel. Quickly, I open up the locker, panic leaping to my throat – but everything is present and correct, nothing's missing. Thank God.

'Guys, did anyone notice the padlock for our locker was broken?' I ask the others, and they look at me blankly. I show them, and Theo shrugs.

'Probably just cheap. We can buy another one today – bring the passports with us? We probably ought to keep them on us anyway. Don't want to get stuck here, do we.'

Briefly, I think of what Saskia said earlier – about feeling as though there was someone else in the room in the night. But surely, they'd have taken something, wouldn't they? Unless they were looking for money, and were disappointed to only find our passports. We've all got our wallets on us, I think.

Saskia grabs the padlock from me, turns it over in her hands, examining it. 'Do you think it's been cut?'

'Of course not,' Theo snorts. 'It's just snapped. Where did you even get that, Hol? It looks like it's from Poundland!'

'We're not all made of money!' I say. 'But I take your point. I'll buy one today, find a shop.'

'I don't like it,' Saskia says, 'we really can't stay here another night, Theo, it's not safe.' She looks uneasily around the room, at the empty set of bunk beds.

'I'll call the hotel once we're out and about,' Theo tells her, and she nods, though she still looks a bit perturbed.

'Don't worry,' I tell her, 'I'll put all of our passports in my bag, look.' I tuck them into the pocket of my rucksack, give her a reassuring smile.

We traipse down the stairs, and as we do I glance back up towards the rooftop, towards the small square of bright blue sky. It looks so beautiful, like a postcard, the azure shape against the white surround. I close my eyes briefly, wishing I could somehow capture everything, a series of mental photographs. *Click click click.*

The entrance to the hostel is busy; the same Australian woman is manning the desk, though she looks more tired today. She taps away at the computer, chewing gum as she does so, *snap snap snap.* The walls surrounding her desk are filled with paraphernalia – postcards stabbed through with neon drawing pins, Post-it notes with love hearts scrawled on them, photographs of travellers, tanned faces shoved close together. *Live fast die young*, reads a slogan emblazoned across the top of a corkboard, and I wonder how many people believe that to be true.

'I plan to,' Theo says, pointing at it, and Saskia nudges him in mock horror.

'Don't say that!'

'See you guys later!' the receptionist chirps – Danni, her name badge says – and Theo raises a hand to her as we spill out of the doors onto the street. Saskia immediately scans left and right up the street, as if checking for something, and I look sideways at her, seeing if she's all right, but she seems fine – her cheeks are a little flushed maybe, but she appears happy enough, her fingers laced through Theo's, her large black sunglasses perched on the top of her head. She always manages to exude glamour, like a movie star.

'Don't worry,' Lucas says, whispering in my ear, perhaps sensing what I'm thinking, 'I prefer your look. Hostel chic, remember.' He squeezes my hand, and I feel a burst of happiness.

'Let's go,' Theo says, 'food market, here we come.'

Suddenly, there's a shout from behind us and all four of us turn to see Danni on her feet, holding something in her outstretched hand.

'Your room key,' she says, 'you left it on the reception desk.'

'Oh,' I say, 'thank you so much. Sorry about that.'

She hands it to me, and I see a frown on her face as she looks at us.

'Be careful, yeah?' she says, abruptly, and I pause, my fingers still clutching the hard metal of the key.

'Of course,' I say, and she nods, tosses her hair back over her shoulder, snaps her gum.

'City like this, you gotta keep your wits about you,' she says, and I nod, thank her again, though Theo is already rolling his eyes at the unsolicited advice. But she's right, I think, as we turn and walk away, and for some reason as we turn the corner I feel a cold shiver go down my spine, a sense of unease that is worsened when I turn back to see that Danni is still looking at us, watching us leave, her hand held up to her forehead, shielding her eyes from the blazing hot sun.

Chapter Seven

Holly

The roads feel dusty and dry as we walk to the market, and I wish I'd brought a hat because the sun is so intense. We're following Theo, who says he knows where he's going, and we're having to walk in single file because of the way the traffic is whizzing past us – I've never seen anything like it. It's a mix of cars, motorbikes and tuk-tuks, and nobody seems to be sticking to the rules, if there even are any. Fumes from the engines beat against my bare legs, hot clouds of smoke, and I squeal as a moped gets too close, the huge thick wheels of it just inches from my toes.

'Can't we go down a side street or something?' I shout to Theo, but he doesn't seem to hear me. There are stalls lining the street, brightly coloured items hanging under lime-green umbrellas. They're mainly selling clothes – sportswear and dresses, the thin, flimsy fabrics fluttering lightly in the breeze caused by the traffic hurtling by. I stop briefly and catch a pair of Nike trousers between my fingers, and the woman manning the stall immediately comes over to me, smiling widely, gesturing at the clothes.

'No, thank you,' I say. 'Sorry.' But she puts a hand on my arm, still smiling, pointing at the rest of the stock she has hanging under the umbrella. I shake my head, feeling guilty, and walk on – the others are up ahead and I don't want to get lost.

'The best prices!' the woman calls after me, 'The best prices in Bangkok!'

I ignore her, hurrying forwards, keeping my eyes focused on the bright pink of Theo's shirt. It's hard, because the whole street is so colourful – huge signs hover above our heads, advertising restaurants, spas, bars and chemists, the vibrant primary colours bleeding into the perfect blue of the sky overhead. A giant red sign for a travel agency looms on my right, and a man in the doorway grins at me widely, his white teeth flashing in his tanned face.

'Looking for a day trip?'

'No, thank you,' I say, firmly, but he just keeps grinning, takes a step towards me, holding out his hand.

'I can show you the best places to go. First time in Thailand?'

'I— Yes, but I'm fine, thank you though,' I say. He pulls a sad face, lower lip out, his eyes twinkling, and I say sorry again, hurry forwards. Suddenly, I can't see the others anywhere – the pink of Theo's shirt has gone, and there's no sign of Lucas's dark hair, Saskia's blonde head. Immediately, adrenaline begins to course through my body, and I force myself to take a deep breath, scanning the crowds for them. Everywhere is just so busy, so alive, but I don't like the sensation of being alone, not in such an unfamiliar environment.

I pull out my phone, but the two little dashes in the top right corner show me that I've got no signal – probably because there are so many people around.

'You lost?' The travel agent is back at my side; he must be able to see the panicked expression on my face. I hesitate

– I could ask him for directions to the food market, but I don't want him to know I'm by myself. Inwardly, I curse myself for not doing more research, for being so reliant on Theo. I'm a grown woman, I ought to be able to handle things myself.

'I'm fine,' I say, rearranging my features into a reassuring expression, and then suddenly, there's a hand on my arm and Lucas is there, warm and familiar, putting his arm around my waist and steering me forwards, telling me the others are just up ahead.

'Sorry,' I say, 'I got distracted looking at some tracksuit bottoms and then you'd all just disappeared.'

'Stick with me,' Luke says, holding my hand, and I clasp his fingers through mine, feeling foolish. The others are waiting for us on the corner of the street, and I feel even more silly when I realise how close by they were, the whole time.

'Oh there you are, Holly. I'm starving,' Saskia says. 'Are we almost there, Theo?'

'Just down here, I think,' he says, and we veer off to the left, down a smaller, slightly quieter street that leads into a big market square, where a white tent covers half the space.

'Whoa,' Lucas says, 'this looks incredible.'

It really does – there are rows and rows of food carts, some covered by the tent and some out in the open air, shaded by brightly coloured umbrellas, purples and yellows and greens forming a canopy above the glistening trays of food. Seafood winks at me from beneath sheets of plastic, nestling in ice; fruit is piled high, ripening in the heat, and meat sizzles and spits in large black pans. The vendors themselves move like insects, hands flying through the air, dicing and slicing and stirring, folding and packing and serving. I watch as a woman folds spring rolls on a skillet, three at a time, her fingers flying with amazing speed and dexterity, her eyes not even watching her own movements. A few stalls down, a man unloads vegetables from the back of a tuk-tuk, sweat forming across his back, his hands unpacking and stacking flawlessly. The smells are almost overwhelming – a heady mix of flavours, sweet and savoury and spicy all at once, and my mouth fills with saliva, despite the fact that it's only a quarter to twelve, barely even lunchtime.

'We're not bound by the constructs of time here in Bangkok, Holly,' Theo says, when I say this aloud. 'We're on holiday! Normal rules do not apply.'

'Well, when you put it like that . . .' I say, grinning back at him, and he winks at me. We wander further into the market, which is full of people – a woman barges past me to get to a stall selling eggs, rows and rows of them neatly lined up on the table, white and speckled and beige, and in front of us, a gaggle of students are ordering what look like pointy pork skewers, accompanied by little plastic bags of sticky rice which the vendor twirls between his fingers, twisting the plastic bag handles tighter and tighter together. At the end of a row, a woman sits on the ground, baskets of bright red chillies in front of her; she catches my eye and smiles, putting her fingers to her mouth.

'God, there's so much to choose from!' Saskia says. 'Though I don't fancy the look of those . . .' She points to a table where a row of what look like rats are lying on their backs, their skin flayed, bodies red and raw.

'Ugh.' I shudder, averting my eyes, and Theo laughs.

'Don't be so daft, girls. It's a local delicacy here!'

'Can we find a pad thai or something?' Saskia says, and we don't have to look far – a few stalls away a woman is stirring a big wok full of noodles, the hot, savoury smell drawing us in.

Lucas is still holding my hand tight as we join the small bustle of people in front of the pad thai stall, our fingers linked sweatily, which I'm glad of because otherwise I worry I'd get lost in the throng. Sweat coats the pad thai vendor's brow and I watch as she wipes it away with the back of her forearm. These places never strike me as being particularly hygienic, but I don't want to appear prudish so I just swallow, smile up at Luke.

'I can't decide what to have!' I say. Now that we're here, I'm hungry too, the tequila from last night causing my appetite to swell. And I don't even want to think about the sambuca.

Theo has reached the front of the queue. He scans the options, written on a blackboard in white chalk: pad krapow gai kai dow, which Lucas says is chicken mixed with chilli and Thai basil, served on a bed of rice with a fried egg. Massaman curry with rice. Plaa neung manow – Theo asks for us, and we're told this is fish with rice. Eventually, we play it safe and Theo just orders us four pad thais, prawn for me, chicken for Saskia, and beef for the others. The woman behind the stall gives a little laugh; perhaps she's used to tourists and their boring tastes. Her mouth is small, and her face creases as she smiles, her own private joke.

I watch as the same woman takes the money – cash only, the bills folded quickly into her palm – and scatters handfuls of chilli across the top of the pans, her eyes watering slightly now from the smoke, the blue hot heat of the flames relentless.

Theo pays. Nobody objects. We didn't really discuss how we were going to split things financially this trip. I guess we'll have to, at some point. He can't pay for everything: it's not fair. I make a mental note to talk to Lucas about it later, make sure we work it all out. I mustn't forget.

There are plastic yellow stools and small, low tables scattered on the street next to the stall and we sink into them gratefully. I pull my sunglasses down over my eyes – the sun is even brighter now than it was this morning – and twist some noodles up using the cutlery they gave us. They're delicious – salty and sweet at the same time. Theo shoves a wooden fork into his food and starts scooping great chunks of it into his mouth, barely pausing for breath.

'Man,' he says between mouthfuls, 'this shit is good. Nothing wrong with sticking to what you know – though this is better than any pad thai I've had back in Bermondsey.' He laughs.

'Anyone fancy a beer to wash it down?' Saskia asks, and Theo gives a little cheer, spraying a drop of saliva onto the table, where it glistens briefly then pops into nothing.

'Great minds,' he says, 'that's my girl!'

'I'll go,' she says immediately, glancing around. There's a corner shop opposite, in the far corner of the square, the neon lettering standing out above the bustle of the food stalls. Saskia abandons her plate of food, pushes back her stool in the dust and heads over. I watch as she walks away, her hips swaying in the purple trousers. She always looks so stylish.

'Someone should help her,' I say, and Lucas volunteers, tousling my hair as he stands up, his fingers pushing my headband out of place.

'Oi!' I say, straightening it, not wanting them to see my greasy hair.

'Your hair looks great,' Lucas says, as though reading my

mind, and I roll my eyes at the obvious lie, then blow him a kiss as he follows Saskia to the corner shop.

'You having fun, Hol?' Theo asks, when they've gone.

'Absolutely,' I say brightly, 'it's amazing, isn't it? Home feels a million miles away.'

'I quite fancy sampling something a bit more adventurous than pad thai while we're out here,' Theo says, nodding to the food stalls. 'Did you know they eat dogs in Thailand?'

'God, not for me,' I say, shivering. 'But be my guest. I'd be curious to know what it tastes like.'

'What d'you think of the hostel?' he asks me, shovelling more food into his mouth. 'I'm still a bit pissed off with the Omni. I could swear I made the booking.'

'I don't mind it, actually,' I say, thinking of the Excel spreadsheet, of our budget. 'Though I didn't sleep that well. I thought I heard people arguing in the night – did you hear anything?'

He shakes his head. 'Nope. Not a thing.'

'D'you think we *are* too old to stay in a place like that?' I ask him, spearing a prawn with my chopstick, driving the wood through the flesh. 'I guess it's set up for teenagers, you know. Travellers. Not two working couples on holiday.' I pause. 'But it is a lot cheaper than the Omni, isn't it?'

'Working couples,' he says, mimicking my words, though not unkindly. 'Thought the whole point of coming out here was to have a bit of fun, you know, reclaim our lost youth.' He ignores my comment about it being cheaper, and I wonder if he even heard, whether the thought of money and what this is all costing even registers in his mind.

He's grinning now, but I can feel the tension underneath, the edge of bitterness with which he says the last two words: *lost youth*. Out of all of us, Theo seems the most worried about getting older – he was the one who pushed forward with this trip, after we had the drunken idea for it over dinner last month. He was the one who made a fantasy a reality, who actually booked everything.

Theo's a management consultant in London now, whatever that means. I've known him almost two years, and never quite got to the bottom of it. I've asked Lucas, but I don't think he really knows either – we joke about it sometimes, lying in bed at night in my tiny Hackney flat with our legs tangled together, trying to imagine what Theo does day to day. 'I know what his *father* does,' Lucas says, 'he basically runs the banks. All right for some, isn't it?'

My job is easier to explain: marketing for a publishing house, promoting the books – mainly non-fiction, lately. Coffee table books, cookery books, lifestyle books – the kind that I take home and put on the shelves but never really read. Saskia works in administration at a law firm, a big, anonymous place with an intimidatingly large office. Lucas has been teaching ever since university – secondary school Biology. Neither Lucas nor I get paid much, to be fair, but we get by, and it's enough – though this will be our only holiday this year, and I know for a fact that Saskia and Theo have booked to go to the Maldives next month, for Valentine's Day.

'Let's have a vote on where to stay when the others get back,' Theo says, scraping his fork around the edge of the plate – he's finished his pad thai already.

There's a sudden sensation on my leg, a soft nudge, and I look down to see a little cat rubbing against my legs, a tabby with a thin, slightly bent tail.

'Aw, look at this little guy!' I say, bending down to stroke him – I love cats. He mewls quietly, and Theo laughs.

'He's after your pad thai, Holly. Don't be naïve!'

'Well, he's got good taste then. You've almost finished yours in about three minutes flat!' I tell him and he pulls a piggy face, puffing his cheeks out wide.

'You'd better finish yours before I come after that too.'

'I suppose we ought to line our stomachs if last night is anything to go by,' I say, reaching down and giving the cat a little bit of prawn, which he nips quickly from my outstretched fingers, his rough little tongue scraping against my skin. 'I didn't know you still had it in you with the tequila, Theo!'

'Your boyfriend is a bad influence,' he says, winking at me, and I laugh.

Both of us know it's the other way around.

'We come bearing goods!' Lucas is back, clutching a couple of cardboard packs of bottled Thai beer: *Chang*, reads the label, which also shows two little elephants facing each other. The green bottles glow in the sun and even with my sunglasses on, I have to squint to see Lucas's face, the light is so bright now. Saskia is following, a few steps behind, picking her way through the tourists. It feels like it's getting even busier here now.

Lucas sets the beers down on the small plastic table with a thud. Condensation slides down the sides, pools slowly underneath. Saskia cracks open a bottle, twisting the lid under her palm, and there is a wet hissing sound as the lid pops off.

'You OK?' I ask her, and she just nods, gives me a tight little smile.

'Yeah. Just finding it a bit overwhelming here – it's so busy, isn't it?'

'It's beautiful though,' I say, and it really is – the colours, the way the light hits the rainbow of umbrellas, the warm smiles of the vendors as they call out to one another across the stalls. Above us, the sky is azure, the sun a dazzling white orb, as perfect as a painting.

'This is the life, isn't it?' Lucas says, putting a hand on my knee, offering me a drink.

'It's amazing,' I say, taking a sip of beer, the cool tang of it welcome on my tongue. The little cat has disappeared from beneath the table and I look around to see where he's gone – I liked him – but he's nowhere to be seen. As I turn back to face the others, I have the odd, prickling sensation on the back of my neck that I had at the airport – as though someone is watching me – and I spin back around, wondering if it's a local, looking for tourists to sell to. I can't see anyone though – just the crowds swarming the stalls, and a young girl standing on her own, clutching a bottle of water, her narrow feet pointed together like those of a ballerina.

After a minute, I sit back on my stool, letting my shoulders slump, and close my eyes, just for a second – the combination of the sun and the beer is making me feel sleepy. I can hear the hiss and sizzle of the pad thai pans, the chatter and laughter of the other people in the market, the blaring of horns and the screeching of brakes on the main road. Somewhere in the background, someone is singing on the street, the voice low and unfamiliar. Behind us, a dog barks; there is something desperate in the sound of it, the animal striving for attention. I think about what Danni from the hostel said, her warning to be careful, and although I can't explain why, I feel as though I need to heed her advice. The city is pulsing around me, unfamiliar and strange, and the sound of the dog barking seems like it's getting louder and louder, more and more desperate.

'Holly! You look like you're a million miles away,' Lucas says, and I give myself a little shake, trying to brush the odd sensation off, telling myself I am just being silly. There's nothing to be afraid of here.

Chapter Eight

Lucas

He's finished his pad thai, though it congealed a bit in the heat when he went with Saskia to the corner shop to get the beers. Somehow, he's on his second bottle already, even though it's – he glances at his watch – shit, only twenty past twelve. Still, they are on holiday, after all, and it's helping him relax. Besides, Theo is on his third.

'So what are we thinking?' Theo says, his voice cutting through Lucas's thoughts. 'I think Saskia is keen for us to go to the nicer hotel tonight, you keen for that too, mate? Holly and I thought we ought to have a vote.'

Lucas shrugs, though inwardly, he knows what he'd prefer – to stay at the hostel. He and Holly had whispered about it last night, comparing the prices between Pho Hostel and the Omni Tower Hotel. But he doesn't want to be a downer, and he doesn't want Theo to think he's being tight.

'I'm easy, really. Whatever other people want to do.'

'Are you talking about moving tonight?' Saskia interrupts – she hadn't been paying attention, had been flicking through something on her phone – Instagram, probably. 'The hotel would be nice, baby. We can't stay at the hostel, really we can't. We haven't even got anywhere safe to put our passports.'

Lucas and Holly exchange glances, but Theo is already pulling out his phone.

He presses a few buttons and puts it to his ear. Lucas pushes the worry away, tips his head back, tilts back on his stool, looks up at the perfect blue sky. A plane glides across it, leaving a white stream in its wake, cutting a trail across his vision. They'll be OK, money-wise, eventually, won't they? They've got their spreadsheet to keep them in check. But he knows even as the thoughts occur to him that he's lying to himself. That he hasn't got enough money to get the kind of flat Holly wants. That he is in more trouble financially than he's been letting on – ever since three months ago, when the school he works for announced the cuts and he was forced to accept a reduced salary to keep his job. The memory of it comes back to him – the sense of shame, the harried look on the headmaster's face. It isn't his fault – but it is a problem, and it's the kind of problem he shouldn't be keeping from his long-term girlfriend. God, he's got to find a way to sort it out.

'You OK there, Lukey?' Saskia is smiling at him indulgently and Lucas suddenly feels embarrassed. He rights his stool, and runs a hand through his hair; it's damp with the heat already.

'Just relaxing,' he says, 'that allowed?' He's teasing her, and her eyes flash back at him, her lips curled around the top of her beer.

Holly is tipping her face up to the sun, letting the warmth play across her features. Her eyes are closed now, her long eyelashes brushing against her cheeks. She looks beautiful, if a bit tired – Lucas remembers her saying she didn't sleep very well at the hostel, so maybe the hotel will be good for her. He wants her to have a good time; she deserves it, they both do.

Theo still has his phone to his ear, clearly on hold with the hotel. Suddenly, Lucas feels a presence above them, momentarily blocking the sunlight, a shadow falling across the table, and looks up to find a street seller, a big bunch of slightly ragged roses in his hand.

'Beautiful flowers for beautiful ladies,' he says, smiling; Lucas sees he has a front tooth missing, a dark gap where the enamel should be.

'Ah, no thank you,' he says, holding up a palm, but the man simply smiles and pulls out a handful of fans from behind his back, little wooden hand-held ones, decorated in a pretty blue-and-pink flowery pattern.

'Ooh, they're nice!' Saskia says, reaching her hand out, and the man beams at her. Holly is clearly keen, too, and he ends up reaching into his pocket, buying them both one, handing the seller the baht reluctantly.

'You guys have to get a bit more savvy, we'll end up buying everything,' he says, and Saskia pulls a face at him, fanning herself with the new purchase. He looks away from them briefly, trying not to be annoyed – he can't let his worries about money affect the group, can he. It's not fair. He swallows, trying to bring back the calm, happy sensation he'd had moments earlier, but there is a slight sinking feeling in his stomach when he pictures the numbers in his bank account. Even Holly doesn't know how tight things are at the moment – primarily because he hasn't told her. She's so excited about the idea of buying somewhere together, and he's never been able to find the right time.

Theo is ending the call, grinning.

'All set,' he tells them, 'we're booked – for real this time – into the Omni for the next two nights. I even managed to get us upgraded, because of the "mix-up".' He does scare quotes with his fingers. 'Knew they'd come round to my way of thinking. So anyway, the rooms should be good.'

'My hero!' Saskia crows, pulling him towards her and giving him a sloppy kiss. Lucas sees Holly watching and reaches out a hand across the hot plastic table to her, enveloping her fingers in his palm.

'Are you feeling OK?' he asks her and she nods, smiles.

'I'm fine,' she says, 'thank you for the fan.' She squeezes his hand, and he feels guilty for being annoyed – it's not expensive, after all. He needs to lighten up a bit. 'That's great news about the hotel, Theo – really great. Thank you.'

'At your service,' he says, taking a sip of his beer, 'it'll be good to be somewhere proper. No more dorm rooms for this trip!'

'Exactly,' Saskia says, 'it's going to be perfect.' She blinks, once, twice, then looks over at the food stalls again, at the crowds of people, jostling into one another, haggling for fruit, selecting bunches of vegetables, tied together with string. Steam from the pans of meat rises into the air, dissipating into nothing, and Lucas sees her scanning the whole scene carefully, almost as though she's looking for something.

Or someone.

Chapter Nine

Holly

'I want to see the Buddha,' Saskia is saying, repeatedly. We've been sitting at the table in the food market for too long, drinking in the sunshine, and Lucas looks like he might be about to fall asleep now; his eyes are all droopy and he keeps yawning.

'Saskia's right,' I say, 'we need to get on, make the most of the day. We can actually just walk to Wat Pho temple, it's not far from here. That's where the famous statue of the Buddha is.' I reach around and rummage in my bag for the guidebook.

'Ooh, the guidebook's out, she means business,' Theo says, reaching over to try to take it out of my hands but I swat him away, focus on finding the right page.

'Here!' I say. 'Twenty minutes' walk, we can do that, easy. Come on.'

'Twenty minutes in this heat!' Lucas lets out a groan.

'Lucas!' I say prodding him. He's resting his elbows on the table with his head tipped onto one palm. 'We've been in the sun too long – come on, let's go and do something cultural. You know we'll regret it if we don't.'

'You're right,' Saskia says, 'come on, Holly, let's get these lazy boys up, or leave them here!' She jumps to her feet, suddenly energised, and I stand up too, pulling my bag onto my back where it sits uncomfortably, making me feel even hotter.

The boys groan and laugh and haul themselves off the plastic yellow stools, which are by now slippery with our sweat. It's boiling; I pull out my sun cream and plaster more across my face, reach up to do the back of Lucas's neck. He never remembers: I can see it reddening already, the skin beginning to burn. I've slathered it on myself; I always burn really badly if I don't. Me and my pale English skin.

We make our way out of the market, turning left into an alleyway of unfamiliar streets. A stall full of leather bags catches my eye, the brown, tan and red colours bleeding into one another, the tassels dangling, and next to it a stall full of silk scarves, flapping gently in the breeze. Saskia reaches out, runs her fingers over one of them, and I do too, the material soft between my fingers.

'You feeling OK?' I say to her – she seems a bit quiet, not quite her usual self. But she nods, looking straight ahead at where we're going, not turning to meet my eye.

'Of course,' she says eventually, 'I'm fine.' But when the stall seller comes out to greet us, she jumps as though she's been electrocuted, her whole body briefly seizing up.

'You seem a bit jumpy?' I ask her, but she shakes her head, tells me again that she's fine, and so I let the matter drop. After a minute or two, she pulls out her phone and begins filming the street as we walk, her thumb held down on the screen of her phone, lifting it up and down to show the breadth of the stalls.

We're passing a flower market, now, on the right; I see bundles of marigolds and carnations, jasmine and gypsophila, the scent of them carrying on the air towards us. There's a woman haggling for an orchid, her hand outstretched, her basket open and waiting for the vendor to give in. Lucas and Theo catch up with us, and Theo points us down a side street that I might not have noticed otherwise.

'You've still got the passports, haven't you, Holly?' Lucas says suddenly, and I swing my rucksack around to my front and feel for them in the pocket, my fingers touching the reassuring leather straight away.

'All good.' I give him a thumbs-up.

We round the final corner and suddenly, there it is – Wat Pho, magnificent in front of us, huge and glowing, so impressive that it momentarily pushes everything else from my mind.

Golden spires reach skywards, and I crane my neck to look up at them as we walk across the flagstones. It's so crowded at this time in the afternoon, we should have come early this morning, but still the beauty of the place is evident. Stone statues are dotted around the outside, and large oval flower-beds bursting with green leafy plants and bright purple flowers mark the entrance.

Pyramid-shaped structures rise up into the air, four or five times my height, and I step closer to one, touch the burning hot stone gently with my fingertips. The detail is incredible; my fingers skim the carvings, the red-and-white layers of it. The complex is much bigger than I thought – a brown wooden sign in the middle points us in the directions of the reclining Buddha, the Sala Karn Parien, the Phra Mondob, and an exhibition on the history of Wat Pho, the English words written in white paint underneath the Thai lettering. A group of American tourists are standing in front of the sign, drinking giant cups of Fanta and fanning themselves with the information leaflets; we sidestep them neatly, trying to figure out where to start.

A red door set in a beautiful white arch flanked by two stone emperors smiling benevolently is in front of us, and Saskia goes straight through, pulling her phone out of her pocket to take photos. I haven't actually taken any yet, though I'm sure she'll have more than enough for the whole group. Last year, she framed one of the four of us out for dinner; I put it up in my living room. Saskia had written our names on the back in her scrawly, loopy handwriting, plus the date and an inscription. *July 2023: the four of us.* I remember running my fingers over the words, relishing them. *The four of us.*

'We need to cover up a bit,' Lucas says, catching up with us and grabbing my elbow. I look around and realise that all the women have coverings over their bare shoulders, so Saskia and I quickly do the same, pulling patterned silk scarves from Theo's rucksack as he fumbles with his wallet, taking out enough baht to pay for entry for us all. Immediately, the scarf is stifling in the heat, and for a moment a rush of claustrophobia comes over me, but I push the feeling away, try to focus on my surroundings.

'This way to the Buddha!' Saskia says, pointing at one of the signs, and we follow her through a hexagonal courtyard surrounded by golden statues, standing guard atop red chests covered in black-and-gold detailing. There are information boards in the shade, lit by little green lamps, but the other three are ahead of me, none of them stopping to read. In the centre of the hexagon is an enormous blue-and-gold structure, with tiled steps leading up to another spire that towers above us all.

'God, it's beautiful,' Saskia is saying, filming it on her phone as we go, no doubt ready for uploading to Instagram as soon as humanly possible. I only use Twitter and Instagram for work, and I deleted Facebook a while ago; it was too much to keep up with – in the office, we use it all the time for marketing books, but I've got no desire to see random updates from the people I went to school with any more. Still, this place is nothing if not photogenic. I'll have to get Saskia to send me the pics, so I can print some for my wall.

'It really is incredible,' I murmur, and for a moment my whole body relaxes. There is a sense of peace here, of calm, and although it's quite noisy due to the constant chatter of people around us, the sound of their voices feels oddly soothing. I can hear a range of languages – flutters of Mandarin, an American twang, a group of Italian students complaining about the heat.

'Wow.' Saskia stops short as we turn the corner and see the reclining Buddha, surrounded by people – a huge golden statue of around fifteen metres high. 'It's awesome,' she breathes, and I stare up at it, feeling small, smaller, as if I could sink down into the ground. The Buddha's face looks down at us, with a long, sloping nose, perfect curving lips, hooded eyes that gaze at the bustling tourists passively, calmly. The light is glinting off the statue's face, casting a golden glow around us, and I feel Lucas come to stand beside me, the soft touch of his hand at my waist, his arm snaking around me.

'Gorgeous, isn't it?' I say brightly. He nods, kisses me on the top of the head, bends his mouth to my ear. He smells faintly of beer and pad thai, and I nestle into him.

'No PDA in the temple!' Theo and Saskia have snuck up behind us and I giggle, move away from Luke.

'Honestly, you guys. Inappropriate!' Theo says, and for a moment the four of us laugh together before we are shushed by a middle-aged couple who give us a very dirty look.

Beside us, a gaggle of Americans are taking selfies, crowding together in front of the Buddha, their smiles white and wide.

One of them, a bit taller than the rest with thick dark hair, steps away from the group and comes straight towards us. For a moment, Saskia looks stricken, and I wonder if he's about to tell us off for doing something wrong, but he's just holding out a phone, asking us to take a picture of him and his girlfriend.

'D'you mind?'

'Of course not,' I say, putting my bag down and taking the phone from him, and the girl next to him puts her hand on her hip, smiling into the camera. I take a few snaps, and when I'm done Saskia has disappeared from beside me. I spin around, but the space behind me is empty – the boys have wandered off too.

'Lost your friends?' the American says, and I smile, shrug. 'It happens. They'll be around somewhere.'

'What d'you think of the Buddha?' he asks me, and I nod, tell him I think it's amazing. His girlfriend has wandered off to the left with the rest of their friends but he stays next to me, hovering, somehow uncomfortably close.

'Are you enjoying Thailand?' he asks, stepping even closer, and automatically I move backwards, putting space between us, not wanting him to come any nearer.

'Sorry, I need to find my friends,' I say quickly, and I move away, not wanting to get into awkward conversation, not wanting the heat of his attention. Perhaps he's just being friendly, but something about him makes me feel uncomfortable. I go into the adjoining room in which a statue of another Buddha, much smaller and with part of its nose missing, stands inside a glass case. My heart feels like it's beating a tiny bit faster and I force myself to take a couple of deep breaths, irritated that a stupid tourist could unsettle me like that.

'There you are.' The others reappear in the doorway that

leads out to a sunny courtyard, and I wave at them, noticing that Saskia looks a little pale.

'I'm feeling a bit sick, sorry guys,' she says, suddenly. 'I think it's just the heat, it was so crowded in there.'

'Poor you,' Lucas says, 'do you want some water?'

'I'm so sorry, I think I just need to go back outside,' she says. 'I'll meet you when you're done, shall I? I'll just go and get some air.'

She turns on her heel before we can stop her and heads into the courtyard, disappears from view.

I stare after her for a second or two, wondering what's the matter.

'Shall I go with her? Make sure she's OK?' I ask the others, and Theo shrugs.

'Up to you. I'm sure she's fine.'

I feel another prickle on the back of my neck as she vanishes, as though someone is watching, but when I turn around, there's just the same group of Americans, the tall guy and his girlfriend. He catches my eye and smiles, and it's just then that I realise – I don't have my bag. My bag is missing. It's gone.

Chapter Ten

Lucas

'Shit!' Holly grabs his arm, her fingers digging into his flesh. 'My bag, Lucas, my little rucksack. I put it down in the other room.'

She's panicking, now, and he puts both hands on her shoulders, trying to keep her calm.

'Hey, hey, don't worry, we'll find it. When did you last have it? Your little brown one?'

She nods. 'Yes, yes – I think I put it down when I took that guy's photo. Back near the Buddha.'

'OK,' Lucas says, 'let's head back that way – Theo, you coming? Holly thinks she's lost her bag.'

He looks up from reading a plaque on the wall. 'Er – yeah, can do. I'm sure it'll still be there.'

'Never mind.' Lucas leaves him to it – there's no point disrupting all of their days, after all, and he can tell his mate doesn't really want to retrace their steps. He and Holly head back into the main room of the temple, where the Buddha gazes serenely down at them, and Holly lets out a little wail when there is no sign of the rucksack in the spot where she left it.

'God, how could I be so stupid? I just put it down for like two minutes, and then Saskia disappeared, and I was looking for her, and there was that creepy American guy – oh God, Luke, what a moron.' She buries her head in her hands and Lucas sighs, pulls her close to him and strokes her hair.

'What was in it? And what creepy American guy?'

She looks up, sniffs. 'Oh, no one, just some tourist who stood too close to me. In my bag – God, my phone, my charger, my sun cream – I think some money, too, though I didn't bring my whole wallet, thank God. And – oh my God – the passports, all four of them.'

'Shit. OK,' says Lucas, trying to think clearly, 'let's go see if there's a lost property, or an information desk, or something. Someone might have handed it in?'

They hold hands and retrace their steps silently, back to the entrance, back out into the sunshine. There's a welcome desk with a slightly bored-looking woman behind it, and they approach, Holly's face taut with anxiety.

Lucas opens with 'Do you speak English?' and the woman nods, as though she is used to this question, raises her eyebrows.

'Great,' says Lucas, 'sorry, we— My girlfriend has lost her bag. Her rucksack.' He gestures idiotically to Holly's back, forming a hump with his fingers, wishing he wasn't being such a typical example of a Brit abroad.

'I left it in the main room, the one with the Buddha,' Holly says. She's speaking very fast and Lucas can see the beginnings of an angry red rash creeping up her neck, the one she gets if she's anxious or upset. The blotches are starting to stand out on her pale skin.

'A bag?' the woman repeats and Lucas nods, trying not to think about the fact that Holly's money is in there, and that if they've lost all four of their passports, it's going to absolutely ruin the trip. His mind races – they'd have to go to the British Embassy, wouldn't they? Explain what's happened. He's sure they'd work it out, but it would mean disrupting their plans entirely, and Theo and Saskia won't be happy either.

'It's a brown leather rucksack,' Holly says, 'it has our passports, my phone, everything. Please, has anyone handed it in?'

The woman holds up a hand as if to stem the flow of words coming from Holly's mouth, and Lucas places a hand on her arm.

'It'll be all right,' he says, 'we'll find it, I promise.'

Chapter Eleven

Saskia

I don't know what came over me in the temple. It was that guy, the tall one, the way he came towards us. I suddenly had a flashback, a bad one, and then I had to get away. It felt as though the walls were closing in on me, getting closer and closer; my throat felt like it was getting really tight. I know I'm just being silly, that all of that was so long ago, but that moment on the first night when I thought I saw – *him* – well, it's just brought it all back, I suppose. I had to get outside, get away; I didn't want Theo wondering what was wrong.

I'm sat outside now, in the courtyard at the back, on a low stone wall that surrounds a big bank of flowers. They're beautiful – pinks and purples – and beyond them is a row of orange trees, the little orbs peeking out from between the luscious green leaves. There are still so many people, even out here, endless tourists holding up selfie sticks and beaming into their cameras, a constant background chatter of people and heat and noise. A blonde woman is dropping coins into a little bronze bowl a few metres in front of me, making a wish, and for a second I wish I was her, wish that I could have another life, another past, one that I didn't have to hide.

But I don't. I have this life, with Theo, with my friends, and I've worked hard to build it. The past is in the past, and that's where it's going to stay.

'Water?' A man with a little cart approaches me. He's selling little bottles of water and actually I do want one, I realise how thirsty I am. But I haven't got any money – Theo's paying for us both, he's got all the cash, and the joint-account bank card.

'Sorry,' I say, spreading out my hands helplessly. 'No money. No cash.' I pat my pockets and shrug, and he wanders off immediately, the little bottles bobbing away from me. My mouth feels very dry.

'Saskia, there you are.' Theo appears in front of me. 'How are you feeling now? The others have vanished, don't know where they've got to. Oof.' He sits down beside me, stretches his long, tanned legs out in front of us. I look at the little golden hairs, his red-and-white leather shoes. He puts an arm around me, lazily, and I rest my head on his shoulder, feel the soft thrum of his heartbeat against my body.

'I'm a bit temple-d out now, I reckon,' he says, 'what about you? Are you still feeling sick?'

'I'm OK,' I say, 'better now that you're here.'

He twists his head, plants a kiss on the top of mine. 'It's probably just the heat, I reckon. I was thinking we ought to go find a swimming pool, if you're up for it? They have some great spas here. You could even get a massage.'

The thought of this does cheer me up slightly; my shoulders feel a bit achy from the tension, and the idea of immersing myself in a pool is glorious given how hot the sun is on the top of my head.

'That sounds great actually,' I tell him, 'shall we go find the others?'

'Sure,' he says easily, getting to his feet and stretching down a hand to help me up, 'come on then, Mrs Sanderson.'

He winks at me, and I feel a rush of love towards him, towards my new name, my new life. Every time I look at him, it cements my decision. I can never tell Theo what happened. Never, ever, for as long as I live.

Chapter Twelve

Holly

I can tell by the look on the woman's face that it's not good news. She disappeared after we described the bag to her, presumably to go look in their lost property pile, but returns empty-handed, with a pitying expression as she meets my eye.

'Sorry, miss,' she says, 'nothing given to us. No bags. Nothing.'

'Are you sure?' I say desperately, but she is shaking her head, her eyes already sliding past us to the next people in the queue, who have been waiting impatiently behind us for the last five minutes, sighing and tutting under their breath.

Lucas puts a hand on my shoulder, steers me to one side and we look at each other, his dark eyes clouded with concern.

'Oh my God,' I say, 'I just can't believe it, how could I have been so stupid! It's the first day and I've lost everything – all our passports, Lucas! What the hell are we going to do?'

'Let's just not panic,' he says, but I can tell he doesn't really have a plan, doesn't have the answers.

'My phone's in there too, everything,' I wail – I can hear my voice becoming whiny and high-pitched but I don't care, all I care about is getting my bag back. I picture someone rummaging through it, putting their hands all over my things, seeing the picture of Lucas and me on the background of my phone, sneering as they pull my credit card out from the case. I ought to phone and cancel it, I'll have to use Lucas's mobile. I try to think what the guidebook said to do if you lose your passport, where to go, but my brain feels fogged with worry. I'm furious with myself for being so careless, on the first day, too. I've ruined the trip for everyone.

We wander slightly aimlessly away from the information desk, come to a stop under an orange tree out in the front courtyard. The sun is so bright, it's dazzling, and I want so badly for us to have a nice time but how can we now that this has happened? I picture myself putting my bag down on the ground, taking the American man's phone to snap the pictures of him and his girlfriend, then turning round, getting distracted because Saskia wasn't there. I walked away without it, didn't I?

'We're going to have to go tell the others,' Lucas says, pulling out his phone, but just as he does so I hear a shout, and spin around to see a guy jogging up behind us, clad in a white T-shirt and black shorts. He's got a bottle of water in one hand, and in the other—

'My bag!' I cry out, and the man comes to a halt in front of us, bends over slightly, clearly out of breath.

'You're Holly Appleby, right?'

'Yes!'

'I found your bag.' He's smiling at us both, his blue eyes sparkling – clearly, he knows how much this means to me. I could hug him.

'Thank you so much, thank you so so much,' I say breathlessly, taking it from him and immediately opening the pockets, feeling for our passports, my phone. It's all there.

'Don't worry, I didn't take anything,' he says, grinning. 'I just looked at your passports to try to find your names. Glad I found you.'

'Seriously, mate, you're a hero,' Lucas says, clapping him on the back. He looks incredibly relieved, and I feel almost weak with the sensation. I'm not letting my bag out of my sight again.

'Where did you find it?' I ask him, and he points back inside the temple. 'Picked it up off the ground, near the Buddha. I did ask around but it didn't belong to anyone who was still close by. I was going to hand it in to reception, but they told me you'd just been, that you'd walked off this way.'

'Well,' I say, 'you're a star, thank you. I'm very grateful. God, I'm such an idiot, walking off like that without it.' I can feel myself blushing, and look away from him, down at the floor. He's nodding, grinning at us both, spreading his hands.

'It's nothing. These things happen.'

'Can we buy you a drink or something, to say thank you?' Lucas asks, and the guy holds up his hands, shaking his head.

'No need, really. I'm just glad I could help. I lost my entire suitcase once, on a trip to Jordan. Total nightmare. I know how easily it can be done.'

'Well, truly, thank you,' I say, 'you've literally saved my life.'

He laughs, catches my eye again, and I feel the heat rise to my cheeks. There's something about him – he's not conventionally attractive, per se – he's got dark hair, shaven closely to his head, and he's quite thick set, with startling blue eyes that seem to pierce right through you. He reaches out to shake Lucas's hand and I notice how wide his hands are, imagine one engulfing my own. He looks like the type of person it would be good to have around, I suppose.

'Caleb,' he says, 'good to meet you both. And hey, enjoy

the rest of your trip. Bangkok is amazing.' He pauses. 'Where you guys staying? Round here?'

'We've actually been in a hostel,' Lucas says, 'but tonight we're moving to a hotel.'

He wolf-whistles, the sound hissing through his front teeth. 'Sounds like an upgrade. Very nice.'

There's a tiny pause as we stare at each other, and then he grins again, raises a hand in the air and turns on his heel.

'Good to meet you, Holly and Lucas. Behave yourselves in Bangkok.' He winks, and then he's gone, disappearing back into the crowds around the temple, his close-cropped hair bobbing away into the background.

'Thank Christ for that,' I say to Lucas.

'Let's just double-check nothing's missing,' he says, and we go sit down on a bench to the side of the courtyard, pull open the rucksack and take out item by item. My phone is here – I've a missed call from Theo, and a message from my mum, asking if I'm having a good time. The charger is here too, and my water bottle, and all of our passports. I prise my phone case off, expecting to see the money and my credit card tucked away, but they're not there.

'Oh,' I say, 'my money's gone. And my bank card.'

Lucas looks surprised. 'Really?'

'Do you think he took them?'

I feel stupid, thinking of him smiling at us. He seemed so genuine, didn't he? And why bother taking the cash but not taking the phone, not taking anything else?

'I guess someone else could have taken it before he picked up the bag,' I say, feebly, and Lucas nods, shrugs.

'Yeah, of course. Well, look. Just cancel your card, and never mind about the cash. It wasn't much, was it?'

'No,' I say, swallowing, 'but Lucas – it's not as if we have much anyway, is it. Do you think we ought to speak to Theo, about the hotel tonight? We could just be honest with them, say we need something cheaper.'

His jaw hardens, sets in a firm, straight line.

'No,' he says, 'no need to do that. Let's just stick to the plan, OK? It'll be fine. Come on,' he gets to his feet, 'let's go find them. Get out of here.' He jumps to his feet. 'Look, call your bank, cancel your card like I said. You don't want anyone using it first.'

Chapter Thirteen

Lucas

God, losing more money is the last thing they needed, but he's trying hard not to mind. It isn't Holly's fault she lost her bag – well, OK, it is, but she didn't mean to – and the main thing is they've got their passports back. He really wasn't fancying a trip to the embassy.

He calls Theo once Holly's finished speaking to the bank, and the four of them reconvene outside the main entrance to the temple. It's almost four o'clock, but the sun is still burning hot, and the atmosphere feels slightly tenser than it did earlier – what with Saskia feeling sick and Holly losing her bag, it hasn't been quite the perfect first day he'd originally hoped for. Still, they're back together now, aren't they. They can still have a good evening.

'So, Theo and I were thinking about going to a spa,' Saskia says. 'What do you guys think?'

Holly's face brightens. She's clutching her rucksack to her chest, like it's a baby, her wrists looped through the handles as though she wants to have it as close to her as possible.

'That sounds great actually,' she says, 'I'd like a de-stress. Is there one you have in mind?'

'There's a place called the Dahra Thai Spa, not far from

here,' Theo says, looking down at his phone, 'we could get a tuk-tuk over, if you're tired of walking?'

'Good plan,' Saskia says, 'my feet are killing me already. We've only done one morning!'

There is a row of tuk-tuk drivers waiting outside, and Theo haggles adeptly with two of them, getting the price reduced by a third. Lucas is impressed, and the four of them clamber into the two carts, he and Holly in the first and Saskia and Theo in the second.

Their knees press against each other's in the back, and Lucas tries to put his arm around Holly but fails. The space is too cramped, so in the end they both sit in silence, their faces turned towards the open sides of the cycle, watching Bangkok roar past in a blur of colour and heat and sound.

Their driver weaves deftly in and out of the traffic and Lucas grits his teeth as they narrowly avoid a yellow taxi. Fumes drift towards him, making him feel a bit sick.

'You OK?' he asks Holly after ten minutes of silence between them, and she nods, gives him a wan little smile. She's upset about losing the money, he knows she is, and cross with herself for being careless in the first place. At least nobody had used her card yet, though – the bank had been able to cancel it quickly, no harm done. There'll be a new one waiting on the doormat when she gets back to London. Still, he can tell the experience has shaken her a bit.

Lucas is relieved when their tuk-tuk driver pulls up outside a large, low white building with wooden shutters, the words 'Dahra Thai Spa' inked in red font on the sign outside. Lucas hands their driver the right amount of money, then feels guilty and fumbles for a few more notes – even though he's acutely aware of how little cash he has at the moment. The driver's smile is wide, and Lucas watches as he drives off, strong, wiry arms turning the steering wheel gently from side to side in time to his music, disappearing into the smog in the distance.

'All right,' Theo says, jumping down from their tuk-tuk and reaching out a hand to Saskia, 'come on then, you lot. Let's go get massaged!'

Chapter Fourteen

Saskia

Inside the spa, I instantly feel calmer. It's darker, and cooler, for one thing, and we're greeted at the front desk by two women, smiling serenely, their soft pink lipstick and French manicured nails somehow comforting after the hustle and bustle of the street outside. There's music playing – panpipes, I think, a repetitive, calming tune, and the air smells of incense – nag champa, or something similar.

'Welcome to Dahra Thai Spa,' the younger looking of the two women says. 'Do you have a booking?'

'No reservation,' Theo says, taking control again, 'but we'd like to book in, if possible?'

I have a sudden worry that they'll be booked up, but she just nods, smiles, runs her finger down the sheet of paper in front of her. There's a bowl of rose petals on the desk, and to the right, there's a fountain, a steady little stream of water running softly in the background.

'Here is our list of treatments,' she says, and hands me a leaflet, emblazoned with the spa's logo, two hands clasped around a lotus flower.

'Wow,' Holly says, looking over my shoulder, 'massage

therapies, herbal treatments, body scrubs, facials . . . What are you going to go for?'

'I think I just want a massage,' I say – I want something to ease the tension in my shoulders, make me feel the way I did before that first night in the hostel, before the memories started to come back. I want to feel like my old self again.

We each choose a treatment – Theo and I both opt for massages, but Lucas wants a body scrub and Holly decides to get a facial – and Holly and I are led upstairs by another woman, a beautiful Thai lady with swept-back dark hair and shiny red fingernails. She's wearing white sandals which clack on the stairs as she leads us up, to where a large room has several doors leading off the side of it. She tells us the men will go to another part of the spa, that they keep the male and female areas separate.

'Please, get changed in here,' she tells me, gesturing to a door on the left, and I glance at Holly.

'I think we're having them separately.' She shrugs, and the Thai lady gently puts a hand on my back, almost pushing me inside the room in front of us. There's a white dressing gown hung on the back of the door, and a pair of thin white slippers, plus a locker which presumably is for my clothes. I look at myself in the mirror as I undress, at the narrow bones of my hips, the slight round of my tummy. There's an old scar on my abdomen, white now, but still visible, and I run my finger over it carefully, then cover it with the flat of my hand, as though by hiding it, I can pretend it doesn't exist.

The dressing gown is too big for me, but the soft folds of it feel comforting, cosy. The Thai lady knocks on the door, then leads me into another room, where a mattress is laid out flat on the floor. The lighting is dim – two candles are on either side of the bed, and there's the sound of rainwater, soft and mesmerising in the background. It smells nice, too, the candles giving off a floral scent.

'Please, lie down on your front,' she tells me, after taking off my gown, and I do as she says, obediently sinking into the mattress. She covers me with a towel, sweeps the hair off the back of my neck.

'Where are you from?' she asks me, haltingly – I sense her English isn't as good as the woman's downstairs.

'London,' I reply, my voice slightly muffled by the mattress; I have to shift my head slightly to be able to speak. She doesn't say anything else, just begins by rubbing my left foot, her hands slick with some sort of oil. It feels amazing – her hands are soft yet sturdy, and I can feel my body relaxing as she works her way up, kneading my back, ironing out the kinks in my muscles. I've taken my watch off, so I don't know what time it is, but after a little while I can feel her standing up, even though my eyes are closed; the weight of her moving off the mattress. Then there is the click of the door opening, a small sliver of light that I can see from behind my eyelids, and then nothing – I'm alone.

It's strange how the energy changes when you're alone in a room. For a moment or two, I lie there, content, listening to the sound of the simulated rainfall, trying to clear my mind like they tell you to in meditation – not something I've ever been particularly good at, to be honest. I wonder where Theo is, if his masseuse is as good as mine. I wish we could've had them in the same room, it would've been fun – romantic, even. After a little longer, I begin to wonder where she is, and the click of the door opening reassures me. I twist my head slightly, open my eyes, expecting to see her shiny white sandals, the flash of red toenails, but instead, I see another pair of feet entirely.

Someone else has come into my room.

Chapter Fifteen

Holly

I'm halfway through my facial when I hear the scream. High-pitched, shrill – and definitely Saskia. I jolt upwards in my chair, and the beauty therapist jerks backwards in shock – she'd just finished placing some rose petals on my cheeks, and my skin is shiny with cream.

'Sorry!' I say. 'I think that was my friend – that scream, did you hear it?'

She stares at me, then says something in Thai, something I don't understand. I'm wearing a dressing gown but I get up and open the door of the treatment room, searching for signs that something is wrong. But everything looks normal – the other doors are closed, and the soft, gentle piping of the music is still going, at odds with the adrenaline that is pulsing through my body.

I'm sure I heard someone scream.

My phone is in my bag, which is in the room – God, I've let it out of my sight again – but as I glance wildly around, one of the side doors opens and Saskia rushes out. She's wearing a white dressing gown but it's flapping apart, exposing her naked torso, and her feet are bare.

'Saskia!' I say. 'Are you OK? What's the matter?'

She's gulping for breath, as though she can't get enough air, and I forget about my bag and rush over to her, put my arms out. She hurtles into them, and I feel her shuddering against me, her tears beginning to wet my shoulder.

'I – I,' she says, but I can't understand her, she's breathing too fast, too hard.

'Come and sit down,' I say, 'tell me what happened.' Behind us, the Thai woman who was giving me the facial is hovering, her expression one of concern, her hands still oily with the stuff she was putting on my face.

We sit down in the room with my bag and the beauty therapist disappears, reappearing moments later with a glass of water for Saskia, which she takes gratefully, her hand shaking.

'What's going on?' I say. 'Please, Sask, you're scaring me.'

She turns towards me, looks me dead in the eye. 'Someone came into my room, Holly. A stranger. A man. He— ' She bows her head, and I feel cold dread running through me.

'Did he – did he hurt you, Sask?'

She shakes her head, clenches her fists in her lap, as though trying to get control of herself, her emotions.

'No,' she says, 'no, he didn't hurt me. But he came into the room, he shut the door, said something to me in Thai. I didn't understand – and then when I sat up, he shouted at me – it was so scary, Hol, I didn't know what was going on, and I felt so . . .' She gestures down at herself, naked underneath the robe, and I feel a wave of sympathy towards her.

'Ssh, it's OK, it's OK,' I tell her, rubbing her back. She feels small under my fingertips, somehow fragile, like a little broken bird.

'You're fine now,' I repeat, 'you're fine.'

'I'm sorry,' she says, 'God, I'm so embarrassed. But I freaked out, you know. I didn't know who he was – I thought – I don't know what I thought.'

I frown. She seems genuinely distraught, and I wonder why she's quite so on edge. I mean, it probably would be a bit confusing if someone came in like that, but he probably worked here, didn't he?

'I understand,' I say, 'it was just a shock, I suppose. A bit of a panic attack, maybe.'

She nods, rests her head wearily on my shoulder. 'Sorry, Hol. Don't tell the boys, will you? Not that they've come leaping to my defence.' She half laughs, wipes her nose with the back of her hand. 'God, sorry, I've completely interrupted your facial.'

'It's fine,' I say, 'don't worry about it, silly. The main thing is that you're OK. You nearly gave me a heart attack with that scream. I thought something bad had happened.'

I regret the words the moment they're out of my mouth, and I see her freeze slightly, her eyes slightly narrowing.

'I mean,' I say, 'something bad did happen, sorry, of course. But I – you know what I mean.'

'Of course,' she says, but there is something a little cooler in her tone, now, and she stands up, ties her robe around her tightly.

'I'm going to go get dressed,' she says. 'I'll see you back downstairs when you've finished your treatment. Sorry again, Holly.'

I put my arm out to try to stop her, then let it fall to my side. Maybe it's better for her to be alone for a minute, to calm down. The beauty therapist is raising her eyebrows at me, and I can feel the cream tightening on my face, so I tip my head back, allow her to carry on. We've paid for it, after all.

Chapter Sixteen

Saskia

Holly thinks I'm a freak, I can tell. But the sensation of the man being in my room was so visceral, so scary – it brought back memories. Unhappy ones. It was something about my lying there on the bed, without my clothes, and him towering over me – that made me feel so unbearably vulnerable. It was as though my body just went into flight or fight mode, as though I lost control of my rational mind, my senses. All I could think about was getting away from him, getting out of that room.

I get changed slowly, carefully, pulling my top and harem pants back on, sliding my feet back into my dusty sandals and dropping the dressing gown and slippers into the large wicker basket in the corner of the changing room. As I slide my hand into the pocket of my trousers, searching for my phone, my fingers reach something else – a piece of paper. I pull it out, figuring it must be a receipt for something that I don't remember buying, but it isn't. It's a little white scrap, it looks like it's been torn out of a notebook. And scrawled across it in red Biro are four words, words that fill my heart with ice.

FANCY A GAME, SASKIA?

I drop the paper as if it's red hot, and it spirals to the floor, landing on the grey tiles soundlessly. I step back from it, as though it might explode, my heart hammering in my chest. I shove my hands back into my pockets and turn them inside out, checking in case there is anything else, but it's just the note, the note that I definitely didn't put there, the note I've never seen before in my life. With trembling fingers, I pick it up again, smooth it out, staring at the blood-red capitals. I know whose writing this is, whose writing it must be. But I don't want to know. I don't want this to be happening. I never wanted to hear those words again in my life. *FANCY A GAME, SASKIA?*

It's what he always used to say. Right before we did it. Which means he's here, in Bangkok, and that I wasn't imagining things. I wasn't imagining things at all.

*

They give me a refund on the front desk, mainly because there's a very sheepish-looking Thai cleaner standing there next to reception, clearly explaining what happened – that he'd come into my room when the masseuse was getting more oil, thinking he was supposed to start cleaning, change the mattress. He'd only shouted at me out of surprise because of the way I got up from the bed – he was trying to reassure me. Apparently.

The receptionist translates all of this for me into rapid English, then apologises profusely and hands me back the full amount in baht, her manicured nails brushing against my palm.

'We are so sorry,' she tells me, and I nod, feeling too exhausted to do anything else. The cleaner wears a hangdog expression, and I try to force a smile at him, convey the fact that I understand it was an honest mistake.

What isn't an honest mistake is the note currently burning a hole in my pocket.

The others don't emerge for another twenty minutes or so, and I decide to wait outside in the street, not wanting to endure the receptionist's apologetic smiles any longer. It's darker now, and I blink – it feels as though we've been inside the spa for hours, even though I didn't even finish my treatment. All I can think about is the note – how it could be him, how he could have put it there, whether I really am going crazy after all this time. Unless— I stand still on the street, listening to the roar of the traffic. This isn't one of the others playing some sort of trick on me, is it?

I dismiss the thought as quickly as it came – none of them could know that that was the phrase he used to use, could they? I've never told anybody, not even Theo. How could I?

If I told anyone, it would destroy my entire life.

Chapter Seventeen

Lucas

The sky when they emerge from the spa is beautiful. The sun is setting, and streaks of red, pink and orange line the sky, infiltrated with purple clouds, as though the whole city is bathing in a pool of molten lava. It actually takes his breath away, momentarily – it feels so far from his small London flat, from the dull English skies where the darkness seems to creep inside the houses, where the office blocks of the city rise up around you like a prison. Here, he feels freer, easier, and the sky is never-ending, luminous. Magic.

Saskia's already outside when they come out, but she doesn't look very relaxed. Theo on the other hand has had the time of his life – he nudges Lucas discreetly on the way out, tells him how hot the woman who massaged him was. Lucas grins back, but it makes him a little bit uncomfortable. Holly's face does look glowy, so he supposes the facial worked – to be honest, he's not entirely sure what a facial is supposed to do, but he hopes it's had the desired effect.

Holly links Saskia's arm the minute they get outside, and the pair of them walk off ahead of him and Theo, heading back in the direction of the hostel. They've agreed to go get their bags, then go over to the Omni Tower Hotel, where they're now booked in for the next two nights.

'My shoulders feel amazing,' Theo is saying, 'she really went to town on them. God, wouldn't it be great if you could just get a massage every day, before work? It'd make getting up in the morning a whole lot easier. Especially if the masseuse looked like that.' He winks at Lucas, sniggers. Theo has always had this streak to him, Lucas thinks, ever since they were young, at university. He'd never do anything – God, no, he loves Saskia, and he's a good guy – but there is this strange lewdness that comes over him at times, and Lucas tries for the most part to ignore it.

'We thought we'd lost Holly's bag earlier,' he says, trying to change the subject. 'She left it in the temple. Luckily, some guy found it, ran up to us just as we were about to come and find you.'

'Oh shit, really,' Theo says, but Lucas can tell he isn't really listening, he's looking at his phone, trying to make the GPS work.

'My phone's not working properly, is yours, mate?'

Lucas pulls out his phone, surprised to see he's got one text message – nobody ever texts these days, it's all WhatsApp or email. He opens it, then feels his stomach drop – it's a text from HSBC, letting him know that he's in his overdraft, that interest will be charged from midnight tonight. Fuck. He really can't afford for this to keep happening. He's already maxed out on his credit card, and now his current account is empty too.

'Mate?' Theo is looking at him expectantly and Lucas quickly closes down the messaging app, navigates to Google Maps, trying not to think about how much phone data he will be using, about the bill from Vodafone that will surely come in as soon as they get home.

'This way,' he says, pointing to the right, 'we want to head north, I think. Back past the market.'

'Oh apparently it's pretty cool at night,' Theo says, peering over to check that what Lucas is saying is correct. 'Shall we walk back through, check it out?'

'Sure,' he says, 'whatever you want, man. I'm easy.' As long as he doesn't have to spend any more money he is, anyway.

Chapter Eighteen

Holly

The boys want to go back through the market square, and they're right – it's got a different vibe in the evening. The sun is just about to dip below the horizon, now, and it feels as though while some of the food stalls have closed, others have opened up – sellers have laid out their wares on the ground, piles of electronics, DVDs and even old VHS tapes, and little souvenirs, glittering golden elephants and light-up wands that they wave at us while we approach. A woman beckons us towards her, she's laid out a row of tarot cards on the ground, and my eye is drawn to them, the black-inked pictures depicting the various forms of fate.

'I can tell you your fortune,' she says to me, as I walk past, and for a brief moment, I feel tempted. What would it be like to know exactly what lay in store for you, I wonder. To know how life was going to turn out, for better or for worse. Would it help? Or would it be unbearable – if you knew something terrible was about to happen, and you weren't able to stop it?

Saskia doesn't seem to have noticed the tarot reader – she's marching up ahead of us, clearly eager to get back to the hostel. I've tried to talk to her since we got out of the spa, but she just says she doesn't want to talk about it, that she's sorry for ruining my facial.

'It doesn't matter about the facial, I just want to make sure you're OK,' I keep saying to her, but she just nods and tells me she's fine, and in the end I leave it. Maybe she's had panic attacks before – I don't know. Lucas has never mentioned it, but perhaps it's not the sort of thing he and Theo would discuss. Surely she has told Theo, though. I hope so, for her sake. Neither of the boys have mentioned it – they can't have heard her scream, if they were on the other side of the spa.

We turn off the main square, back through the maze of side streets, and Theo and Lucas go up ahead, following the directions on Lucas's phone. My skin feels tight and a bit odd from the facial, as though it's a little sore, and I'm looking forward to getting to the Omni, now, washing it in the cool water and putting my usual moisturiser back on. Maybe I don't react well to whatever the Thai lady used on my skin. Or maybe it was left on too long when I was trying to console Saskia.

Back at the hostel, we traipse back up to the dorm room. The other bed has been made, and all evidence of the other person has gone – the discarded bottle, the phone charger, all of it disappeared.

'Looks like we'd have had it to ourselves after all,' Lucas says, wryly.

'I'd still rather move,' Saskia says, quickly, and Theo nods. 'Of course.'

We gather up our things, shoving them quickly into our bags and suitcases, and it's as I'm shutting my case that I see it. There's a photograph, taped to the locker where we originally stored our passports, before the padlock snapped. It looks like it's been torn from a newspaper, and stuck to the scratched red metal of the locker with Sellotape. I frown.

'What's that?'

Theo notices it too, and goes across, pulling it off the locker in one swift movement.

'Huh. Weird.'

All of us gather around him, peering over his shoulder. The photo is faded, as though it's quite old, but it's discernible as a dark-haired man, wearing a suit. His face, however, is scratched out – quite harshly, too, as though someone has taken the time to really scrape an implement across his features, leaving just a white messy space where his expression should be.

'Looks like it's been clipped from a paper?' Lucas says. 'How weird.'

'Probably some prank,' Theo says, dismissing it, handing it to Saskia who has her hand outstretched, wanting to see. I stare at it with her. I can't help but feel a bit unnerved – there's something sinister about the fact that we cannot see his face, but that someone has left it here, in this room that only the four of us are occupying.

'Who would do that?' I say, trying not to sound freaked out, but it's been a long day and I don't like the thought of somebody coming into our room, sticking this up, taking the time to do so. Standing here, right where I am now, so close to all of our things. Quickly, I go to my suitcase, zip it open again, do a quick check to make sure that everything is there. It is – my clothes, my toiletries, nothing is missing.

'Maybe they got the wrong room,' Lucas says, shrugging. 'It doesn't mean anything to me.'

'Me neither,' Saskia says, but she looks pale, and when she hands me the photo, I notice that her fingers are slightly trembling. An after-effect of the panic attack earlier, I think. I turn the picture over, in case it says anything on the back, and to my horror, there are four words stamped on it, in block capital letters, written in thick black marker pen.

I AM WATCHING YOU.

I yelp and drop the photo in shock.

'What?' Lucas says, alarmed, and I point at it.

'Look what it says on the back!'

He picks it up, turns it over. There's a moment of silence while we look at it, the four of us. Lucas raises his eyes to meet mine.

'That is a bit creepy,' he concedes. 'But look, it can't be aimed at us. Nobody knows us here. And this is just a pic of some random guy, isn't it.'

'Yeah, just chuck it in the bin,' Theo says. 'Come on, we need to get across to the Omni, then get some dinner. And maybe even a late-night swim?'

I crumple the photo up in my hand, shove it into my pocket. But I still can't get the words out of my head: *I am watching you.* I think about the feeling I had in the night, the sounds of people outside the room, and an involuntary shiver runs through me, as if someone has walked over my grave.

I'm glad we're moving now. Despite the money, the sooner we get out of here, the better.

*

It's a relief to be back at the Omni Tower Hotel. It's a different man who greets us on the reception desk this time, and he finds our booking at once.

'Welcome,' he says, smiling, 'we look forward to hearing what you think of the Omni.'

The air-con is a welcome change from the heat of outside, and the lobby is cool and calming, especially compared to the hostel. I take a deep breath as I look at the pink flowers; their heads are drooping a little more than before, but they're still giving off a beautiful scent, and I try to push the horrible photo from my mind.

As if on cue, two more Thai men appear to take our bags, lifting them with ease and ushering us to a bank of golden elevators – I see one of them hurtling down from floor sixteen, descending towards us at speed, the little red electronic numbers in the display on the top changing rapidly. I wonder how high the building is, how many storeys – the views from the top must be incredible, and I make a mental note to ask if there is a roof terrace, or even a bar up at the top where we can watch the sunset one evening.

Inside the lift, we stare at ourselves in the mirror that spans the back wall. The other three walls are covered in a dark blue, plush, velvety material that gives the space a hushed, muffled feel – as though if you screamed, nobody would hear you. I look a bit dishevelled, I think – my face is shiny from the facial – and Saskia still looks pale. The boys seem a bit tired, but not too bad overall – perhaps we all just need a shower and a change after the day we've had, and then we can get something nice to eat.

We ascend with speed and I feel my stomach lurch slightly. I must look a bit anxious because the two bellmen exchange a glance as though perhaps they're thinking how silly I am. I catch one of them smirking, slightly – though maybe I'm just imagining it. We come to rather an abrupt halt on floor eleven, and the doors slide open with a ping.

'Please, this way,' the first of the men says, and they lead us to the left, down to rooms 1101 and 1102.

'Oh great, we're next to each other,' Theo says. We're given keycards and Lucas and I make our way into 112.

Our room is equally as impressive as the lobby downstairs. Lucas slides the card into the little black scanner by the entrance, automatically illuminating a large, glossy room, dominated by a four-poster bed, with one wall entirely made of glass. Blackout blinds hang above the tall French windows, and a balcony opens out from the doors. We immediately cross the room to look out – it's almost dark, but you can just about see the glimmer of a pool below, winking in the twilight. It looks huge, surrounded by white padded sunloungers and dotted with stripy umbrellas. A pop-up bar is situated on one side of it, advertising cocktails, ice and beer – a neon-blue sign making it stand out in the darkness.

'Wow,' I breathe, 'this is incredible.'

Lucas is grinning. 'No more slumming it for us, eh? Jesus, how much is it per night here?'

I don't answer; I'm busy pushing open another white door to an en-suite, where I'm met with a huge rainforest shower, four black knobs on the grey tiles surrounding it, and piles of neatly folded towels, hand soap cut into the shape of coral. There's a candle, not yet lit, perched on the side by the mirror and I pick it up idly, lift it to my nostrils. It smells like summer, somehow – fresh and flowery – and I spy a bottle of hand lotion, too, rub some of the fig-scented cream into my palms.

There's a little white card folded and placed on top of the towels, and as I pick it up, my heart gives a stupid little lurch, thinking of the photo at the hostel, but it's just a typewritten note asking us to re-use our towels if possible, to help the environment.

'It's gorgeous in here,' I call to Lucas, but he doesn't answer. I wash my face, dry it with a small, incredibly soft hand towel embossed with a golden O, then untie and re-tie my ponytail, trying to make myself feel a bit less dishevelled. Now that we're here, I'm keen for a quick swim – the pool looked inviting in the half light, and I quite fancy sampling a poolside cocktail, too.

I poke my head back around into the bedroom, and see that Lucas is lying on the bed, his eyes closed.

'Lucas?'

He opens one eye, half smiles at me.

'Just wanted to test the bed.' He pats the space next to him and I jump on, invigorated by the new surroundings.

'Want to come for a swim with me?'

He groans. 'I think I might need a quick power nap to be honest, Hol. Sorry, I know that's boring.'

I pout at him. 'I'll see if Saskia wants to come instead.'

'Good idea.' He kisses me briefly on the top of the head, pulls me lazily towards him. His limbs feel heavy on mine, and I wriggle free, pick up my phone from where I've dropped it on the side table. It vibrates – a message from my mum again – and I squint at the screen, noticing as I do so that my battery has drained right down, which seems to keep happening since we got here. Weird: I only charged it this morning, I think. Perhaps I'm remembering wrongly. Or perhaps being abroad eats up the data and therefore the battery far more quickly.

Lazily, I WhatsApp Saskia – the walls are probably too thick for her to hear me if I shout.

Want to go for a swim?

She replies immediately. *Yes! Let me just get changed.*

I heave myself up off the bed, unzip my suitcase and pull out my swimming costume – an old black one that I really should have replaced years ago. It's lost its elastic slightly, and I resolve to buy a new one if we see a stall where they're going cheap. I deserve to treat myself every now and again, don't I? I bet Saskia's will be brand new, specifically bought just for this trip.

Lucas wolf-whistles as I strip and I laugh.

'Sure you don't want to come?'

'Nah, you girls head down. Theo and I can get a beer in the bar downstairs, once I've lain here for a bit.' He smiles at me, and I bend down to kiss him quickly on the lips.

'You look great,' he says, and I roll my eyes.

'This costume is about a thousand years old.'

Grabbing a dressing gown from the bathroom – big, white, fluffy, delicious – I slip on my sandals and go out into the corridor, ready to knock for Saskia. Just as I'm about to, though, I hear raised voices, and pause, my hand held aloft.

It sounds like Theo, which is weird because I don't think I've ever really heard him raise his voice, not in the whole time I've known him. I can't quite hear what he's saying – the words are too muffled, but it's definitely him. Then Saskia says something in return, but again the words aren't clear, there's just an unintelligible noise, although something about it makes me think it's a row. There's a cadence to their sentences, an edge. Suddenly, there's a bang – a thudding, as if someone's slammed a fist down in frustration – and I manage to catch the words 'if you don't TELL me!'

Then there is silence. I hesitate, not knowing what to do, my arms beginning to goose-pimple under the corridor's air-conditioning. I wrap my robe more tightly around me, biting my lip. She must know I'm about to knock for her, given our message exchange. Maybe I've misinterpreted things, or they've put the TV on or something? There was a big black one attached to the wall in our room.

I lift up my hand to knock but before I can do so, it flies open and Saskia is there, clad in a bright red bathing suit, a towel slung casually over her arm.

'Oh you're ready!' she says, brightly, 'let's go, shall we? Theo's staying here.' She pulls the door closed behind her before I can even catch a glimpse of him, then sets off rapidly along the corridor, leaving me with no choice but to follow, my sandals slapping loudly along the tiles.

Chapter Nineteen

Lucas

Lucas yawns, his jaw clicking slightly. He shouldn't have had those beers at lunchtime; he feels sleepy now, a combination of sun and alcohol. He knows he ought to probably have gone with Saskia and Holly, that the pool would be nice, all that blue, but he just wants to close his eyes, just for one minute, just for a second . . .

When he wakes up, the hotel room is completely dark. Lucas fumbles for his phone to check the time, then swears when he can't find it – he'd thought it was beside him, but it must still be in his bag.

It feels so late, like the middle of the night, though surely, he cannot have slept for that long.

'Holly?' he calls out, wondering if she's back, but his voice just bounces back at him. It feels a bit echoey. Lucas reaches for the lamp at the side of the bed, switches it on, and immediately the room is flooded with yellow light, bathing it in a slightly eerie glow.

'Hol?' he shouts again, wondering if she's in the bathroom, but still, there's no answer. She must have come back though, because the blackout blinds are down, and he's sure he didn't close them before he drifted off. Maybe she forgot something in the room. The blinds are certainly effective – there's no light coming through from outside at all, and now he feels weirdly disoriented, in this hotel room in Bangkok on his own, luxurious though it is. He wonders where Theo has got to – maybe they can go for a drink, see where the girls are, if they're still in the pool.

Lucas gets up, walks over to the blinds and pulls. Below him, the lights of the pool come into view, but the sun has pretty much gone. It gets dark so early here too, only a little later than it does in the UK at this time of year. He can never get used to it, the weird feeling that it's time to go to bed, when in fact the night is young.

Lucas blinks, stretches. He needs to shower, his skin feels sticky and a bit gross. Padding into the bathroom, he strips and twists on the water, feeling the hot rush of it immediately relax his shoulders, the pound of it easing out any knots that are lingering from carrying a rucksack all day. God, that business with Holly's bag. He's so glad they found it. There are bottles of expensive-looking shampoos and shower gels lined up on a little shelf set into the tiled wall and Lucas squeezes some into the palm of his hand. It smells woody, earthy, and he rubs himself clean, then tips back his head and lets the water cascade through his hair. He thinks briefly of the photograph taped to the locker at Pho Hostel – it was a bit weird, to be honest, but Theo had seemed so unbothered, and he hadn't wanted to overreact in front of Holly. He closes his eyes, the water thrumming on his forehead, picturing those aggressive black letters: *I am watching you.*

Just as he's remembering, there is a banging on the door – sudden and loud, urgent. Lucas shuts off the water, stands still for a moment, listening. The sound continues. His heart begins to beat a little bit faster, almost imperceptibly, but he tells himself not to be so paranoid.

Wrapping himself in a towel, he runs a hand through his wet hair and shakes his head briefly from side to side, like a dog, spraying the mirror with tiny drops of water. Then he goes to answer the door.

But what he sees isn't what he was expecting at all.

Chapter Twenty

Saskia

The pool is deep, deeper than it looked. I submerge myself underwater, allowing my body to drift downwards, enjoying the feeling of being weightless, free. When I come up for air, Holly is stood in front of me, holding two cocktails with little green umbrellas and metal silver straws in.

'Ta-da!' She grins at me, the water up to her waist, hands me one of the drinks. 'Mojitos. Thought they'd be refreshing.'

The ice clinks as I take the glass from her – it's stuffed full of mint, but when I take a sip it's surprisingly strong.

'Why can't all swimming pools have cocktail bars on the side?' she sighs, taking a long slurp of hers. 'Mm. Delicious.'

The pool is heated – it must come on at night, God knows there's no need for it in the day time, so even though the temperature is beginning to drop a little bit now that the sun's gone down, it still feels lovely in the water. I'm wearing my bright red swimming costume, but it is a bit too tight around my thighs, and my wedding ring seems loose on my finger, perhaps because my hands have cooled down. I transfer my cocktail to my right hand and clench my left hand tightly, pushing it back into place. I'd be devastated if something happened to it.

We wade over to the side of the pool, set the glasses down on the side. The pool is surprisingly quiet – there were a couple of other women here earlier, reading on the sunloungers, and one couple splashing around in the shallow end, the man's arms circling the woman as he pulled her close to him, whispered in her ear. I should have persuaded Theo to come down with us, but it didn't feel like he wanted to. Better to let him cool off a little bit; we had a small argument before I left the room.

It was the same thing we always argue about, really. He told me he could tell something was wrong, that I was a bit off, and asked me to talk to him, to open up. As usual, I didn't. I couldn't. He got frustrated, then, like he often does – and I felt terrible. But opening up to Theo, much as I'd like to, is simply not an option.

Especially after the photograph that was taped to the locker at the hostel. Because even with his face scratched off, I knew who the man in the suit was. It would take more than that to erase his features from my nightmares.

What I don't know is why someone had put his photo in our dorm room.

Chapter Twenty-One

Holly

Saskia and I end up having two cocktails each, and I'm feeling nicely buzzed by the time we emerge from the pool. Glittering silver fairy lights have come on around the cocktail bar and the railings that surround the far side of the pool, and the stars are coming out, too – the whole place feels magical. I've tried to ask Saskia if she's all right, after what happened at the spa, and then what I thought I heard in the hotel, but she just brushes me off, tells me she's fine. She does seem OK, I think – she hasn't mentioned any argument with Theo and I'm starting to think that maybe I misheard the whole thing. It's hard to tell through doors and walls.

'I'm getting hungry,' I say after we've finished off the dregs of our cocktails. 'My fingers are starting to go a bit prune-like. Shall we go shower, find the boys, get some food? I wonder if we ought to have booked anywhere for dinner, or if we can just turn up.'

'I think Theo had somewhere in mind,' Saskia says, and we make our way up the steps of the pool, back into the hotel. I slide my feet into my sandals, trying not to slip, and we go through the stairwell to the lift that will take us from the pool back up to our rooms.

'That was weird, earlier,' I say, as we're ascending, 'you know, that photo in the room.' I give a little laugh. 'It freaked me out a bit, to be honest. I'm glad we're not at the hostel any more. I have sort of felt it, a few times, you know – it sounds silly, but that sensation of being watched. It must just be because we're in an unfamiliar country, I guess. People are probably looking at us thinking we're an easy target, tourists, you know.'

There's a tiny pause. I wait for her to answer.

Then she nods, vigorously. 'Yeah, I expect it's just that, Hol. Theo's right, it will have been someone playing a prank, someone who got the wrong room.' Another pause. 'I do know what you mean though, I have felt . . .' She breaks off. 'I don't know. Just, you know, earlier, in the spa – and when we left the airport, in the car, I felt like there was someone behind us, following us, you know. But it's ridiculous, it sounds mad when I say it out loud.' She half laughs, though it doesn't quite meet her eyes. 'I've probably watched too many films about Brits abroad and all the horrible things that can happen!'

I meet her eyes in the mirror of the lift. 'We'll be fine,' I say, slightly more confidently than I feel. 'We just need to make sure we stick together, that's all.'

The lift dings, and the doors slide open. Saskia and I step out into the corridor, then promptly to one side as a couple sweep past us. They're older, and dressed up – the woman in a long, silky green dress and her partner in a dark blue shirt. I wonder briefly what has brought them to Bangkok – they look out of place somehow, as if they wouldn't fit in with the hustle and bustle outside.

'See you in ten?' Saskia says, as we reach our rooms, and I nod.

'Yep – meet you downstairs.' She smiles at me, then slides her keycard into the door and disappears.

I knock on the door to our room, expecting Lucas to pull it open, but nothing happens.

'Luke?' I call, but there's no answer. Damn. He must have gone downstairs, but I didn't bring my keycard with me. In fact, I didn't bring anything with me – I haven't even got my phone.

'Sask?' I rap on her door, still clutching my towel around me. I'm starting to get a bit cold, and I'm hungry, too – the cocktails are starting to swirl a bit uneasily in my stomach.

'Saskia?' I try again. There's a scuffling sound and then the door opens and she's there, hair dripping wet, small smudges of mascara under her eyes, having clearly just hopped out of the shower.

'Sorry,' I say, 'I forgot my room key and Lucas isn't here. Is Theo?'

'No,' she says, 'they're in the bar downstairs, he messaged to let us know. Where's your phone?'

'Also in our room.'

She steps back to allow me inside and tells me she'll be two minutes in the shower, that I can get in after her.

I sit down on the edge of their bed as the hiss of the water comes back on, glancing around the room. Their bags are on the floor, their contents spilled out already, though Theo has hung up a couple of shirts which I can see dangling in the half-open wardrobe. Saskia's phone is plugged in to charge by the bed, and it lights up as I look at it, the screen filling with what look like Instagram notifications. I wonder what else she's been posting.

Theo's side of the bed is dimpled, as if he's been lying on it, and there's a half-drunk glass of water on the table, next to a blue packet of paracetamol. I wonder if he'd mind if I had some; my head is beginning to hurt a bit, a combination of sun and cocktails and the beers we had earlier.

Standing up, I go over to his side of the bed and pick up the painkillers – but the box is empty. I sigh, then see a white pill pack poking out from just underneath the bed; he must have dropped it. Bending down, I scoop it up, but my fingers brush against something else, tucked just underneath the edge of the bedsheets, where they hang down close to the floor. Frowning, I pick it up, hold it between my fingers. It's a black marker pen. For a moment, I can't work out why this bothers me, and then it comes to me – the photograph taped up in the hostel room, the writing on the back. It was written in thick black ink.

'Holly?' Saskia has reappeared and her voice startles me – quickly, I drop the black pen onto the floor and nudge it slightly with my foot until it's back out of sight, feeling as though I have been caught doing something I shouldn't.

'Just wanted some paracetamol,' I say, holding up the pills, and she nods.

'Of course. Help yourself. And the shower's free. D'you want to borrow something of mine to wear, 'til you can get back in your room?'

'If you don't mind,' I say, and she grins at me. 'What's mine is yours.'

In the shower, I let the hot water wash away all the chlorine of the pool, tilting my head back under the flow of it, enjoying the sensation. But my mind keeps coming back to the marker pen – why would Theo have it in the room, have one with him? It's an odd thing to take with you to Bangkok, isn't it? I squeeze shower gel onto my hands, rub it over my limbs into a lather. I'm just being silly. There are loads of reasons he might have a pen with him, it's hardly as though I've found a nuclear bomb. It must just be a coincidence that the note was written in the same sort of ink. Anyway, why would Theo have written those words himself? It wouldn't make any sense.

I shut off the shower, wrap myself in a large white towel and pick up my discarded swimming costume from the floor, hang it over the side of the bath to dry off. In the mirror, my skin is flushed from the heat, and I wipe the steam away so I can see myself more clearly, my hand squeaking on the glass.

'Good shower, isn't it? A lot better than the one at the hostel looked,' Saskia says when I emerge. She's applying lipstick, her lips pursed in front of the mirror in the room – a beautiful gold-edged cheval one, positioned over by the window. She's changed into a backless black dress and low silver heels, and her hair hangs in thick wet tendrils on her shoulders.

'You look great,' I tell her, and she turns to face me, pressing her lips together to rub in the colour.

'I thought you could wear that,' she says, pointing at the bed, where a yellow dress lies, slightly crumpled. 'You've always looked great in yellow. It's one of your colours.'

'Are you sure?' I say, picking it up gingerly – it feels expensive, the fabric soft and slippery between my fingers.

'Of course,' she says. 'Oh, and if you need some underwear too – here you go.' She bends down, rummages briefly in her bag then chucks me a pair of knickers, white with a pink frill.

I get changed with my back to her, trying to position the towel so that it's still covering most of my body. I'm comfortable around Saskia, of course I am, but we've never shared a room before or anything, and I suddenly feel a bit self-conscious. She sprays perfume on us both – a dark, musky scent – and I slide my feet back into my sandals; they'll have to do for now.

'I knew it'd suit you,' Saskia says, looking me up and down appraisingly, and I feel a flash of pleasure at her obvious approval. It's not that I don't have nice clothes, they're fine, but there's something about wearing a dress of Saskia's that makes me feel different – as though I've shucked on a newer version of myself – a prettier, more glamorous one.

'Let's go find the boys,' she says, with a last glance in the mirror. She picks up a little black clutch bag from the bed and checks for her phone, her lipstick, her room key.

'Right,' she says, 'let's get out of here.'

I follow her out of the room, my sandals clicking on the floor. At the last moment, I glance behind me, taking one last look around – at the rumpled bed, the discarded towels we've left on the floor, the smudge of mascara Saskia's made on the mirror. My mind flickers to the marker pen, lying hidden beneath the bed, but I dismiss the thought as quickly as it came. Whoever wrote that note must have intended it for somebody else. Not for us.

Chapter Twenty-Two

Lucas

They're sat in the hotel bar that adjoins the restaurant of the Omni, the three of them. He'd been surprised when he'd opened the door to find Theo and Caleb together, but they've all been sat down here for an hour or so and Lucas is enjoying the new dynamic.

'I ran into Theo in the lobby,' Caleb had explained, 'I recognised him from looking through your passports earlier, when your girlfriend – Holly, isn't it – lost her bag.'

'I'd just popped down to ask about reserving a table for tonight,' Theo had said, 'they've booked us in for eight. Thought the menu looked good, that we may as well eat here instead of traipsing around again. Feels like it's been a long day.'

'Let me buy you that drink,' Lucas had said, and when Caleb had held his hands up in protest, he'd shaken his head, insisted. 'Literally, we'd be spending the night in the British Embassy if it weren't for you. A pint is the least I can do.'

Now the three of them are perched on bar stools, enjoying a beer together as they wait for Holly and Saskia.

'So you're staying here too?' Lucas asks Caleb, and the other man nods.

'Yep, had it recommended by a colleague of mine, actually. Nice, isn't it? Though I feel a bit weird being here on my own. Doesn't have the same traveller vibe as some of the other places I've stayed – though it is good to have a bit of luxury. Showers are amazing.'

Lucas nods. 'They're the best bit so far.' He wonders, briefly, whether he'd told Caleb that they were staying here, if he'd mentioned it earlier, but decides that he can't have done. It had all been such a quick moment, and all he can remember is the relief he'd felt at the sight of Holly's bag, complete with their passports.

'How long are you out here for?' Theo asks, and Caleb shrugs, rubs a hand over the top of his head.

'Two months or so, all in all. I'm on sabbatical from work, wanted to see where the wind took me. Thailand's an amazing place – I was meant to move on, move around a bit more, but I've been in Bangkok for ten days now. The city gets to you, you know? Always feels like more to do.'

Theo is nodding enthusiastically. 'Absolutely. We love it so far.'

Lucas takes a sip of his beer. A sabbatical – God, he wishes. The only decent chunk of time he gets off is in the school summer holidays, but at that time of year, everything is so expensive that he can barely afford to go anywhere outside of the M25.

'So what else have you guys been doing, apart from the temple today?' Caleb asks. Earlier, Lucas had thought he was their age but up close he can see that he's actually a little bit older, perhaps late thirties, even forty. He's always found it quite hard to judge people's ages but there's something more experienced-looking around the other man's eyes – small creases that offset the bright blue of his gaze, and there's an air of confidence, too, that seems to set him slightly apart from him and Theo. Lucas feels a strange urge to impress him, and he can tell that Theo feels it too – can tell from the way his friend is behaving – his voice slightly louder, brasher, his gestures wider and more expansive.

'We went to one of the food markets,' Theo says, 'sampled some of the local delicacies. Man, those rats are something, aren't they? Bit of an acquired taste.'

Lucas frowns – why is he pretending they ate more adventurously than they did? But it's working – Caleb is laughing, and Lucas finds himself joining in. He glances briefly at his watch – where are Holly and Saskia? They must be done with their swim by now.

As if on cue, he feels a hand on his shoulder and spins around to find Holly, grinning at him in a bright yellow, expensive-looking dress that he hasn't seen before.

'Hi!'

'You made it,' he says, 'here, sit down. You look nice. Where's Sask?'

'Well, you locked me out of our room, so this is Saskia's dress, she's just nipped to the loo,' she says, plucking at the yellow fabric with her fingers. Lucas sees the flash of recognition on her face as Caleb raises a hand in greeting.

'Oh! Hi! You're the guy who found my bag!'

He places a hand on his chest, dips his head. 'Guilty as charged. The very same.'

'How funny!'

'We ran into each other,' Lucas explains, and Holly smiles, pulls up another bar stool so that she is perched a little precariously beside him.

'It's so nice to see you again,' she says, politely, 'honestly, I was so relieved to get my bag back. It had *everything* in it.' As she says this, Lucas remembers that actually, when Caleb returned it, Holly's money and bank card were missing – he'd forgotten that, until now; she'd been able to sort it out with the bank so easily. He wonders if they ought to somehow ask him about it, but he can't think of a way of doing so without it seeming insulting, like they're accusing him of stealing from her. He wouldn't do that, would he? He feels a flicker of unease as he looks at Caleb, wondering. But no, he reasons, if he had been the one to take it, it's hardly like he'd have come to have a drink with them, is it? No, it must have been someone else who went through it before he picked it up.

Holly seems to have come to a similar conclusion, because she appears to warm to Caleb very quickly. He *is* charming; Lucas finds himself chuckling as Caleb regales them of his first night in Bangkok, a night on which he'd mistakenly found himself flirting with a Thai woman who turned out to be married to the owner of the hostel.

'Honestly, the look on his face, it could have killed,' Caleb says, doing an impression of it – narrowed eyes, dagger-like stare. He's finished his beer and Lucas notices that Theo has too, whereas he still has just under half left. Holly's ordered a glass of white wine, which the bartender brings over on a small silver tray, a thick white fabric napkin slung over his arm.

'Where's my lovely wife?' Theo says, looking around the hotel bar, and Holly frowns.

'She said she was just coming – she just went to those bathrooms over there.' She points across the room to a set of twin doors, an image of a smartly dressed man and woman on each. As if on cue, the left door swings open and Saskia emerges and Holly waves, calling out to her across the bar.

'Sask, over here!'

The bar itself is quiet, the kind of refined quiet that money brings, and Lucas feels like Holly's voice is echoing a little around the room. There's an older couple in the corner, sipping cocktails, and a man working on a laptop, but other than that, they're the only ones there. Chandeliers hang from the ceiling and the walls are covered in striped maroon-and-white wallpaper, edged with a gold trim. There's only one waiter – the guy who served them behind the bar – but Lucas imagines that it will get busier soon, with residents coming down for dinner, because the surrounding tables are all laid out carefully with glinting silverware and upturned wine glasses, waiting to welcome the hotel guests.

'Saskia, this is Caleb,' Theo is stretching out an arm to her, pulling her close. He kisses her on the side of the head and Lucas watches as Caleb stretches out a hand to her.

'Pleased to meet you. Your husband has been singing your praises.'

Lucas wonders if he is imagining the flicker on Saskia's face. He must have been, because it vanishes as quickly as it came and she reaches out to shake Caleb's hand, her lips stretched open in a smile.

Chapter Twenty-Three

Saskia

My heart is thumping as I take his hand, even though it goes against everything in me to do so, even though my insides are screaming at me not to. The sensation of his skin against mine is almost surreal, because it has been so long, so long since I looked into those eyes, so long since I heard that voice. And now here he is, sitting with my husband, sitting with our friends, drinking a beer in a hotel bar in Bangkok as though we are strangers.

'Nice to meet you.' The words come out of my mouth, but I don't really recognise them – my voice sounds alien, like it's coming from someone else. The weirdest thing is that nobody seems to notice – Theo asks me what I want to drink, and Holly asks me what the toilets down here are like, whether they're posh. Lucas says something about Caleb finding Holly's bag, earlier at the temple, about bumping into him again here at the hotel. I'm nodding, but my mind is whirring, trying to make sense of this situation, trying to find a way through.

'Caleb, you ought to join us for dinner!' Theo says, and I turn to look at him, try to communicate with my eyes, make him see somehow that this is a bad idea. More than a bad idea. But it doesn't work, he just grins at me, asks if I like the wine that the waiter has just brought over.

'It's fine,' I say, woodenly, and Holly raises her eyebrows in surprise.

'I think it's yum. But what do I know. I'm not exactly a connoisseur.'

Caleb laughs, and I see a flicker of pleasure cross Holly's face. I remember when I used to make him laugh, occasionally. Before it all happened.

The restaurant is starting to get busier, now, the tables around the bar beginning to fill up. A Thai woman in a black-and-white suit comes up to us, tells us that our table is ready, and Theo puts his hand on her arm, asks if she'd mind terribly if we could switch it from four people to five.

'Of course,' she replies, smoothly, and we follow her away from the bar, threading our way through the tables to one towards the back, near the windows that look out over the city. Theo pulls out my chair for me – a heavy, dark wood chair with a high winged back and a red velvet cushioned base – and I drop into it, close my eyes briefly as Caleb inevitably takes the seat beside me, just as I knew he would.

'Ooh, this looks amazing,' Holly says, picking up a menu; when I reach for my own, I see that my hand is trembling, and quickly I clasp both hands together in my lap, hoping nobody has noticed.

'Some water for the table?' The waitress has reappeared, holding a large glass bottle full of water, which she pours out meticulously into our glasses, her grip steady and still. I watch as the stream fills my tumbler, then take a gulp quickly, forcing myself to swallow, to keep breathing.

'Shall we get red or white?' Theo asks, picking up the wine

list from the centre of the table. He always chooses the wine whenever we go out, and I see his eyes skimming to the bottom, the most expensive part of the list.

'I'm a red wine guy myself,' Caleb says, and Lucas nods. Images come back to me, of the two of us drinking a bottle of Merlot, heads huddled together, planning, plotting. The splash of it on the table, scarlet as a bloodstain. I dig my nails into my hand to distract myself, bring myself back to the present.

'Same. If that's OK.'

'Saskia?'

Theo has to say my name twice before I respond.

'Red is fine,' I say eventually, 'sorry, I was miles away. Whatever you guys want.' Theo looks at me slightly quizzically for a second, but then the waitress is here and his attention disappears. Part of me wants to reach for my husband's hand, hold it tightly and pull him away from here, away from this table, back up to our room where we can slam the door and lock it and hide, and part of me – the other, bigger part – knows that I mustn't do that, that I mustn't let on, that I must ensure that everyone here thinks tonight is the first time I've ever set eyes on Caleb.

Only I know what is at stake if they realise the truth.

Chapter Twenty-Four

Holly

I can't decide whether to go for the scallops or a good old-fashioned curry. I know Lucas is worrying about the prices here, but everything looks and sounds so delicious, and I figure that while we're staying in this hotel, we may as well enjoy it, make the most of it. Plus, I'm having fun – Caleb is a good laugh, and he seems to be getting on really well with the boys. I'm always encouraging Lucas to make more friends, be a bit more outgoing – and so I'm pleased to see how easily he's getting on with this guy.

'So before Bangkok I spent some time in India,' Caleb is telling us, 'I did the usual golden triangle, you know – typical tourist – but then I went off track to a town called Varanasi, too. Incredible place. Very spiritual.'

Theo is nodding, his face animated. 'I've always wanted to go there, actually. Heard great things. Maybe that should be our next trip! We could make this holiday an annual thing, couldn't we? That would be so much fun.'

I swallow, dart a glance at Lucas. It wouldn't be fun for our bank balance.

'Sorry to interrupt – are you ready to order some food this evening?' The waitress appears and we all place our orders – I plump for the scallops in the end – and she tops up our wine glasses, too, all of which seem to have been diminished rather rapidly. I rub my tongue across my front teeth, conscious of getting red-wine mouth, and take a sip of my water. Across the room, it looks like they're setting up for some live music – there's a woman in a red velvet dress clutching a microphone, tapping it with two fingers to test it, and a guy next to her unzipping what looks like a saxophone or a trumpet case. The restaurant is much busier than it was when we first came down, and there's a great atmosphere – the perfect blend of background noise so that we can still hear one another speaking.

'We should go take a day trip tomorrow,' Theo says, 'I've been reading about this waterfall, in the national park. Erawan Falls, it's called. Meant to be beautiful, there's a tour bus that leaves from the end of our road, I think.'

'Sounds great,' I say, 'I think I saw it in the guidebook too. I love waterfalls. Remember that one we saw up in Yorkshire, Lucas? Tallest in England.'

'I'm up for a waterfall trip,' Lucas says, 'long as it's not too far, I don't want to spend ages on the bus.'

'Plan then,' Theo says, 'it'll be good to explore outside the city before we move to the island.'

The waitress reappears, bringing us a basket of bread and a little ceramic bowl of oil. I break a piece off, dip it into the oil – it tastes delicious, the bread crumbling in my mouth, the oil slick on my tongue.

'So,' Caleb says, 'Theo, Saskia – you guys just got married, right? How did it all go?'

I look at Saskia, expecting her face to light up like it usually does whenever anyone mentions the wedding, to get out her phone and start showing him the photographs, but to my surprise, she doesn't say anything, and after a second or two, it is Theo who jumps in.

'Ah man, it was the greatest day of our lives, wasn't it, babe?' He reaches and squeezes her hand across the table. 'We did it in a place called Butley Priory, out on the Suffolk coast – my family are from around there, originally. Beautiful place.'

It had been – a gorgeous old priory, one of the most lavish weddings I've ever been to. It must have cost a small fortune, but everyone knew they could afford it – well, Theo's father could anyway. To him it was probably a drop in the ocean. They paid for us all to stay for the weekend, had over a hundred and fifty guests.

'Sounds wonderful,' Caleb says, 'really special. Both your families there?'

Theo laughs. 'My family practically orchestrated the entire event.'

Lucas snorts. 'Remember the size of your mum's hat?'

The food arrives, all at once, and Theo orders us another bottle of red wine, waving his hand dismissively when Caleb offers to buy a round.

'My treat,' he says, 'by the sounds of it, you saved our bacon today. We owe you.'

'Excuse me.' There is a clatter as Saskia pushes back her chair, gets to her feet quickly. All of us look up at her.

'You OK?' I ask her, and she nods.

'I'm fine, I'll be back in a minute. Excuse me.'

I stare after her as she hurries away from the table. Theo is looking at her retreating back, too, and I catch his eye, frown.

'D'you think she's OK?'

I'm expecting him to share my concern, but his gaze slides away from me, and he takes another gulp of red wine. 'I'm sure she's fine. Why wouldn't she be?'

*

It's been almost ten minutes and Saskia still hasn't returned. The three boys are laughing at something, and we've almost polished off the second bottle of red wine, now, but I can't shake the feeling of unease. I'm about to get to my feet, to head upstairs to the rooms and see if I can find her, when there's a hand on my arm and I turn to find Caleb, sitting very close to me, his blue eyes piercing into mine.

'Don't worry about your friend,' he says, quietly, as if he can read my thoughts, 'she'll be OK.'

Lucas and Theo are looking at something on one of their phones, giggling together as though they're teenagers. Caleb sees me looking at them and grins.

'Boys and their toys, eh?'

I smile back at him, taking a sip of wine, even though I probably don't need any more. The scallops were delicious but not very substantial – I possibly ought to have a dessert or something, to soak up some more of the alcohol.

'Exactly.'

'How long have you all been friends?' he asks me conversationally, and I bite my lip, trying to think.

'Well, Lucas and Theo have known each other forever, since school. And I met Luke about three years ago. Saskia and Theo have been together about . . . five years, I think? I can't quite remember, now.'

He's nodding, looking interested. I wonder if he's been a bit lonely, travelling out here on his own – I'm not sure I'd like it. But then again, people do, don't they – maybe it's nice to have that kind of freedom.

'What else have you got planned for the rest of your trip?' he asks me, and I tell him about going to Koh Samet, the beach villa. He's got quite an intense stare, I think after a while, but actually it's nice to have somebody's full attention, to feel like he's really listening to me, seeing me. It's not that Lucas isn't attentive – he is, most of the time – but we've both been so busy and stressed in our everyday lives that often it feels like we're not paying as much attention to each other as perhaps we ought to be.

Saskia still hasn't returned and I break from Caleb's gaze to look around the restaurant, checking for her.

'I just don't know where Saskia's got to,' I say, a little awkwardly, feeling as though I am perhaps being dramatic, overly worried. My mind flits back to the note on the back of the photograph in the hostel, the eerie sensation she described to me earlier when we were in the lift, that feeling that someone could be watching us. Why isn't Theo bothered too?

'I'm going to find Saskia,' I say firmly to the table, but just at that second, my phone buzzes in my lap. It's a phone call – my mother's calling me from the UK and I hesitate, knowing that I need to look for Saskia but wondering why she's calling me when she knows I am away.

Caleb sees the word 'mum' flash up on my phone and holds up a hand.

'Don't worry – you take it. I'll go look for her, back in a minute. I'll just check if she's in the lobby or anything.'

Before I can say anything, he's got to his feet and is

striding away across the room. Theo and Lucas eventually look up from the phone screen and I press my own phone to my ear, placing one finger against my other ear to try to hear better.

'Mum? What's the matter? Is everything all right?'

Chapter Twenty-Five

Saskia

He finds me by the lift bank. For a minute, I think about running – but where would I go? A sense of inevitability comes over me as I see him striding towards me, that familiar walk, and I lean back against the wall, waiting. Trapped.

'You can't leave the table in the middle of a meal,' he says, when he's standing in front of me. 'It's bad manners, Saskia. Surely you know that.' His voice is lilting, jokey, as if this is all one big game to him. Which I suppose in some ways it is.

He's so close that I could reach out and touch him, push him, but I don't. My hands remain clenched by my side, two tightly closed fists.

'What are you doing?' I say quietly. I can't meet his eye – those piercing blue eyes, that stare.

He shrugs, and I hate the casual way he has, the devil-may-care attitude. He knows how much I care. He knows exactly what he's doing, because that's the kind of man he is. Always has been.

'I'm not doing anything, Saskia. I just wanted to see how you are. It's a coincidence, darlin'.' His voice, away from the others, is different, altered – back to how I remember it. He always called me 'darlin''. For a while, I found it a comfort. Now it just brings me fear.

'Was it you, at the hostel?' I whisper, even though I already know the answer, and he nods.

'I couldn't believe it when I saw you.' He takes a step closer, so close that I can smell him – that musky, animal scent. 'And then you never replied to my note.' He tuts, shakes his head like I am a naughty schoolgirl.

I close my eyes. He comes closer still, dipping his head so that our foreheads are almost touching. The memories are crowding around me, closer and closer. I don't want to think about it. I don't want to think about it.

'I asked you before, and I'll ask you again,' he says, and then there's a pause, a beat of silence, and the hotel around us seems to shimmer and dissipate, until there are only the two of us standing there, locked together, the energy between us threaded with danger.

And then he says it, and the words fill me with dread, because they are his way of reminding me that in this situation, I am trapped by his will. I have no power at all, because he knows my secret. Whatever happens, that secret, the one that binds us, it can never come out. So I need to know what he wants. And whether I can give it to him.

'Saskia,' he says, his mouth inches from mine, 'it's been a while. Do you fancy a game?'

Chapter Twenty-Six

Lucas

He can tell that Holly's on the phone to her mother from the tense set of her shoulders and her jaw. She's on her feet, now, leaving just him and Theo at the table – Saskia still hasn't reappeared, and he thinks Caleb said he was going to have a quick look for her. Theo has been showing him the new ad for their friend Mike's business on his phone, and he'd got distracted – but Holly is returning to the table now, her face creased with the anxiety that always accompanies an interaction with her mother.

'You OK?' he asks her, and she nods, unsmiling.

'Yep. I'm fine. It's just the usual.'

He reaches out a hand, pulls her back into her seat then leans across and rubs the back of her neck, trying to help ease the tension that he knows will be knotting its way across her spine. Her mother has had a drinking problem since Holly was twelve, and these phone calls are not unusual. He is endlessly impressed by her patience with them, but he knows the toll it takes on her, too.

'Is there any more wine?' she is asking, and Lucas reaches for the bottle, shakes it slightly from side to side.

'We're out. But we can get some more.'

Theo flags down the waitress and they order another bottle – their third, which Lucas worries is a bit excessive but then tells himself not to – they're on holiday, after all.

'Where have the others gone?' Theo says, looking around as if he's only just realised that his wife is missing. Lucas shrugs.

'I don't know. Oh – actually, there they are.'

Saskia and Caleb are making their way towards them, and Lucas sees Holly's eyebrows knit together slightly as her eyes flicker between them.

'Where've you been?' Theo asks. 'We almost sent out a search party.'

'Sorry, babe,' Saskia says, sliding back into the chair beside him, reaching over and kissing him quickly on the lips. 'Did you get more wine?'

'I just don't understand why she does it!' Holly bursts out suddenly, and Lucas braces himself, knowing this was coming.

'What?' Saskia says, startled, and Holly sighs, rolls her eyes. She's picking at the skin around her fingernails in agitation; Lucas can see the little red raw strips around her cuticles.

'My mother,' Holly says, 'she rang when you weren't here. Drunk, as per. She knows I'm on holiday with you guys. She *knows* that. I mean, it's one thing doing it when I'm at home, but when I'm abroad, with my friends . . .'

Caleb winces sympathetically. 'Parents, right. Who'd have them?'

Holly sniffs, and Lucas can feel her frustration, can tell she is trying not to let it overwhelm her.

'Holly's mum can be a bit . . . difficult,' he says, by way of explanation, but Caleb is nodding as though he understands, as though he empathises.

'Say no more,' he replies, 'I get it. Christ,' he leans back in his seat and exhales loudly, blowing his cheeks out like a monkey, 'it's only when you get to this age that you really realise, isn't it? We have to start parenting them, not the other way around.'

Holly nods. 'That's exactly it. I'm tired of it. It's – she – is exhausting sometimes.'

'You sound like you're a very patient daughter,' Caleb says, and she half smiles, blushes very slightly.

'It doesn't feel like I am.'

'Of course you are,' Lucas says, squeezing her hand, gently stopping her from pulling at her skin. 'Of course you are.'

'You're lucky that your mum at least shows her emotions every now and again,' Theo says, unexpectedly. 'My parents have basically spent their whole lives being extremely repressed.' He snorts, picks up his glass of wine and takes a big gulp, the colour flushing to his cheeks. There's a tiny speck of food on the collar of his shirt, Lucas notices, and his eyes look a little blurry now. He wouldn't have said anything like that if he hadn't been drinking.

'Repressed but rich,' he says, before he can stop himself, and Theo looks at him, his gaze suddenly sharpening. For a moment, the table seems to hold its breath, but then the moment breaks, and Theo laughs loudly, slams a hand flat down on the table, making the wine glasses shiver.

'That's right!' he says, 'That's right. Repressed but rich. Ha. I like that.'

Across the table, Lucas sees Caleb and Saskia look at each other – just a short glance, but there is something in it that sticks in his mind. Later, as they're paying the bill, Theo gets out his credit card and proposes a toast.

'To my repressed but rich parents. This one's on you.'

They clink glasses, the five of them laughing, and Lucas feels only a twinge of disloyalty to Theo's family, who, it must be said, have only ever been welcoming to him over the years. He pushes the thought away as quickly as it came, downs his drink, and glances around the table, at the four flushed faces looking back at him, the glitter in their eyes, the secrets within their smiles.

Chapter Twenty-Seven

Holly

I wake up and the sunlight is streaming into the room. I have a vague memory of opening the blackout blinds last night, drunkenly saying I wanted to see the city, of pressing my body up against the glass, looking down at the glitter of the pool below, the lights of Bangkok beyond it. I remember Lucas wrapping his arm around my waist and pulling me backwards onto the bed, the two of us kissing for a bit before we both passed out in a red-wine haze.

He's sprawled out next to me in his boxers, his arms flung above his head, snoring very slightly. I lick my lips, swallow, and push off the white blankets, stretch my arms out and pad to the bathroom. In the mirror, I'm horrified to find that my mouth is almost black – a crusty red rim on my lips, a blackberry hue to my tongue. I scrabble around in my make-up bag for my toothbrush and smear some toothpaste onto it, twist on the cold tap. My hands are shaking slightly and my heart is beating too fast. God, how much did we drink?

'Ughhhh. Can you get me a glass of water?' Lucas's voice floats through from the bedroom and I spit my toothpaste into the sink, rinse my mouth out one more time.

'Coming.'

I fill up one of the tumblers next to the sink and take it to him, smiling as he hangs his head down to his chest and groans.

'I feel ill.'

'I know,' I say, 'that last bottle of red was most definitely a mistake.'

He gulps the water quickly, his Adam's apple bobbing. 'Good night, though, wasn't it? That Caleb bloke's a laugh.'

I nod. 'Yeah, it was great. Sorry I got so ranty about Mum.'

He waves a hand, sets the water glass down and pulls me towards him. 'Don't be silly. You don't need to apologise. I know how it is.'

'Yeah.' I nestle into his chest, into the warm familiarity of him.

'I can hear your heart,' he whispers in my ear and I half laugh, nod against his torso.

'No wonder. It feels like it's about to beat out of my chest. I hate hangovers.'

'What shall we do today?'

'God, I think Saskia and Theo wanted to do that waterfall tour, didn't they?' I pick up my phone from the side, press the screen but it's black, flat battery yet again. I fumble around for the phone charger.

'My phone keeps dying so fast,' I tell Lucas, and he shrugs.

'Maybe you need a new one.'

I frown. 'Maybe. Or maybe I ought to just keep it switched off, stop Mum from being able to ring me with non-emergencies.'

He grins. 'That is another option, yes.'

There's a knock at the door and I get to my feet, swing it open to see Theo on the other side, clad in a dressing gown emblazoned with the Omni Tower Hotel logo. He comes in without my inviting him, throws himself dramatically onto the foot of the bed.

'Maaaaate. I feel like death.'

Lucas laughs. 'Don't we all.'

'Where's Saskia?' I ask and he jerks his thumb to the wall.

'In the shower. She seems OK. Don't think she drank as much as the rest of us.'

'She's a wise woman, your wife,' Lucas says. 'Shit, why did we have that last bottle of wine?'

'Ah, fuck it,' Theo says, 'it was worth it, wasn't it? We had a good time.'

'D'you still want to do this waterfall tour today?' I ask him. 'Only didn't you say it started at ten thirty if so?'

Theo glances at his wrist, then frowns. 'My watch.'

'It's nine forty now,' Lucas says, checking his phone, but Theo isn't listening, he's still got one hand circling his bare wrist, a worried expression on his face.

'I had it on last night,' he says, 'and I don't usually take it off unless I'm in the shower.'

'Not to sleep?' I ask him, but he's shaking his head.

'No. I'll have to go check the room. It's worth about forty grand.'

He's gone within seconds and Lucas and I look at each other.

Forty grand! I mouth, pulling a face. 'I'm getting in the shower.'

*

The shower helps to wake me up and ten minutes later, I'm dressed – in my own clothes today – and ready to go. Lucas is fiddling with the fancy coffee machine on the table, trying to get it to work, when there is a hammering on the door. I open it, and Theo comes storming in.

'My bloody watch,' he says, 'I can't find it anywhere.'

'Your Rolex?'

'Yes,' he says, 'I've looked all over, honestly. It's gone.'

'Don't panic, mate,' Lucas says, 'are you sure you had it on last night? Let's go ask in the bar downstairs.'

'Saskia's gone to ask,' he says. 'Fuck, do you think someone's taken it?' He squeezes his eyes shut briefly. 'Christ, my head is banging. I can't really remember what happened. But I know I had it on when we were eating.'

'One of the staff will probably have picked it up,' I say, uncertainly, and he looks briefly mollified, but inside, I feel a twist of unease. First my bag, the money, and now this. Somehow, it feels like a bad sign, an omen. I think of the picture taped up in the hostel, the black marker pen under Theo's bed. They are small things, but they are adding up, and for the first time, I find myself feeling a bit homesick, wishing briefly for the comfort of my own little London flat, the safety of my home.

Chapter Twenty-Eight

Lucas

Downstairs, Saskia is talking to the waitress from last night, but it's clear from their expressions that it isn't good news.

'They haven't seen it,' Saskia says, 'I'm so sorry, babe.'

Theo is shaking his head. 'I don't get it,' he says. 'How can it have just vanished?'

Lucas looks over to the reception desk, where Praew, the guy from the very first night, when they couldn't get in, is watching them all, expressionless. He feels a wave of embarrassment, wonders what the staff here are thinking about them, panicking over a too-expensive watch. He wonders how much Praew and his colleagues get paid.

'Maybe we should ask Caleb, too?' Holly suggests, and Theo nods.

'Yeah, of course. Has anyone got his number?'

'No need,' Lucas says, seeing a familiar figure loping into the lobby from the direction of the elevators. 'You can ask him in person.'

'Morning all.'

To Lucas's surprise, Caleb looks fairly fresh-faced – he'd been as plastered as the rest of them, Lucas had thought, but this morning he looks clean shaven and bright, as if he's slept well.

'How are we?' he says, clapping a hand on Theo's back, smiling at the others. 'Thanks for letting me gatecrash your dinner last night guys. Much appreciated.'

'No problem,' Holly starts saying, at the same time that Theo abruptly asks him if he's seen his watch.

'Your watch?'

'Silver Rolex.'

Caleb shakes his head. 'Sorry, mate. Did you definitely have it on? I don't remember seeing it,' he laughs, 'but then, I don't really remember much after bottle numero duo.'

'I definitely had it on,' Theo mutters, and Saskia rubs his back, her wedding ring glinting slightly in the bright lights of the hotel lobby. Lucas can feel Praew's gaze on them all, the back of his neck is prickling and he turns, angling his body away from the reception desk.

'What do you want to do?' Saskia asks Theo, in a low voice. 'We could stay here, keep looking?'

Theo glances up and Lucas sees the flit of embarrassment cross his face when he sees Caleb watching him.

'Nah,' he says, 'it'll turn up, I'm sure. Let's stick to the plan.'

'So, waterfall tour?' Holly says. 'We can probably just about make it if we head there now. Doesn't the tour van pick up from the end of this road?'

'You guys are still planning on doing the waterfall today then?' Caleb asks, and Lucas nods.

'Yeah, should be good.'

Caleb nods, and Lucas wonders if perhaps they ought to ask him along. He's good company, after all, but they did spend the whole evening with him, and it'd also be nice to have a bit of time alone, just the four of them.

'You don't mind if I join you, do you?' Caleb says, and

Lucas feels a jolt of surprise – he's not sure he'd have asked quite so directly, but still, each to their own. There is a tiny pause, during which time he expects Caleb to jump back in, to say not to worry, the usual social nicety that might smooth out a moment of awkwardness. But he doesn't – he just stands there, looking at them all, his blue eyes clear and expectant. Lucas feels bad.

'Of course, sure,' he says, and Caleb grins, claps him on the back.

'Brilliant. Lead the way.'

Theo catches Lucas's eye, just briefly, and Lucas gives an infinitesimal shrug, as if to say, *what can you do?* The girls don't seem to mind – beside him, Holly links her arm through his and Saskia pushes open the door to the hotel, her sunglasses covering her eyes as they step out into the burning bright sun of Bangkok, the five of them. *And then there were five*, Lucas thinks. The line reminds him of something, an old Agatha Christie story maybe – he can't remember, he was never particularly well read at school. It comes to him later, as they're standing in front of the waterfall, the thunder of the water in their ears. *And then there were none.* It's a murder mystery, he remembers. How odd that he should think of it now.

*

'So it's called the Erawan waterfall,' Holly is saying excitedly, the guidebook open in front of her as they sit on the bus – which is, thankfully, air-conditioned. Their knees are pressed together, there isn't much room, and Lucas is starting to feel nauseous as the vehicle rounds corners at considerable speed. 'Or no,' she says, 'sorry, Erawan *Falls*.'

'Great,' Lucas says, 'it's kind of further away than I thought it was, though.'

'Only an hour to go, guys.' Caleb leans across the aisle of the bus to them, tapping his watch. 'It'll be worth it, you'll see.'

Lucas frowns. 'I thought you'd never been?'

There's a brief pause. 'No, I haven't,' he says at last, 'but I mean, it's meant to be amazing.'

In the seats behind them, Saskia and Theo are silent, as they have been for most of the journey, since they left Bangkok. Lucas knows Theo is stressing about his watch, and Saskia has barely said anything all morning. None of them had realised the falls were this far away – they're going to spend half the day on this bus. Still, at least it's not too busy. There are five others on the bus with them, but the other seats are empty. Three teenagers are sat at the back, and there is another, older couple too, sitting up nearer the front. Lucas keeps hearing snatches of their conversation; the woman is talking about a true-crime programme she saw, about a man who drugged and killed travellers. It's not exactly what he's in the mood for hearing as they speed away from the city, the scenery around them changing, growing lush and green. The roads are much quieter out here – they have passed the odd motorbike, but it is a far cry from the chaos of Bangkok.

He thinks he must have closed his eyes for a moment because when Lucas wakes up, the bus has slowed right down, and they are pulling to a stop. To his surprise, Holly is no longer next to him – she's moved and is now sat with Caleb, talking, their heads bent close together. As he looks across, she laughs – a proper laugh, as if he has said something really funny, and Lucas feels a little twinge in his gut. The bus pulls to a halt and the driver appears with a small microphone, telling them they've arrived, asking them to bring any valuables with them rather than leave them in the bus.

'Not likely,' Theo mutters, grabbing his bag, and Saskia rubs his arm sympathetically.

As they disembark, Holly grabs his hand.

'Sorry,' she hisses, 'you were asleep!'

'It's fine,' he says, shortly, but still, he wishes she hadn't laughed like that, and feels a flash of annoyance towards Caleb. Why has he come with them, anyway? Yes, OK, he rescued her bag, but they've paid him back now, haven't they? Theo bought him that hugely expensive dinner, all that wine. Lucas frowns. Did Caleb even offer to pay?

'All right, mate?' As if he can read Lucas's mind, Caleb is slapping Lucas on the back, grinning at him widely. There is something in the grin that Lucas doesn't quite like, as though the other man has somehow got one up on him – but he's probably just being paranoid, isn't he. He's hungover, tired, in a bit of a bad mood. There's no reason to take it out on this bloke.

'All good. Looking forward to this,' he replies, and Caleb nods enthusiastically.

'It's a beautiful place.'

Again, the words jar him – it sounds like he has been here before. But if he has, Lucas thinks, then surely he wouldn't be tagging along with them to see something he's seen already, would he?

'This way please,' their tour guide tells them, and he and Holly link hands, follow the three students and the older couple down a tarmac path surrounded by trees. There is a tall wooden sign at the side of the road, framed by yellow swirls, with the name Erawan Falls at the top, followed by a load of information in Thai, none of which he can understand.

'Basically, don't fall in,' Caleb says, winking, and Holly laughs.

Lucas grits his teeth. 'I'm not planning on it.'

Behind them, he can hear Theo and Saskia arguing – he is talking about his watch, again, and Saskia is trying to placate him. Lucas feels sorry for her – Theo can be like a dog with a bone sometimes. He lets go of Holly's hand, hangs back a bit, falling into step with them both.

'You guys OK?'

Saskia smiles at him, but her face is pale and she still has her sunglasses on so he can't really read her expression.

'We're fine, Luke, thanks. Theo's just worried about his watch.'

'It'll turn up, mate.'

Theo grunts, but looks slightly mollified, and Lucas winks at Saskia, trying to force a smile. Up ahead, Holly is walking next to Caleb, and as he watches, they round the corner and disappear.

'Don't you think it's a bit weird that he's tagged along with us today?' he asks in a low voice, and Theo shrugs.

'Don't really care, to be honest. Seems like an OK guy.'

Lucas frowns. 'Yeah, I guess so. I don't know. There's just something . . .' He tails off – he can't really explain what he means, even to himself. So he's flirting with Holly a bit. It's not exactly a crime, is it? And he doesn't need to worry about Holly reciprocating – he's never worried about that kind of thing, not with her. Their relationship has always felt solid, the most solid thing in his life for the last three years. He doesn't need to get jealous. But still . . . His mind flickers to Holly's stolen bank cards, Theo's missing watch. Perhaps they are being too trusting of this man, this stranger. Or maybe he's just being paranoid.

'What d'you think of him, Sask?' he asks, unable to help himself, and she seems to blanch slightly, unless he is imagining it.

'I'd rather be on our own,' she says, at last, but her voice is very quiet and he almost has to strain to hear. They round the corner, and for a moment, all thoughts of Caleb are pushed from Lucas's mind because there in front of him are the falls.

Seven tiers of waterfall tumble through the forest, cascading over the rocks, surrounded by a jungle of green. The water pooled at the bottom is a crystalline blue, and the students from the bus are already pulling off their shoes and socks and wading into it, their chatter carrying on the air towards Lucas and the others as they stand staring at the majesty of it.

'Whoa,' Theo says, 'amazing.'

'It's beautiful,' Saskia agrees, and Lucas waits for her to lift up her sunglasses, but she doesn't. The rushing of the water is loud, a roaring white noise that seems to encompass them all, wrapping them up together, and for a moment or two he just stands and stares at it, marvelling at the way the gushes tip towards the earth.

'There's a walk we can do around the falls, it's about a kilometre and a half.' Caleb has appeared next to them, and Lucas feels a splash of irritation at the 'we'.

'Actually, I might see if Holly wants to do it, just the two of us,' he finds himself saying, not stopping to hear an answer or to check to see if Caleb registers the slight. Instead, he goes to where Holly is standing on the slippery rocks, gazing up at the water, mesmerised.

'Come for a walk with me?' he asks her, and she slips her hand into his, smiles up at him as they begin to ascend the path that leads up through the jungle, along the side of the highest waterfall. Lucas can feel someone's eyes on him as they get higher and higher, and when he turns back around, he can see Caleb watching them, can feel the heat of his gaze even as the sound of the waterfall drowns out everything else.

Chapter Twenty-Nine

Saskia

Theo's in a terrible mood because of his missing watch, and I can feel Caleb watching him, noticing everything with those bright blue eyes. I wonder what he's done with it, the Rolex – imagine it sitting in his hotel room, or tucked away in his rucksack, or even in his pocket right now. It's probably the latter – it's the sort of thing he'd enjoy, a little game just for himself.

I could try to ask him for it, or slip my hand into his pocket somehow, but realistically, I know him well enough to know that there is no point. The watch is small fry to a man like Caleb. What he's after is something much bigger.

I'm desperate not to be on my own with him, but Lucas and Holly walk off together and then Theo says he's going to find the toilets and I am left with him, standing on the rocks by the foot of the waterfall, watching as the water cascades down over the emerald-green shrubbery, feeling the tiny splashes of water on my face, a fine mist of spray.

I decide to just say it.

'What do you want, Caleb?'

He smirks at me. He's standing too close to me, as usual, but I'm right near the edge of the rock so there is nowhere for me to move to, nowhere for me to go.

'You know what I want, darlin'.' His voice has changed again – it becomes rougher the minute the others are out of sight, slips back into the drawl I know of old. The real Caleb, not the imposter trying to pull the wool over the eyes of my friends. The man I know is ruthless, utterly self-serving. Even if he pretends not to be.

'I don't have money,' I say, and at that he actually laughs, picks up my hand in his. I squirm, but he holds it tight, lifts it so that my wedding ring sparkles against the backdrop of the waterfall. Anyone watching us from afar might think he'd just proposed to me. The thought makes me shudder.

'It's not mine,' I say, 'I mean, the ring is mine, obviously, but . . . you know what I mean. The money. If that's what you want, I can't give it to you.'

He doesn't let go of my hand, and I glance anxiously upwards and around, checking to see if the others can see us.

'I don't understand how you can even need it,' I say, keeping my voice as low as possible, even though there is surely no way anyone could hear us over the sound of the falls. Behind Caleb, I can see a group of tourists posing together for a photo; their big smiles make me want to cry. A couple of children are splashing in the shallows, their mother watching them carefully. The scene makes me feel grubby, like I want to dive into the water below and scrub myself clean of all this, of my past, of what I did.

What we did.

'You think the money you gave me lasts forever?' he says, shaking his head, a small smile playing on his lips. 'No, no, Saskia. Turns out, it doesn't go as far as you might think.'

I swallow. My breathing feels shallow, raw. I want him to let go of my hand. Theo could reappear any minute.

'I'm not the same person any more,' I tell him, through gritted teeth, and I wrench my hand away from his, crying out slightly in pain as he twists my fingers.

'Have you forgotten what I did for you?' he asks me, and his voice has an extra edge to it now, a darkness that frightens me. I move away from him, but lose my balance and I slip slightly, my right foot sliding on the wet rocks. He reaches out, grabs onto me, stopping me from falling, and I clench my jaw tightly. I'd rather he let me fall into the water. As it is, this will be just another thing that he can hold over me.

'We were so good together, Saskia,' he says, and I want to close my ears, stop the words from seeping in. Memories come back to me, a heavy body over mine, harsh breathing against my neck. Bruises on my arms; shopping for long-sleeved tops. The endless cycle of it all.

'Please,' I say, 'I can't give you what you want. I'm not the same person any more.'

He releases his grip on me and I step back from the edge of the rock. Behind us, the waterfall roars.

'That's right,' he says, 'you're not, are you? You're not little Saskia Green. You're Saskia Sanderson. Married to Theo Sanderson, son of George Sanderson.' He grins, wolf-like. 'Do you think I don't know how much money you've married into, darlin'? Do you think I don't know how much Theo Sanderson is worth?'

I stare at him, my heart thumping.

'I won't do it,' I tell him, forcefully this time. 'I love Theo.'

'You loved someone else before him,' he says, his face very close to mine, so close that I can see the whites of his eyes. I'm frightened to look into them, to lose myself in his words, the way I did before. Before I knew how dangerous it could be.

'That was different,' I say, and he just looks at me. There's no panic in his eyes, no uncertainty. He knows exactly how much power he has, how much I have sacrificed, what I would have to do to keep him happy. It's not even a question in his mind.

Chapter Thirty

Holly

'Are you OK?' I ask Lucas, for what feels like the hundredth time. We're right up at the top of the waterfall, and the view from up here is spectacular – the silvery water flowing down in an endless stream, the trees all around us, stretching upwards to the sky, their leaves forming a protective halo around the falls. Below us, I can see people underneath the overhang of the rocks, behind the water flow, but they look tiny from up here, and I can't see Theo, Caleb or Saskia anywhere.

'I'm fine,' Lucas says, but I can tell he isn't, I can sense when something is up.

'Did you fall out with Theo, or something?' I say, but he shakes his head.

'Of course not.'

We continue walking, and for a moment, I try to just let myself enjoy how beautiful the national park is, how stunning the falls really are. I pull out my phone, take a couple of photos, but it's impossible to capture the way the water glitters and the movement of it all. The air feels purer up here, fresher somehow, and I take a few deep breaths, hoping it clears the last remnants of my hangover.

'You seem to be getting on well with Caleb,' Lucas says, suddenly, and at last, the penny drops.

'You're annoyed because I went to sit with him on the bus?' I say, and Lucas says nothing, confirming my suspicions. I want to tell him he's being ridiculous, paranoid, and I'm about to but there is a tiny twinge of guilt in my stomach that stops me. I *was* flirting a bit with Caleb, he was making me laugh, and OK, if I'm totally honest, I do think he's quite attractive. But still, it's not like anything would ever happen. I'm with Lucas, and I love Lucas, and that's the end of it. But I suppose he isn't totally imagining things.

'Lucas,' I say, 'look, I'm sorry. I was just having a bit of a laugh, that's all. You know that.' He's walking slightly ahead of me, a few paces in front, and I half run to catch him up, grab his arm and pull him around towards me, so that we're facing each other.

'I love you,' I tell him, sincerely, and I see the features of his face soften at the words, the familiar crinkles form around his eyes. I reach up to kiss him, gently, and eventually he responds, pulling me towards him and wrapping his arms around my waist. After a minute or so, I laugh, pull away.

'It's actually too hot to hug, isn't it?' It *is* hot – the trees are shading us a little bit up here but it's still very warm, and with Lucas on one side and my backpack on the other, I feel like I can't breathe.

'I'm sorry for making you worry,' I tell him, and he looks sheepish.

'I'm sorry for being a dick.'

I shove him sideways as we walk on. 'You're not a dick.'

I'm relieved that the tension between us seems to have passed, but after a few minutes, as we begin the downward descent on the other side of the waterfall, he starts up again.

'Don't you think he's a bit weird, though? Caleb, I mean. Coming here with us today. A bit clingy, almost?'

I frown. 'I mean, not really. I like him. Don't you?'

He shrugs. 'He's all right. A bit intense, maybe. I just thought we could have had today to ourselves.'

'Well, we have got time to ourselves,' I say, gesturing around to the clear path ahead of us – it seems not many tourists are actually bothered to do the walk, and are mostly content to splash around in the pools below or amuse themselves in the café, which is attached to an information centre that I can see over to the right of the falls. I pull out my phone, take some more photos – the view from up here is incredible. I tip the camera down so that I can capture the flow of the water down to the pool below, zooming in a little to get the right shot. As I glance down, I catch sight of two figures standing further out than everybody else, on the edge of one of the rocks, and squint at them, narrowing my eyes against the sun. It looks like Saskia – I can see the flash of her blonde hair, the pink of her top. She's standing with Caleb, and as I watch, he reaches out a hand, and it looks to me like he grabs her waist. I frown. I must be misreading things.

Lucas follows my line of gaze and I see his eyes come to rest on the two of them too.

'Is that Caleb and Saskia?'

I nod. 'I think so.'

'Why is he holding onto her like that?'

I shake my head. 'I don't know. Maybe he's stopping her from falling? I can't see properly.' We both look back down at them, squinting – I'm almost sure he's holding onto her, and their heads are close together, too, his lowered to meet hers. I feel a twist in my stomach, a sick feeling. I use my phone camera to zoom in a bit, hoping we're wrong, but when we look at the photo, his hand is clearly visible on her waist.

'What the hell,' Lucas says, and I can hear the edge of anger in his voice. 'He needs to get away from her.'

'Luke,' I say, 'we're so far away from them, come on, it's probably nothing. Let's just head down and see. There'll be an explanation.'

'Where's Theo?' he says, storming ahead of me along the path, and I have to tear my eyes away from Saskia and Caleb and follow him, my backpack bouncing painfully against my spine.

'I don't know,' I gasp, 'but Luke, please. Don't overreact, don't say anything.' I grab hold of his arm, force him to come to a stop. 'Promise me, Luke.'

He sighs, runs a hand through his hair. 'It looked like – I don't know what it looked like. But there's something weird about him, Hol. I can feel it.'

'Well, maybe there is,' I say, 'but we don't have to ever see him again after today, do we? I'm sure he'll get the message if we don't invite him to hang out. And Saskia adores Theo, you know she does. It won't be anything.'

He looks at me, as if weighing up what I'm saying. 'I want you to be right,' he says at last, and I breathe out, give him a reassuring smile. It's not like him to get so agitated, but he's been a bit on edge for this whole trip, now that I think about it. I'd put it down to the fear of flying, at first, and then a bit of a hangover, but perhaps there is something else.

'Is there anything else you want to tell me, Lucas?' I ask him, prodding, and he opens his mouth, his lips parting as though he's about to say something. I stare at him, my heart rising in my chest – but then he closes it again, lowers his gaze from mine.

'No,' he says, 'of course not, Holly. Come on, let's go find the others.' He puts his hand in mine and squeezes it, but I can feel how clammy his skin is, can feel the sweat on his palms. Nerves. Lucas is nervous about something, and I don't know what it is.

Chapter Thirty-One

Lucas

He'd nearly told her about the money, then. It had been right on the tip of his tongue. To tell her about the pay cut, the text from HSBC, about the overdraft, about how actually, all of it was much worse than she knew. About how much it was playing on his mind. To the extent that they ought to press pause on the idea of buying a flat.

But he hadn't; he hadn't wanted to look weak, to upset her. So he'd kept quiet, told her it was nothing. But he couldn't quite meet her eye.

One thing Lucas does know, is that he wants Caleb to stop hanging around with them. What the hell was that, with Saskia on the rocks? He's tempted to tell Theo, but the sensible, rational part of him knows that Holly is right, that it will just cause trouble, that they don't really know what they saw. Saskia does love Theo, he is sure of it – you only had to look at the pair of them at their wedding to know that. He finds it very hard to believe she'd ever be tempted by anyone else, but then you never know, do you? Caleb has a certain charisma – even Holly's taken in by it.

Down at the bottom of the waterfall, they see the other three ankle-deep in the water, their shoes and socks in a pile on the bank.

'The water's lovely,' Saskia calls out to them, smiling. She's taken her sunglasses off now, they are perched on the top of her head, and Lucas eyes her suspiciously, trying to work out if there's anything going on, any hint of guilt lurking in her eyes. But she looks the same as she always does, and besides, Caleb isn't anywhere near her – he's waded further in, the water lapping around his calves, which look thick, tanned, sturdy. The water is a startling turquoise close up like this, and he and Holly kick off their shoes and go in. Theo is clearly still pissed off about his watch but has perked up a little bit – he's gazing up at the waterfall in awe, his hands planted on his hips, his brown, slightly hairy feet visible through the clear water.

'How was the walk?' he asks Lucas, and Lucas nods.

'Yeah, great. Lovely views from up there.'

Theo nods. 'I bet. Not sure I can be arsed, though. Think my hangover is actually starting to get worse.'

'Hair of the dog when we get back,' Lucas tries, and Theo laughs.

'If we make it back.'

For some reason, the hairs on the back of Lucas's neck stand up at this comment, and despite the heat of the day, a cold sensation trickles over him, sliding down his spine.

'What d'you mean? Why wouldn't we?'

Theo grins. 'No reason.'

'What's the view like from up there?' Saskia asks, pointing to where he and Holly have just been walking, and Lucas nods.

'Amazing.'

'It's meant to look like an elephant's head at the top, that's why it's called Erawan,' Saskia says, 'it's the name of the three-headed white elephant in Hinduism.'

'Guidebook?' Theo asks, and she nods.

'Nice.'

'What time does the bus leave?' Lucas asks, and Theo scowls.

'I'd tell you if I had a watch.'

Saskia groans, puts her arm around his waist, comforting him. Lucas is watching Caleb, searching his face for any kind of flicker as he looks at Saskia and Theo together, but the other man's expression remains impassive, unreadable.

Maybe he and Holly imagined what they saw. They must have.

Chapter Thirty-Two

Saskia

It's on the bus ride home when it happens. I'm sat with Theo, watching the landscape change out of the window, the lush green of the national park fading as we drive back towards Bangkok. Tiredness is seeping into me, partly from the heat of the day and the walk, and partly from the mental strength it is taking not to panic, not to let on to Theo that anything is wrong. My phone vibrates, the sensation against my leg making me jump, and I pull it out to see a WhatsApp message from Holly, even though she's sat right here, just a few rows ahead in the bus, in front of the older couple who are on the tour with us.

Saw you and Caleb standing together at the falls.

I freeze in my seat, immediately tilt my wrist slightly so that Theo cannot see the message. Looking forward, I can just about see the top of Holly's head, the little mound of dark hair, but I can't see her face. I hesitate, my fingers hovering above the keyboard of my phone, unsure whether to reply. What did she see, exactly? I think about him holding my hand, grabbing my waist. What it might have looked like. Stealthily, I glance over at Theo but he's staring at his own phone, not paying attention to what I am doing at all.

Holly is typing, the little dots appearing at the top of my screen. I'm holding my breath. The next message comes through.

Everything OK?

I allow myself to breathe out, relieved that she's checking on me, rather than accusing me.

Everything's fine, I type back, quickly, and I press send before I can think about it for too long. I see the top of her head tip downwards in the seat in front, and two blue ticks appear next to my message, showing she's read it immediately. I wait, to see if she'll type any more, but although it says she's still online, nothing happens.

I take a few more deep breaths, close WhatsApp and shove my phone into my bag, pushing it into the darkness where it can't torment me. There is no way I can let Holly in on what's happening, even if she thinks she might be able to help me. She can't help me. No one can.

As the bus bumps along, another thought occurs to me. I replay Holly's message in my mind: *Saw you and Caleb standing together at the falls.* The way it's phrased – could it almost be a threat? What if Holly isn't trying to help me at all?

But as soon as the thought comes, I tell myself I'm being paranoid. Holly is my friend, she's just looking out for me. I can't let Caleb's toxicity affect my thinking. I'm not the person I used to be any more, and I'll do everything I can to keep it that way.

Chapter Thirty-Three

Holly

There's a bit of an uncomfortable moment when we get back to the hotel. The bus drops us off at the end of the street, where we were picked up this morning, and Lucas and I scramble out first, thanking the driver and waving goodbye to the three students and the older couple who were on our trip. The older couple raise a hand in response, but the students barely acknowledge us. Away from the air-conditioning, we find the city streets stiflingly warm again, the air thick and soupy. Theo wants to go to a rooftop bar he's heard about, a few streets away, back through the main market square.

The five of us walk back to the hotel together – Saskia doesn't quite meet my eye, and briefly I wonder if perhaps I shouldn't have sent that text message, but I just want her to know I am here for her if she needs me, in case she *does* want to talk. I thought about replying again after she'd told me everything was OK, but then decided it would be better to leave it. I don't want her to think I'm spying on her. Or judging her. On the bus home, I looked again at the photo of them I took. They definitely appeared more intimate than they should. I was only trying to get a clearer view, to be sure, I tell myself, but I save the photo anyway. Something stops me from deleting it.

Caleb walks off ahead with Theo, the two of them falling into step together, and I can hear him asking Theo questions, about his father, his family, joking about the kind of wealth the Sandersons have accumulated.

'You ask a lot of questions, don't you?' I hear Theo say, jokingly, and Lucas looks at me meaningfully, and then I wonder if perhaps he is right, whether there is something a little predatory about Caleb. But then I think about the bus journey, how kind he was being – asking me about things with my mum, really listening to what I was saying, and I think perhaps he's just someone who cares about people, who is interested in them and their lives.

Back at the hotel, there is a pause as we hover in the lobby. I need to go back up to the room, get changed before we head to this rooftop bar tonight, and I need to charge my phone because the battery is flat again.

'Excellent day-tripping, people,' Theo says, one arm slung around Saskia's shoulders. There's a tan line where his watch was – Theo is one of those people who will get a bit of colour after only a few hours in the sunshine, whereas it would take me weeks to go even a tiny bit brown.

'So meet back down here around seven thirty?' he asks. 'Then we'll head to the rooftop place, yeah? It's called The Loft, sounds epic. We should get some amazing views from up there.'

'Sounds good,' Caleb says, easily, without pause, and that's when Lucas steps in. I can almost feel him vibrating with the need to say it, the energy radiating off him in a way I haven't seen before.

'Sorry, mate, I think it'll just be the four of us tonight,' he says, and only I can tell that his body is tense, and my own body tenses as a result. God, couldn't he just let the man come? Does it really bother him that much? He isn't usually someone who gets jealous like this, at least I didn't think he was, but I feel as though I am seeing a new side to him now, and to be honest, I don't really like it.

But Caleb seems completely unperturbed – he simply raises his eyebrows, his blue eyes innocent-looking, and shrugs.

'Oh, sure,' he says, 'only Saskia invited me earlier, that's all.' He looks across at her, and she's smiling back at him, her face slightly flushed. Curiosity bubbles in my stomach. Could there be something between them? Surely not – but there is something that looks a bit different about her, something in the flash of her eyes, in the way the two of them connect.

Lucas is wrong-footed and I feel embarrassed for him. He's behaving like an idiot. Quickly, I grab his hand and squeeze it, pull him slightly towards me, as if I'm covering him up, shielding him.

'Of course you should join us,' I say, brightly. 'Come on, Luke, let's go upstairs. See you guys back down here in an hour.'

Without giving Lucas the chance to respond, I tug him away towards the lifts – luckily, one has just reached us and we can get in straight away, so I don't have to look back at the other three.

'Honestly,' I say, as the doors shut behind us, 'Luke, that was really rude. There's no need to be like that.'

'I don't like him!' Lucas bursts out. 'We don't need him hanging around with us all the time, flirting with you and Saskia. He's a playboy, you can see it. I want a bit of time to ourselves. You didn't need to step in like that, like you were ashamed of me!'

'He's just a bloke on his own who probably gets a bit lonely out here,' I respond, 'you're being silly, Luke. Come on. It's beneath you.'

The elevator jolts, suddenly, and for a horrible moment I think we're going to stop. But then it shifts back into life and we continue the ascent, Lucas and I staring at each other angrily, our reflections bouncing back at us.

We don't speak for the rest of the elevator journey.

When we get back to the room, Lucas gets straight in the shower, without speaking to me. I throw myself onto the bed, plug in my phone and turn it on to find three messages from Mum, the first apologising for ringing me in a state last night, the second asking me to respond, the third angrily telling me that she knows I don't care about her. Frustration pounds through me and I feel tears prick my eyes. We've still got a bit of time before we need to meet for the bar and I'm filled with the sudden urge to be in the pool, to distract myself, to leave my phone up here and give myself some time to de-stress.

I grab my things, remembering the keycard for the room this time, and head back down to the pool. I could see if Saskia's around but I want to be alone for a bit, and thankfully, the pool is pretty quiet. There are some girls reading Kindles on the sunloungers, a family complete with bored-looking teenager, a woman with a small baby who looks like she is about to expire from the heat. And a couple, sitting at one of the tables, sipping bright orange cocktails. I can see from the way they are sitting that they've had a row of some sort – she looks tense, her shoulders tight. He is upright, stiff, angry. I wondered what they've argued about.

The sky is beginning to turn into evening, the sun giving us a burning orange finale, and I slide into the shallow end of the pool, feeling my body relax as my limbs submerge in the water.

I duck my head underneath the surface, my eyes immediately stinging slightly with the chlorine. It feels good to immerse myself like this, just a dark, curled-up shape in the pool, my hair flying all over the place, my body weightless. I've always liked the water. I come up for air and swim a couple of lengths, up and down rhythmically, letting the tension seep out of me – Mum's messages, Lucas's snappiness, the strange, unsettling feeling I had in Theo and Saskia's room when I found the black marker pen. The odd photograph, taped to the locker door. Caleb and Saskia, stood together on the rocks, too close to each other. I start imagining them together, replaying the moment I saw them, when it looked like they were holding hands. Memory is a strange thing, isn't it, it distorts things, it doesn't always tell the whole truth. I wish I could relive the moment properly, wish I could know for sure, see objectively whether there was something going on or not. I do a couple more lengths of the pool, trying to force myself not to think about it, to relax. We're on holiday, after all. Maybe tonight will be nice, the rooftop bar.

Somehow, this trip isn't turning out quite how I wanted it to – it is starting to feel brittle, as though it could break at any point.

When I pop up at the end of another length, everyone else from around the pool has disappeared. I wonder what time it is – I ought to go back upstairs and get ready, Lucas will be wondering where I am. But it's nice having the pool to myself and for a moment I starfish out on my back, look up, trying to take deep breaths and stop my thoughts from racing. The sky feels huge above me, endless. I picture our dream flat, the one I've been looking at online, imagine Lucas and me walking through the rooms, unpacking our things onto the shelves, making it our home. I want that to happen so badly, but at the moment, it feels so out of reach.

'Holly!' There's a shout above me, and I push myself upright, my feet cool on the bottom of the pool, then lose my balance slightly and gasp for air as my head disappears under the water. I right myself again, rubbing my eyes – they're stinging properly now, I've been down here too long, so it takes me a minute to adjust to what I am seeing.

Caleb is at the side of the pool, sitting on a sunlounger, watching me. He's got a beer in his hand, and his figure is outlined against the setting sun. It's growing darker now, and something about the shadow surrounding him makes him look slightly menacing.

'Caleb?' I say, surprised.

Water bubbles up in my throat, and I cough, spluttering slightly, then make my way to the edge of the pool. He's really staring at me and for some reason, I begin to feel a little bit self-conscious, I think because of the swimming costume, my lack of clothing. I adjust the straps of the costume, pull it down at the thighs. One strap has slipped slightly down one shoulder and I hike it up, smooth my hair back down against my skull and wrap both arms around my waist.

'I was just marvelling at your ability to hold your starfish,' Caleb says. His voice is strange, more serious than it was earlier on the bus, and I wonder if Lucas's behaviour has upset him more than he let on before.

'Oh,' I say, 'yeah. Well, I love swimming. Always have.'

There's a small silence, then, a pause that feels somehow loaded. I wish the others were here, it feels a bit odd being on my own with him, but he's smiling at me and I tell myself not to be so silly, that it's not as though I'm doing anything wrong.

'Where are your friends?' he asks me, as though he can read my mind, and I glance upwards, to where the windows of the hotel rooms shine blankly out at us.

'I left Lucas in the shower,' I say. 'Look, I'm sorry if he was rude earlier, he didn't mean it. He can get a bit . . .' I trail off, trying to think of the right word.

'Territorial?' Caleb asks, raising one eyebrow, and I smile, feeling disloyal as I do so.

'He didn't mean it,' I repeat, 'it's fine for you to join us.'

I move slightly in the water; it's growing colder now that I'm no longer swimming, and I shiver, rub my hands up and down the tops of my arms.

'D'you know what the time is, I'd better go up to see—' I start to say, but Caleb cuts me off.

'Can I ask, Holly, how you get on with Theo?' he asks. 'He's an interesting guy, isn't he? Different league to the rest of you.'

He gets up, still holding his beer, and comes to the side of the pool, crouching down so that he is right in front of me. I grip the side, my legs out behind me, keeping the majority of my body underwater. My heart is beginning to hammer inside my chest, like an alarm system to my brain.

'Why do you ask?' I say, but Caleb just keeps looking at me. His bright blue eyes seem darker, somehow; they are almost black in the half light. I can see the water of the pool reflected in them.

He places the beer bottle down next to him on the side; it makes a little chink as it touches the tiles.

'I like Theo a lot,' I say, 'we've been friends for ages, he's always been a great friend of Lucas's.'

'It doesn't bother you, the money thing?' he responds quickly, and I hesitate.

'What do you mean?'

He shrugs, not breaking eye contact even though I feel uncomfortable, exposed now. 'Well, you don't have to be a genius to know he likes to flash the cash,' he says, 'this place isn't cheap.'

'We all wanted to stay here,' I say, and he nods, like he knows I'm lying. He's perceptive, intelligent. Able to read people.

'Actually,' I say, standing up in the pool, feeling the water rush off me, 'I'd better get back inside, Caleb – we're going to that bar, aren't we, and I need to get changed, let Lucas know I'm OK. I left him a bit abruptly!'

'Saskia and Theo's wedding venue looks like it was nice,' he says, suddenly. 'Were you a bridesmaid?'

I hesitate. How does he even know where they got married? Did they tell him?

'Did Saskia show you the venue?' I ask him.

He gives me a half smile. 'Something wrong with that?'

I stare at him, trying to work him out. There's something odd about him this evening, something that wasn't there earlier. He's seemed innocuous to me, just a nice guy on his travels – OK, a good-looking guy, but still just a guy – but now for the first time I'm wondering why he's travelling alone, why he doesn't seem to be with any friends. He doesn't really know us, after all, does he? We don't really know him. I feel wrong-footed, like the ground beneath me is shifting. Maybe Lucas is right about him. Maybe he's created a false sense of intimacy between us, by listening to me earlier, asking about my mum – but it's an intimacy that I ought to try to stop.

'I really do have to get inside, actually, sorry, I don't mean to be rude,' I say, firmly, though my fists are clenched tightly by my sides and I can feel the odd, rubbery texture of my fingers; my skin is prune-like, I've been in the water for too long.

'Hey, of course,' Caleb says, 'sorry, no worries.' He looks at me for a moment longer, and then the tension between us seems to snap and he is more like his normal self again. He gets up from his haunches and pads back over to the sunlounger where I've left my towel, a dark shape bundled up on one end.

'Here,' he says, 'you must be getting cold. And look, sorry if I startled you. I'm just trying to be friendly, that's all. I've had a rough . . .' he trails off, then seems to right himself. 'A rough few months, I guess you could say. Perhaps I've forgotten how to be.'

I don't know what to say to that – a bloom of sympathy hits my chest and the ground shifts beneath me once again.

'Don't worry,' I say, 'of course. I'm just getting cold, that's all.'

Maybe he is just lonely. Maybe I'm imagining things again.

I turn away from him as I clamber out of the pool, embarrassed by how much of my skin is on show, leaving trails of water behind me. Wrapping the towel firmly around myself, I turn to face him again. He's smiling properly now, all traces of strangeness evaporated, and I feel a small sense of relief.

He picks up his beer and tips it towards me, then takes a big sip. I watch his Adam's apple bob in his throat. He's so tall, at least a head above Lucas.

'I'm sorry you've had a tricky few months,' I say, trying to be kind, and he stands stock-still for a moment, looking at the pool, at the water, now completely still.

'Thank you,' he says at last. 'I appreciate that.'

184

I'm walking away from him, my towel firmly around me, when he calls out to me again.

'See you inside,' he says, 'I'll buy you a drink on the roof. As long as your boyfriend doesn't mind.'

I pause, feel the weight of my wet hair heavy on my neck, dripping coldly down my back.

'What?' I turn around, see that he's much closer to me than I thought, only a pace or two behind me. Is he following me inside?

'Only kidding,' he says, winking, and I nod, force a smile that I know doesn't quite meet my eyes.

I can feel him watching me as I walk away, but I don't turn around again.

I wonder what he meant by *a rough few months*. I wonder what he's really doing out here.

Chapter Thirty-Four

Saskia

He sits opposite me at dinner. He's got changed, into an ink-black shirt and blue jeans, and I can just see the edge of a tattoo poking out of the end of his shirtsleeve. It's not familiar; it must be a newer one. He catches me looking at it and winks; I turn away, focus on Theo, who is devastatingly handsome tonight in a white T-shirt and khaki shorts. He's showered and he smells fresh, of the woody-scented shower gel from our room. I know he's upset about his watch but he's cheered up a bit now, is laughing at something Lucas is saying, his smile wide and happy. I can feel tears rising in my throat and I blink hard, swallowing the emotion down.

I can't afford to lose control.

'This place is amazing,' Theo says, and it is – it's beautiful – but I can't enjoy any of it because of what's going on, what Caleb is trying to persuade me to do. The bar looks directly out over the city, the Chao Phraya River stretching out beneath us. The tables are lit up by small golden cones that glimmer in the growing darkness, and the benches we are sat on are covered with midnight-blue velvet, dotted with gold scatter cushions. The whole place feels opulent, luxurious, and the food looks incredible – Theo ordered starters for us all, and two bowls of oysters sitting in ice appeared, surrounded by glistening chunks of lemon. We've got cocktails, too – I've got some sort of negroni with an additional twist, although all of it tastes like ash in my mouth.

'So tell me,' Caleb says, loudly, his voice cutting through the sound of the bar, the clinking of glasses and the hum of chatter. 'Whose idea was it to come to Thailand? Who's the decision-maker in the group? I'd love to hear.'

There is a slight pause; the restaurant seems to still for a second. I feel as though I'm holding my breath.

'I think we'd rather hear about you, actually!' Holly says. 'You're an enigma, Caleb.' There's something slightly clipped and colder to her tone, it surprises me, and I turn to look at her questioningly, but she doesn't meet my eye.

Theo agrees, seemingly oblivious to Holly's tone. 'Yeah, not much to say here, mate. Known this one' – he gestures to Lucas – 'since school. Met these two in a bar. Separately, I should say. Tell us about your good self. What d'you do when you're not taking pity on unsuspecting tourists and saving their lives?' He grins, flashing his teeth, one arm around my bare tanned shoulders. Completely relaxed. Theo likes Caleb, I can tell, he likes having someone around that he can try to show off to a bit. But he doesn't know how dangerous that is.

'Me?' Caleb says, and I can almost see the cogs turning in his mind, choosing which story to tell. He once told me that he had a whole roster of stories, that I could take my pick, choose-your-own-adventure style.

'Yes,' Holly says, her eyes focused on him, laser-sharp, 'tell us about *you*, Caleb. What brought you to Bangkok? What d'you do back home? I mean,' she laughs, looking around at the rest of us as if it's one big joke, as if she's only just realising something, 'we hardly know anything about you!'

Caleb shrugs, but he looks a bit on edge, shifts in his seat, and places both elbows on the table, resting his chin on his interlinked hands then lifting his head up again, as if he can't quite get comfortable.

'Not much to tell, really,' he says, eventually. 'London born and bred. East London, to be precise. I do a bit of everything back home. Whatever people need.'

He looks at me as he says this last bit, and I glance away, feel the burning heat of my cheeks begin to spread through the rest of my body. Memories crowd my vision and I take a sip of the negroni, feel the alcohol hit the back of my throat.

A waiter appears beside us, sidling up silently. His voice makes me jump.

'More drinks while you wait for your mains?'

Theo responds enthusiastically, ordering beers for the three boys, and another cocktail for Holly.

'Saskia?'

I'm lost in a memory, of hands around my throat, spittle on my face. Anger, everywhere. There was always so much of it.

'Saskia? You OK? Want another drink?'

I shake my head. 'I just want some water, actually. Thanks.'

There's a pause, broken only by the sound of a group of women at the next table laughing. I pick up an oyster, the black shell fragile beneath my fingers. My hands are trembling.

Chapter Thirty-Five

Lucas

So he's just got to put up with it, then. Lucas sips his drink, the bad mood hovering over him like a dark cloud. The restaurant is great, but he is beginning to find Caleb's presence intensely annoying, as if he's a persistent fly that Lucas cannot quite swat. There is something a bit odd about his voice, too – he's only noticing this tonight, but when he was talking earlier it sounded as though his accent was lilting a bit, tipping back into a rougher, heavier drawl than the tone he's been using for the last two days.

The girls are still lapping it all up, seemingly interested in his back story, his life, of which there doesn't seem to be much, in Lucas's opinion, anyway. Theo seems relatively oblivious to any issues, too, and Lucas feels a rush of frustration at his friend, at the easy-going way he handles life – except for when it comes to missing Rolex watches, it seems.

The thought circles back to him. *Could* Caleb have stolen the watch? He'd been there that night, after all, and perhaps that's why he insists on hanging around with them – perhaps he's a thief, preying on innocent travellers. Lucas frowns, staring at him, at the hint of a tattoo poking out from underneath the edge of his sleeve.

'What's your tattoo of?' he says, suddenly, and the table turns to look at him – he hadn't realised he'd interrupted something that Holly was saying, lost in his own world, coming up with theories about Caleb.

'Me?' Caleb asks, and Lucas snorts.

'Well, yeah. None of us have got tattoos.' He looks around at the other three, expecting them to laugh or smirk alongside him, but they all appear a bit uncomfortable, as though he's said something wrong.

'Nothing wrong with a decent tattoo, mate,' Theo says mildly, and Lucas feels shame heat up his cheeks, takes another long sip of his drink. His head is starting to spin a bit, to go fuzzy at the edges.

'It's just a design I liked,' Caleb says, unfazed, and he rolls up his sleeve to reveal a serpent's head, the long, forked tongue snaking out, the eyes like slits. Lucas stares at it – it's horrible, he can't understand why anyone would want to voluntarily do that to themselves. Saskia seems mesmerised by it, too, as if she can't look away, and Lucas feels annoyed with himself for drawing more attention to Caleb.

'How much did that set you back?' Theo asks, and Caleb shrugs, his shoulders rolling backwards.

'Not much. Fifty quid or so?' He grins, winks. 'Nothing to you, mate.'

Lucas tenses; it's an odd thing to say, inappropriate. Theo doesn't say anything in response, and there is a slight lull in the conversation, a silence that borders on awkward.

'I'm going to go look out over the city,' Holly says, breaking it, and she gets to her feet, pushes back her chair and heads over to the railings that surround the restaurant.

'I'll come with you,' Lucas says, but she's out of earshot

already, having threaded her way through the other tables to the side. He sees her reach the barriers, her dark silhouette outlined against the inky blue-black of the sky. He reaches her, circles his arms around her waist, puts his head against the nape of her neck, breathing in her familiar smell. It's slightly different tonight, though – must be the hotel shampoo. It has an edge to it, somehow.

'You all right?' he says, and he feels her nod against him, though she doesn't say anything. Together, they gaze down at Bangkok below – the glittering lights of the city, the silver shimmer of the river wending its way through the urban landscape. Eventually, she turns towards him.

'I think maybe you were right about Caleb,' she says, hesitantly, glancing over his shoulder to check that they are alone. He checks too – but the other three are still sat together at the table, too far away to hear what he and Holly might be saying.

'There's something weird about him, isn't there?' Lucas says, and she hesitates again, before nodding, biting her lip.

'I don't quite know what it is. I mean, I liked him when we first met, and obviously, he found my bag, but . . . I don't know. There's something I can't quite put my finger on. There was a moment, earlier, when I was in the pool . . .'

Lucas stiffens. 'What happened?'

'No,' she says, shaking her head, 'nothing bad, nothing at all, really – but I was swimming and then I realised he was there, sat on one of the sunloungers, just . . . watching me. And then he asked a few questions, you know – nothing that would sound odd on its own, but it's just . . .'

'You're wondering why he's so interested in us,' Lucas finishes the sentence for her, and she nods, biting her lip again.

'I feel bad,' she says, 'I keep thinking that maybe he's just a lonely guy, you know, someone who just wants a bit of company, but it is a bit rude of him to keep coming with us everywhere, isn't it? I think maybe you were right, earlier, when you asked him not to come.' She pauses. 'I'm sorry I was grumpy with you about it.'

Lucas tightens his arms around her. 'It's fine, it's OK. I probably did sound like a bit of a prick.'

She laughs, and the moment lightens between them a little.

'We're probably being paranoid, aren't we,' she says, sighing. 'I'm just starting to get an odd feeling about him, that's all. A gut feeling, I guess you'd say. Women's intuition.' She half laughs.

Lucas smiles grimly. 'It's not women's intuition if I've got the exact same feeling, is it? It's something we ought to pay attention to.'

Both of them turn to look over at the table, where the outlines of Saskia, Caleb and Theo sit close together, their faces hidden by the dark lighting.

'Well,' Lucas says, 'we're going to Koh Samet tomorrow, anyway. We'll just tell him goodnight, tonight, and that will be it. It'll be the last we see of him. We'll shake him off.'

'OK,' Holly says, 'OK, yes, you're right. He can't come with us to the island. I'm sure it'll be fine, won't it? We don't need to be rude, but we can just . . . disengage.'

'Absolutely,' he says, feeling a wave of relief, relief that she's come round to his way of thinking, can see how weird the other man has been behaving. He pulls her closer, kisses the top of her head.

'Everything will be fine,' he says, 'don't worry.'

He puts his arm around her, and they turn back to face the restaurant. Holly doesn't say anything else, but Lucas feels a triumphant sensation in his stomach when they return to the table, when he sits down across from Caleb, meets the other man's eye.

'All right, mate,' Caleb says, nodding, and Lucas just looks at him, his insides burning, his hand securely in Holly's underneath the table. *I'm not your mate*, he thinks, *none of us is.*

Chapter Thirty-Six

Saskia

Lucas doesn't like Caleb. I can tell. I watch his face as he sneers at him over the table, and anxiety curdles in my stomach. Lucas does not want to get on the wrong side of Caleb: he has no idea what he's capable of.

I reach out to grab my drink, and as my left hand touches the glass, I realise with a horrible, lurching sensation that my wedding ring is no longer in place. The silver band with the glittering, precious diamond, the ring that I love so much – it's simply gone.

I let out a little yelp, and everyone turns to look at me. Heart hammering, I pull my hand back into my lap, hiding it from view, desperate not to let Theo see.

'Sorry,' I say, 'I'm fine, sorry. I think a mosquito got me.' With my right hand, I rub my arm unconvincingly, wincing, and the other four seem unbothered, resume their chatter. They're talking about the recent election, back in the UK, and I let the words wash over me as I try to think. Has it fallen off, maybe when I went to the bathroom? I try to remember washing my hands, whether it was there then, picturing my fingers under the gush of hot water, the lavender-scented soap. It's worth a huge amount of money – if I've lost it, Theo will go absolutely crazy. And I'll be devastated, too. That ring means everything to me – it's a symbol of our love, but it's also a symbol of my new identity, as Saskia Sanderson, a new woman, a woman who is worthy of loving. Tears prick my eyes as I stare at my hands, the empty space below my knuckle taunting me.

'I'm just going to the loo,' I mutter, pushing my chair back – I'll have to check the bathrooms, check if anyone's handed it in. I don't look at anyone as I walk off, keeping my left hand hidden beneath my right, and the restaurant feels like it's tilting before me as I stumble towards the toilets, tears blurring my vision. I feel lost without it, as if part of me has gone missing too.

The bathrooms are, luckily, empty – I get down on my hands and knees on the tiled floor, peering underneath the cubicle doors, under the sink, checking each of the three toilets, running my hand over the tops of the cisterns. I stare wildly into the mirror above the sink, see my own panicked, exhausted expression staring back, and for a moment it feels like she's behind me, the old Saskia, the ghost of her, darkening my reflection, pulling me back into a past that I've tried so very hard to forget.

There's nothing on the tiles that surround the sink, and I'm about to turn and leave when there is the sound of footsteps behind me, then the unmistakable noise of a door closing softly, of a bolt being drawn across. The slow slide of metal.

I am trapped.

'Looking for something?' Caleb asks me, and when I turn to face him, he holds out a hand, his fist closed, clenched around something that I cannot yet see.

Dumbly, I watch as he opens his hand, reveals the glint of

my ring, nestled in his palm. I hate seeing it there, among the creases and crevices of his skin, out of place – it makes me feel violated.

'How did you . . . ?' I say, unable to stop myself, but he just smiles at me, closes his hand around it again.

'Come on, Saskia,' he says, 'you know me well enough by now to know how I operate.' He shrugs. 'I've been practising, too. Since we last saw each other. Honing my skills.' He smiles, winks at me. 'Though you really ought to be more careful. This kind of ring don't come cheap. And your husband's not made of money.' He stops, laughs. 'Oh no, wait, he *is*.'

I clench my teeth, my eyes shifting past him to the door. I was right – he's pulled the bolt across, locking us both in.

'I'm not scared of you,' I say, and he tuts, as if I've said something ridiculous.

'I know you're not, darlin'. You've no need to be.' He steps closer to me, puts one hand – the hand that isn't holding my wedding ring – on my chin, tilting my head up towards him, forcing me to look into his eyes. 'I'd never hurt you. You know that. That's not my game.'

He lets go of me and I reach up, a reflex, touching my skin where he did as if it is a burn.

'Lucas doesn't like you,' I say, the words bursting out of me in a rush. I don't quite know why I say them, except that I want to find a way to hurt him, to exert some sort of power, but he just laughs.

'Shame,' he says, 'I like him. I like all of your friends, Saskia. Like I say, you're onto a good thing. I'm genuinely impressed.'

I don't say anything. I wonder how long it will take for the others to notice that we've been gone a while, whether any of them might come looking for me. Holly, perhaps, might be suspicious judging by her text messages earlier. Theo should want to know where I am, but I can't see him until I've got the ring back, safely in place on my finger.

'Give me the ring back,' I say to Caleb, calmly, firmly, holding out my hand. It's demeaning, like a child asking for a sweet, but I don't care at this stage. I just want it back.

'You know I will, Saskia,' he says, 'it's not the ring I'm after, is it?' He shakes his head, makes a tutting sound with his mouth. 'That's not the prize here. I'm after a little more than that.'

Tears fill my eyes. I think about the photograph, taped to the locker in our dorm room at Pho Hostel, the one I had to pretend not to recognise.

'What do you want?' I ask him. 'What will it take for you to leave me alone, to walk out of my life again?'

He smirks. 'I think you know what I want, Saskia. I want round two. A repeat act, as it were, of what we did before. Only this time, my payout is a bit bigger. Substantially bigger, you could say.'

Even though I knew – dreaded – that this was what he would say, my heart drops, icy tentacles reaching their way around it. I'm trying so hard to force the images out of my mind, but they're coming thick and fast now – a collection of belongings in a clear plastic bag, returned to me with a blood smear on; conversations in a dark London pub, our voices hushed; a sense of pervading terror, each and every day, that built and built and built until it stopped.

'You don't mean it,' I say to him, swallowing. My lips feel very dry. My right hand automatically goes to the gap on my left finger where my wedding ring should be – my touchstone, and its continued absence only makes me feel worse. When I'm anxious, I sometimes play with it, twisting it round and around my finger, but now I let my hands drop uselessly to my sides.

'I do mean it,' he says, grinning, as if this whole thing is funny. As he speaks, there's a knock on the door, and a woman's voice calls out something in Thai. My eyes dart towards the lock. Neither of us responds to her.

'They'll come in soon,' I say quickly, 'they'll realise the bathrooms shouldn't be locked.'

'Fine by me,' Caleb says, 'we can't stay in here forever, Saskia.' He smiles again, casually, and I feel hatred burning up inside me.

'Look,' he says, 'you know what you owe me, Saskia. Let's face it.' He steps towards me again; I can smell the alcohol on his breath, though I know he isn't drunk, that he rarely gets drunk, because he has to keep his wits about him. 'You owe me your life.'

'Things are different now,' I say, through gritted teeth, 'and I paid you what I owed you. You know I did. It's not my fault you've burnt through the money, that you can't hold down any other lifestyle than that of a criminal.'

Something passes across his face, then, a quick, momentary flash of anger, and I know I've got to him.

There's a hammering on the door again, and this time there's a male voice, too, speaking in English, saying something about getting a set of keys, the master key.

'The lock must be jammed,' I hear him say, 'is anyone in there?' There's a pause, and we stare at each other.

'Go ahead,' Caleb says, but I can't, my throat feels like it's jammed; I can't get the words out.

'Look,' he says, 'I like you, Saskia. Always have. I want us to be friends, like we used to be. Remember? I *helped* you. Now it's time for you to help me.' He opens up his hand, stretches out his fingers so that my ring is exposed again, the beautiful diamond glittering in the harsh light of the bathroom.

'You can have this back,' he says, 'but I want you to think about what I'm offering, here.'

I reach out, take the ring quickly with trembling fingers, ram it back onto my finger before he can change his mind. His gaze doesn't leave mine, and the room feels like it's holding its breath along with me. Our reflections shine back at us in the mirrors, so for a moment it looks as though there are two of him, two Calebs, as though he is multiplying, as though he is everywhere, and I cannot escape him. My chest feels tight with anxiety, as if the walls of the bathroom are closing in, and I'm suddenly desperate to get out, to get some fresh air, to see the sky.

'You don't want your secret coming out, Saskia,' he says, 'do you? You don't want the world knowing what you did. God, think of the headlines. And I'm happy with that, I'm happy for it to stay that way, for you to keep your new name, your new . . . persona.' He looks me up and down as he says this, and I want to run, to hide in one of the cubicles, slam the door behind me and not come out until he's gone. But I can't.

'The only condition,' he says, 'is for you to help me get what I want. Last time, it was what you wanted, and I helped you out. Big time. And now, well,' he spreads his hands, 'think of it this way. Fate has brought us back together. It's given you a chance to repay me, properly. All you have to do, Saskia, is play your part. I know you can do it, because you did it so well the first time. I actually think it suited you, back then.'

'Unlock the door,' I say to him, 'please, Caleb. Unlock the door.'

'I will if you agree,' he says, and there's an impatience in his voice, now, a darker, gruffer tone. He's annoyed that I haven't given in already, that I haven't caved. But how can I? When what he's asking of me is so horrific, so unimaginable?

'I can't do it,' I say, 'you know it's different this time, Caleb. You know that.'

He nods at my clasped hands, the ring. 'You know how easily I can take from you, Saskia,' he says. 'You didn't even notice me doing it. I'm not the kind of guy who messes around. I want a job done, and it gets done, right? I rang the insurance company; I had his passport. I know how much the life insurance is, who the benefactor is. It's you, Saskia. And I want that money. All you have to do is play along. Like you did last time. I know you have it in you, Saskia, because you did it before.'

I let out a little moan at his words, and my whole body begins to shake.

'No,' I say, 'no, Caleb, please. You have to understand. It was a completely different – I wasn't thinking – it's not . . .'

But he doesn't let me finish. There's a loud banging noise, and the door of the bathroom flies open. A waiter bursts into the room, having clearly shouldered the door open. I rush out past him before he can see my face, and Caleb follows; I feel his hand grasp my elbow tightly, pull me to the left, out of sight of the restaurant tables, where the others must surely be wondering where we are.

'Get off me,' I cry out, trying to wrench myself out of his grip, but he is far too strong for me, and his hold is vice-like, immoveable.

'Saskia,' he says, 'I'm not going to let this go.'

There's a pause while we stare at each other, both panting slightly, my breath coming thick and fast, my thoughts a terrifying jumble. And then he says it, the words I never wanted to hear, the very worst thing I did, come back to haunt me in the worst possible way.

'You killed your husband before, Saskia. I want you to do it again.'

Chapter Thirty-Seven

Holly

'We were about to send out a search party!' Theo says when Caleb and Saskia finally return to the table. I watch her face carefully, but it's a mask – she tells us she got stuck in the bathrooms, that Caleb had to call a waiter to help her out.

'God, poor you,' I say, 'I hate small spaces. I once got stuck in the bathrooms on a family trip to Devon, when I was a child. Nearly screamed the place down.'

'Lucky you were there to help, right?' Lucas says to Caleb, but he says it in a way that's obvious he doesn't mean it – deadpan, with no authenticity behind the words.

Caleb doesn't seem to pick up on it, he raises his eyebrows, takes a sip of his drink, and nods. 'I'm always happy to help out a damsel in distress.' He winks at Saskia, and somehow, the sight of it makes the hairs on the back of my neck stand up.

'I've already settled up,' Theo says, and Lucas says that he's added what we owe to an app on his phone, assures Theo that he's keeping a tab of everything he's paid for.

'Don't worry about it, mate, I've told you,' Theo says, but Lucas insists, gets the app up and shows Theo the list of numbers.

'We'll just transfer it over,' I say, putting my hand on Lucas's arm; I can feel how tense he is, and I don't want this to become awkward, not while we're at the table, not in front of Caleb.

'What time does the boat leave for the island tomorrow?' Theo says. 'Can anyone remember? I booked a cab to take us to the pier in the morning.'

There's a smashing noise and Saskia leaps up – her cocktail glass has tipped over on the table, the glass shattering into shards that fly out across the remnants of our meal.

'Oh God, sorry,' she says, and as she picks up a big piece of glass I see the moment that it slices into her flesh, a sliver of bright red blood immediately blooming on her finger.

'Don't touch it,' Theo says, raising his arm in the air to attract the attention of a waitress, 'oh babe, come here.' He wraps a white serviette around her hand; immediately, a red spot begins to grow, the scarlet spreading over the thick material.

'Just a surface cut, it'll stop bleeding soon,' he says, bending to kiss her; Saskia's face looks stricken at the sight of the blood. The waitress appears and says she'll clear it all up, wishes us a pleasant rest of the evening, thanks us for dining with them.

I feel bad as we walk away, leaving her to clean up our mess – the dirty cocktail glasses, the smears of food on the plates, the broken glass. Someone else's problem. Not ours.

As we descend the spiral staircase that leads down from the roof, I manage to pull Theo to one side.

'Look,' I say, 'I'd rather we didn't tell Caleb our plans tomorrow. Luke and I think he's a bit weird, a bit clingy, you know. I'm worried if he knows when the boat is, he'll try to come with us or something.'

Theo looks blank. 'What? Really? I like him, he's a good laugh.'

I hesitate; he's making me doubt myself, but then I think of Caleb and Saskia, standing by the waterfalls, of the way he stared at me when I was in the pool.

'I dunno, Theo – he's making me feel uncomfortable. I just want tonight to be the last we see of him, OK?'

Theo shrugs. 'OK, sure. Whatever. If that's what you want.'

We continue going down the stairs, and I breathe a sigh of relief. We'll go back to the hotel, get a good night's sleep – the boat leaves early tomorrow, at just after nine, and Caleb will stay here in Bangkok, carry on without us. That way, Lucas will relax a bit and we can enjoy the rest of the week, just the four of us, like we were supposed to.

On the walk back to the hotel, I catch up with Saskia, thread my arm through hers. It's late, now, almost midnight. On the main street, the city still feels alive; music blares out from the tuk-tuks whizzing past, and a drunk man stumbles past us, his feet bare, a bottle of something I can't make out in his hand. Briefly, I think of my mother, and pull out my phone to check whether she's messaged, but the battery is flat yet again and I swear under my breath.

'I've got to get a new phone,' I say to Saskia, 'this one keeps dying on me.'

She doesn't say anything, and I squeeze her arm, trying to get her attention.

'Sask? I know my phone battery isn't *particularly* interesting to you, but still . . .' I smile at her, but she doesn't respond, just looks straight ahead as we walk.

'You OK? Is your hand hurting?' I ask her, feeling a bit awkward – there's something odd in her eyes, a sort of misty blankness, as if she isn't really here beside me, as if she's somewhere else entirely, lost in her own thoughts.

'Saskia?' I ask her again, and this time she hears me – she turns to face me and it's like a switch flicks on in her eyes, and suddenly she's there, her usual self again.

'Sorry! I was miles away. I think my hand's fine, it's stopped bleeding now. But I'm really tired, I can't believe how late it is already. Today has flown by.'

'I know,' I say, 'it has, hasn't it? To be honest, I feel ready to leave the city now – I'm keen to have a more chilled time out on Koh Samet. I haven't even started reading the book I brought with me.'

'Definitely, I can't wait to see the villa,' Saskia says. As we round the corner, she twists back, looking behind us, and I do too. The three boys are a few metres behind – Lucas is on the roadside, and I feel a stab of worry – he ought to get on the pavement, the way the traffic is here – and Theo and Caleb are beside him, talking about something, Theo gesticulating in the slightly wider way he does when he's had a drink.

'That must have been horrible, getting stuck in the loo like that earlier,' I say, and Saskia nods.

'It was. But luckily Caleb helped me.'

I look sideways at her, trying to work out if there's anything else going on, but she looks impassive, and I decide that I must be imagining things. If there were something going on between her and Caleb, it'd be more obvious. I think of her at her wedding, how happy she and Theo looked. There's no way she'd do that to him, not with some random guy we've only just met. Still, it'll be good to get away from him, to be on our own. It'll make everything easier.

Back at the hotel, we cluster in the lobby, and I'm about to start worrying again about how we'll get rid of Caleb but to my surprise he raises a hand almost at once, tells us he's heading up to bed.

'Thanks for a great night,' he says, grinning at the four of us, and we all watch as he turns and heads off towards the bank of elevators, his shoes slapping against the marble floor of the lobby.

'Night, mate,' Theo echoes, when he's almost at the lifts, and Caleb turns, smiles at us again, then disappears into the waiting elevator. The doors slide closed behind him, and I breathe a sigh of relief. Beside me, I can feel Lucas's body exhale too – it's as if we were all waiting for something that hasn't happened, and the moment Caleb is out of sight, I start to wonder if Lucas and I have been ridiculous, as if this whole worry over him is entirely in our heads.

'Well, I'm off to bed too,' Theo announces, 'see you guys in the morning, yeah? The car I booked will pick us up at eight forty-five, then the boat leaves Nuan Thip Pier at one, so . . .'

'Meet out the front at just gone eight thirty?' Lucas suggests, and I groan slightly at the thought of the early start.

'We'll need to be packed up too,' Saskia says, and Theo nods.

'Yep. Out the front with our bags at eight thirty latest. We can grab something to eat down at the pier, I reckon. Maybe grab a quick coffee here at the hotel before we get in the car.'

The four of us head upstairs, make our way down the long corridor to our rooms. Briefly, I wonder which room Caleb is in, then push the thought away – it doesn't matter, does it. We'll be out of here in eight hours' time.

'Goodnight, guys,' I say as we reach the room, 'sleep well. See you tomorrow. Koh Samet here we come!'

Lucas slides our keycard into place and opens our door, saying he wants a quick shower before bed.

'Night,' Theo says, raising a hand and going into their room, the door closing behind him with a soft click, but Saskia to my surprise reaches out, pulls me into a hug.

'Sleep tight,' she says, as she pulls away, and I nod, taken aback by how small she feels, how fragile. Did she eat much at dinner? I try to think back, but all I can see is the glass shattering, the bloom of blood on her hand.

'You sure you're OK?' I ask, in a low voice, but she nods quickly and gives me a little wave, before opening the door to their room and disappearing inside. I stand there in the corridor for a few seconds after she's gone, listening, but there is only silence, and after a minute, I go into our room, close the door firmly behind me.

But as I lie in bed next to Lucas that night, willing sleep to come, I find myself thinking back to her expression as we walked home from the restaurant. There was something about it, something odd. If I didn't know better, I'd say she looked scared.

Chapter Thirty-Eight

Lucas

He doesn't sleep well. In the night, he thinks he hears the sound of someone shouting – raised voices coming from one of the rooms nearby. He wakes up at 3am and opens up his phone, reads through the list of things Theo has paid for, checks his bank account online as if somehow there has been a surprise injection of money – but of course, there hasn't.

He's got to talk to Holly about it, let her help him work out a plan. He knows he has to. Keeping it in is making it worse. Or maybe – the thought occurs to him as he flips his pillow over, tries to get comfortable again – maybe he could own up to Theo. He doesn't want to be in debt to his friend, but at least it would stop HSBC charging interest every day, which is what they're currently doing. If he could just get back in the black, he could figure out a way to make some money and then sort it all without Holly ever having to know. Could he take on another job? His heart sinks at the thought – teaching is full-on enough. Could he move to a smaller rental, save money that way? He almost laughs at the thought – it's not as if the place he currently has could get much smaller. Could he and Holly move in together now, into one of their existing places? He pictures it – but the thought of them cramming their stuff into one of their tiny flats is so depressing, and so far from what he'd imagined when they'd first started talking about buying somewhere together, that for now, he dismisses it from his mind.

His alarm goes off at eight, and he wakes to find that Holly is already up; he can hear the hum of the shower and on the floor her suitcase is half open, most of her clothes already packed neatly inside. Groaning, he rubs his gritty eyes and throws back the sheets, the stale taste of last night's alcohol in his mouth. The sooner they get to the villa in Koh Samet, the better – but he's not relishing the idea of a cab ride and then a boat.

'Morning, sleepyhead,' Holly chirps, coming back into the bedroom wrapped in a towel, her hair in wet tendrils around her shoulders. 'You looked so peaceful sleeping that I didn't want to wake you, but we need to hurry if we're going to be downstairs by eight thirty.'

'You seem cheerful this morning,' Lucas manages, and she grins at him.

'Just excited to move on. I don't know about you but I feel like we haven't had a chance to properly just chill on this trip. I mean, Bangkok's been great, but . . .' she tails off, an odd expression crossing her face, and Lucas knows she's thinking about Caleb.

'No, you're right,' he says, getting to his feet. 'It'll be amazing to be somewhere new.'

He feels stiff as he wanders around the room, throwing things into his bag. Holly is singing under her breath, some pop song he's never heard of, and he wonders if he ought to just tell her now about the money situation, get it off his chest. She seems like she's in a good mood so she might take it well, but then again, is it selfish to burst her bubble when she seems happy?

'Holly,' he manages, and she stops what she's doing, turns to look at him, her see-through toiletry bag in her arms with what looks like half the hotel freebies inside it now, too.

'Yes?' She's standing half illuminated by the sunlight coming in through the huge windows, and her expression looks so light and hopeful that he just can't bring himself to do it, to tell her something that he knows will cause her to worry. He has a sudden flashback to her sitting beside Caleb on the bus to the waterfall, of her laughter drifting back to him, of the way she looked at him before it all started to go a bit weird. Something hardens in Lucas, a resolve stiffening. He's not going to tell her. He's going to sort this out on his own, stand on his own two feet. He's going to be the kind of man who can give her what she wants.

'I love you,' he says, instead, and her face breaks into a smile.

'Silly. I love you too. Now come on, let's get going. I won't love you if you make us miss the boat.'

Chapter Thirty-Nine

Holly

There's no sign of Caleb downstairs. I do a quick sweep of the lobby with my eyes as we come out of the elevator, but it's fairly deserted – just the hotel staff behind the reception desk, and an older couple having a coffee in two of the seats over by the window.

Saskia looks as relieved as I am when we've checked out successfully and the car approaches to pick us up outside the hotel; we all get in quickly and Theo once again goes in the front, confirms with the driver that we're off to the pier.

'Did you enjoy the Omni?' the driver asks, and we nod, tell him it was great. Secretly, though, I'm not sad to see the back of it – and the further we drive away, the more relaxed I feel.

Saskia seems to be feeling the same – she's quiet for the first twenty minutes or so, and I notice her checking her phone a lot, but once we're out of the city and back on the motorway, she seems to visibly perk up, winding the window down and letting her hair flutter a little in the breeze, even singing along to a song that comes over the radio.

'Now that we're shot of him, can we all agree that Caleb was a bit of a weirdo?' Lucas asks, and we laugh, though part of me wishes he just hadn't brought him up at all.

'I don't know what the problem was, he was fine,' Theo says from the front, twisting round to look at us, and I wonder if maybe he's right, but then I stop thinking about it and let myself relax, leaning back against the seat, picturing the sandy beach waiting for us, almost able to feel the sensation of the sea lapping against my toes.

We arrive at Nuan Thip Pier just after twelve – the taxi driver tells us the traffic has been relatively good for Thailand, and we've got about half an hour until we need to board the ferry.

'We're getting one of the fast ones,' Theo announces. There are a range of boats bobbing in the turquoise water – larger ferries which I assume are the slower ones, and some smaller ones that look more like speedboats. A big wooden structure covers half of the entrance to the pier, and a queue of tourists are already lined up, paper tickets in their hands, waiting to board one of the larger boats. There's a little café underneath the wooden roof and I volunteer to go get us all coffees – God knows I could do with one.

The Thai man behind the counter greets me warmly, his English perfect, and asks me if I'm having a good time in Thailand.

'The best, thank you,' I say, and he hands me the coffees in a cardboard cup holder, his fingers accidentally brushing mine as he does so.

I head back to the others, who are all sitting on their suitcases; Saskia's got her sunglasses on, shielding her eyes from the glare bouncing off the water, and she takes the coffee from me gratefully.

'Not much in the way of food options at the café,' I say, and Theo shrugs.

'We can get food when we're there. It only takes about fifteen minutes to cross.'

My stomach growls in protest but it's too hot to traipse around looking for lunch so I agree and plonk myself down next to Lucas, reach out to touch the back of his neck.

'You're burning up,' I tell him, fumbling in my bag for the sun cream then smearing some onto his skin. 'Honestly, Luke, you need to be more careful. We don't want you getting skin cancer before we've even moved in together!'

He looks a bit odd when I say that, and I frown, trying to catch his eye. 'Everything OK?'

'Everything's fine,' he grunts, and I decide to leave him – he's probably just hungry.

We sit in relative silence for the next ten minutes, sipping our coffees – Theo is playing with something on his phone, and Saskia is staring off into space, her elbow resting on her knees, her chin in her palm. Her wedding ring catches the sunlight, winks at me, and not for the first time, I wonder how much it might have cost.

'I'm going to have a quick wander round,' she announces, suddenly, 'my legs feel stiff from being in the car.'

I'm about to suggest that I come with her but she's up and off before I have time, disappearing into the throng of tourists that crowd the port. I shrug and dig out the guidebook from my bag, start reading up about Koh Samet.

'Did you know there are mermaid statues on one of the beaches out on the island?' I say, to nobody in particular, but neither of the boys reply. I roll my eyes and decide I'll go for a quick wander, too – the scenery is actually quite picturesque, the brightly coloured flags on the boats rippling in the breeze, the luminous orange buoys dotting the water, the luscious green trees set back from the pier surrounding us all. Mum hasn't been in touch for the last day and a half and I start to feel guilty, think maybe I'll go take a couple of pictures, send them over and update her on our travels.

'Back in a minute,' I say, getting to my feet, and I walk off towards the edge of the pier, wondering if there are fish in this part of the water, what might lie beneath the surface.

I'm standing by one of the larger ferries when I see her, her blonde hair glinting in the light, her figure unmistakable against the bright blue sky. She's got her head in her hands, her shoulders slumped, and as I watch it's obvious that she is crying, great heaving sobs that seem to wrack her whole body. I'm too far away to hear, but I keep watching as Saskia cries, then seems to stop, take a deep breath, and visibly try to pull herself together. She takes out her phone and stares at it for a moment, then I watch in horrified fascination as she reaches out, holds it aloft above the water, then drops it deliberately into the ocean, the little black rectangle disappearing from view.

With that, she turns on her heel and starts coming towards where I'm standing – quickly, I move away, into a gaggle of young tourists who are queuing at one of the electronic kiosks to buy tickets for the boats. My heart is thudding. What is she doing? Why would she throw her phone away like that – it's a brand new one, I know it is, and she loves her phone – loves Instagram, documenting everything, showcasing her and Theo's lavish lifestyle. It doesn't make any sense.

One thing is obvious, though – there's something she is keeping from us. The question is, what?

Chapter Forty

Saskia

I feel better as I watch my phone sink into the blue depths of the sea. I don't trust Caleb one inch, and for all I know, he'll be using it to track me somehow. My only hope is that he doesn't know where we're going today – I've been racking my brain to try to remember whether anyone actually mentioned Koh Samet to him, but try as I might I can't recall. I know we mentioned going to an island, but there are tons of islands off the coast around Bangkok, and I'm praying that he doesn't know which one.

What he's asking me to do isn't something I can even consider, and our moving on today is my only hope of losing him – if I can get through the rest of this week without him knowing where we are, and then get back to the UK, I can carry on as though none of this has happened. Put it down to the terrible twist of fate that it is. After I parted ways with Caleb five years ago, I never planned to set eyes on him ever again. And from now on, that's the way it's going to stay.

I re-join the others; Holly gives me a bit of an odd look as I do so but I ignore her, pushing my sunglasses back down to cover my eyes, which will no doubt be red and puffy from crying. But the breeze on the boat will clear that up, and from now on, I've got to stay focused. The last thing I want is Holly digging around, suspecting something is up. No – I've done my crying now, I've let it all out, and when we get to Koh Samet I'm going to put these horrific last few days behind me. I've come so far in the last five years. I can't let Caleb take that all away.

I won't let him do that to me.

We board the boat together, my hand in Theo's, and the moment the engine starts I feel better, safer. There was no sign of Caleb anywhere near the port, and by the time he must have woken up this morning we were long gone, hours away from Bangkok. We wave at a couple of young boys standing on the edge of the pier as the speedboat cuts away, leaving a bright white trail in the water behind us, and Theo wraps his arms around me as we watch Nuan Thip disappear.

'Let's have some time on our own when we get to the villa,' Theo murmurs, and I nod against his chest, turn to kiss him on the lips.

'Of course,' I say, 'that would be lovely.'

Holly and Lucas have gone to the front of the boat, are facing out to sea, watching as the water foams around us. It feels slightly choppy, and I grab onto Theo as we lurch from side to side. He holds me tightly, his warm, safe arms a huge comfort.

'I love you, Theo Sanderson,' I tell him spontaneously, and he pulls me tighter, resting his chin on the top of my head.

'I love you too, babe. Always.'

I'll have to pretend I left my phone on the boat.

*

The speedboat pulls up to Koh Samet island, and I scan the other passengers carefully as we file up, ready to disembark – it's a smaller boat so there are about twenty of us, but still I examine them all. There's a tall guy in a blue baseball cap pulled low over his face, but his build is all wrong – he's much skinnier and wirier than Caleb, and I breathe a sigh of relief as I realise he isn't among us. One of the cabin crew tells us to throw our luggage into a smaller, long-tail boat waiting in the shallows and I hesitate for a second, not wanting to let go of my possessions, but the man gestures to me impatiently and I obey. Our luggage is heaped on top of one another's, and we're told to climb down into the water, to wade through the few metres or so of shallows to get to the shore.

'God, they could have warned us,' Lucas grumbles, kicking off his sandals, and Theo takes my hand to help me down, the cool turquoise water a welcome sensation after the heat of the boat. The staff pull the long-tail boat gently to the edge of the sand, and we pick our bags back up – Theo takes mine for me, and hands the two Thai men a tip, the money crumpled from being in his pocket. I watch carefully as the last person reaches the shore, helped by her boyfriend, his hand in hers. Caleb is nowhere to be seen.

'Thank God for that,' I mutter, under my breath, but I must have said it louder than I thought because Theo turns round to look at me quizzically.

'What was that, babe?'

'Nothing!' I say brightly. 'Just glad to be here, that's all. Did you say we can walk to the villa?' I put my sandals back on, my wet feet slipping slightly against the warm leather, and pull my water bottle from my bag, taking a long drink.

The relief of being away from Bangkok, of knowing Caleb wasn't on the boat, is immense.

'I did indeed. Follow me, guys, just a fifteen-minute walk,' Theo says, and we do, the three of us trailing after him, down a long path made of wooden decking and straight onto the most magnificent beach. The sand seems to stretch out for miles and miles, acres of gold, and I kick off my sandals, hold them in one hand as we pick our way from the shore, loving the sensation of the warm sand on my bare feet.

'This is beautiful,' Holly breathes, behind me, and on impulse, I reach towards my pocket for my phone before remembering that of course, I don't have it with me any more. I'll get a new one when we're back in the UK.

I twist around to check whether the speedboat is still there – if it is, Theo will insist on going back if I say I've left my phone on the deck – but luckily, I can see it zooming off already into the distance, gone to pick up the next tranche of tourists.

'Shit,' I say out loud, 'I think I left my phone on the boat.'

'Oh no!' Lucas says. 'Do you want to go back?'

'Too late,' I say, arranging my face to try to look rueful, 'Theo, you're going to have to let me take pics on yours!'

I'm doing a convincing job, I think, and besides, there's no reason any of them would possibly imagine that I'd dropped my own phone into the ocean, is there?

'What's mine is yours,' Theo says, 'I can order you a new one once we get to the villa. You should cancel your Apple Pay, though.'

'Will do.' I nod, although I don't think there's much need – I can't imagine the fish of Nuan Thip having much use for Apple Pay.

We walk further up the beach, passing a few wooden signs advertising snorkelling, banana boating and jet-skiing.

'I wouldn't mind doing some snorkelling,' Holly says, pointing to one of the signs, and I notice Lucas frown slightly, wonder if he's thinking about the price, daubed next to it in bright green paint that glistens on the wood.

'Let's see how we feel when we get there, we can make a plan,' I say, and we continue up the beach. The sand is sticking to my slightly damp feet, and the thought of snorkelling right now makes me feel a bit exhausted. The beach seems to be getting quieter the further we walk, and most of the passengers who shared the boat with us seemed to have headed off in the other direction, towards the east.

'The island is made up of a few different beaches,' Theo tells me, 'some are known as more party beaches, especially Sai Kaew, but the one I've chosen is quieter, more secluded. Thought it'd suit us better after a hectic few days in the city.'

'Definitely,' I say, 'secluded sounds perfect.'

We walk up and around a bump on the headland and onto another stretch of sand, this one with a couple of large white buildings situated right at the back, surrounded by palm trees.

'Almost there,' Theo reassures us, 'we're just in one of these.'

'I wouldn't call this fifteen minutes,' Holly mutters under her breath, but she's mollified when we get closer to the villas, when she sees how beautiful they are.

'Wow,' I breathe, 'Theo – it looks amazing.'

'Part of the Paradee Resort,' Theo says, proudly. 'Four private villas, each with its own pool. Our home for the next few days. I think we're the farthest on the right.'

'Incredible,' Lucas says, 'we're right on the beach!'

We make our way up to the final villa on the right – *Flamingo*

Villa, it says on an engraved wooden sign on the wall by the door. There are two golden flamingos flanking the main entrance, too, and Theo flips open a key box to the left of the door, squints at his phone and punches in a four-letter code.

'Here we are,' he says, lifting out a little silver key, complete with a pink flamingo keyring, and he pushes the key into the lock and opens the villa, standing back to usher us all inside.

'Eek, it's beautiful!' Holly says, and it really is. For a moment, I forget about Caleb, about everything, as we enter the main living room, a huge, light-filled space with burnt-yellow walls, long draping red-and-white curtains, with two pristine white sofas facing a central table with wrought iron legs and a polished wooden top. In the middle of the table sits a green crystal vase, full of bright orange flowers, their buds half-opened, stretching up towards the ceiling. A large flat-screen television sits on one wall, and the opposite wall faces outwards onto the beach, two large glass doors giving way to a set of three concrete steps that lead down onto the sand. We wander through to an equally large kitchen, housing a giant silver fridge and sparkling tiled worktops, where another table is laid out with four champagne flutes, and a welcome note informing us a bottle is chilling in the fridge.

'Just what the doctor ordered,' Theo says, taking the bubbly out straight away, but I want to see the rest so I go ahead, through the next door which leads into a big double bed-room, again with a set of doors facing out directly onto the beach. The bed is huge – covered in a white, fluffy duvet, and someone's twisted two towels into swans, their heads tipping forward to form a heart shape. There's an en-suite, too, all sparkling grey tiles, a huge mirror with his and hers sinks, four drawers underneath full of coconut-scented hand creams and little folded flannels. I smear some cream on my hands and wander back into the bedroom, staring out at the view.

'Saskia, look at this!' Holly's calling me from the next room, and I walk in to find her pointing out of the second bedroom window to where a private pool glistens, surrounded by four covered sunloungers. Palm trees surround it, giving us the extra privacy, and a blue parasol covers an outdoor dining table.

'Beautiful,' I say, and she nods, then glances sideways at me, frowning.

'A shame about your phone,' she says, and I nod.

'Yeah. But it's OK, I can get a new one.'

'Of course,' Holly says. There's a slight pause – and am I imagining it or is there a bit of tension between us? – our bodies close together as we stare out at the pool, not looking directly at each other.

'Wasn't it brand new?' she asks, her voice casual, and I hesitate.

'Yeah,' I say eventually, 'but like I say, these things happen. I must have just left it on the seats on the top deck of the boat.'

'Mmm,' she says, but there's a little bit of an edge to her voice, and for a moment I wonder if she can possibly have seen me throw the phone into the sea. But I was far away from them, wasn't I? She can't have done.

'Where are you ladies? Who fancies a poolside drink?' Theo calls from the kitchen and I feel a wave of relief.

'Me please,' I call back, and I leave Holly standing by the window, make my way back through the rooms to the kitchen, where Theo has poured us each a tall glass of champagne, the bubbles fizzing.

'Delicious,' I say, taking one, then chink my glass against his with a smile.

'This place is great, Theo. Thank you so much for sorting it all out.'

'Your wish is my command,' he replies, giving a little bow, and I laugh, take a sip of my drink. The bubbles zing on my tongue. For a second, I feel a spike of something almost like happiness. Maybe everything is going to be all right, after all.

Chapter Forty-One

Holly

Clearly, Saskia isn't going to tell me the truth about her phone. I watch her as we sip champagne by the pool, enjoying the sensation of the sun on my skin, my head covered by the shade of the sunlounger, which has a little covering that slides out from the headrest. Everyone is in a good mood, it seems – there's a more relaxed atmosphere among us now, and the beach villa feels so calm compared with the fast pace of Bangkok.

I can't decide whether to tell Lucas what I saw, or whether it would be better to just leave it, let Saskia's decisions be her own. But I feel like a bad friend for not at least trying to find out what's the matter with her, and my mind keeps running through possible scenarios as to why on earth she'd throw it away. Option one: she really just got sick of it – of the pressure to look at work emails, the Instagram notifications – I remember her screen lighting up with them when I got changed in her room back at the Omni, the night I got locked out of ours. But Saskia isn't like that, not really – she's always embraced the online culture, and surely throwing it in the sea would be a bit of a drastic step. Option two: there was something on there that she didn't want any of us to see.

Messages from Caleb, perhaps? I look over at her now – she's sitting in between Theo's legs on one of the other sunloungers, both of them sipping champagne, her long, tanned legs stretched out in front of them, her body nestled between his thighs. They always look so happy together. I can't imagine her cheating on him – but then perhaps that's me being naïve.

'All right?' Lucas is looking over at me, and I nod, smile at him. He knows Theo and Saskia better than I do, ultimately – maybe I ought to just tell him, find out what he thinks. But then I think of Saskia crying, her head in her hands, and wonder if to tell Lucas would be the wrong move. What if there is something wrong between her and Theo? I think of the night I heard them arguing, the way she burst out of their room, slamming the door behind her. You never truly see inside someone else's relationship, do you? Maybe there's something else going on entirely, something I don't know. I don't want to inadvertently make things worse.

It's just after two thirty, now, and Lucas suggests a walk along the beach.

'There are some great-looking cliffs over to the right,' he says, 'I wouldn't mind exploring a bit.'

'There's a restaurant on the beach I thought we could go to this evening,' Theo says, 'Saskia and I might stay here and chill if you two want to check out the cliffs? Right, babe?'

He squeezes her gently with his legs, and I watch her expression, trying to check whether the thought of being alone with Theo worries her at all. But she looks fine, and I tell myself that it can't be that, it just can't be. Theo is a good guy. He'd never do anything to hurt her.

'Come on then, you,' Lucas says, getting to his feet and stretching out a hand towards me, setting his champagne glass down on the floor, near the edge of the pool. 'Shall we go for a wander?'

I let myself be pulled to my feet and we wave to the others before setting out onto the beach. I see the cliffs in the distance, dark grey shapes jutting into the azure sky, with a row of trees along the top, swaying slightly in the wind.

'It's lovely here, isn't it?' Lucas says, taking my hand as we walk, and I agree, swinging our hands gently in time with our footsteps. It's quieter than I thought it would be, there's hardly anyone else around. An older man is walking along the sealine, his head down as though looking for something, and in the distance, a couple of people are swimming, their bodies just tiny outlines in amongst the waves.

'It's nice and peaceful,' I say, 'and hopefully, a few days chilling out will be a lot cheaper than all the stuff we were doing in Bangkok – nice as that was.'

'Yeah,' Lucas says, but at the mention of money he frowns a little.

'Don't worry,' I say, 'we're a bit over budget according to the spreadsheet, but I think we still ought to be OK.' I squeeze his hand three times, our little code, but he doesn't squeeze back. Instead, he looks more worried than ever.

'Look,' he says, 'Holly, about the money. I just . . .'

We stop walking and I turn to look at him. 'What?' I say. 'What's the matter? You look really serious.'

For a moment he doesn't say anything, and there's just the sound of the ocean roaring behind us, the waves crashing relentlessly onto the shore. The wind seems to be picking up a bit, and a strand of hair flits across my face, into my mouth; I extract it carefully, licking my lips.

'About the flat,' he says, and I feel a jolt of worry. I've been looking forward to moving in together so much – don't tell me he's having second thoughts?

'Are you having second thoughts?' The words burst out of my mouth before I can stop them, and I hold my breath slightly. I don't know if it's all the worrying about Theo and Saskia but suddenly I feel paranoid, as though Lucas might be about to end things with me, as though he's about to tell me he doesn't want to live together at all.

'Of course not,' he says, and I breathe a sigh of relief. I'm just being ridiculous, aren't I? Lucas and I are solid.

'What then?' I say, but he turns away from me, carries on walking up the beach.

'Nothing,' he says, 'it's nothing, Hol, I promise. Forget I said anything. Come on.'

He holds a hand out to me, and I trot to catch him up, feeling silly. It's obviously *not* nothing, because otherwise he wouldn't have brought it up, but I want so badly for it to be nothing that I keep quiet, swallow my fears down, and take his hand as though nothing has happened.

I'm frightened to hear the truth. Which makes me a coward, I know. The truth is out there. How for long can I turn away from it?

Chapter Forty-Two

Saskia

Theo and I lie tangled on the bedsheets, breathing heavily. It's actually nice having the villa to ourselves, being away from Holly's watchful eye, and I lay my head against his chest, feel his heartbeat thundering to match mine.

'It's hot in here,' I say, aloud, and he laughs, the soft, familiar thrum of it.

'Not much gets past you, does it?' he says, and I poke him in the side, sit up and reach for his phone to check the time.

'We're not doing very well with possessions on this trip, are we?' he says. 'First my watch, then your phone. We'd better start being more careful.'

I nod, not meeting his eye. It feels horrible, keeping things from him, but I don't know what else to do. I get up and go over to the curtains, pull them back – we'd closed them to give ourselves a bit of privacy – and jump when I see a face looking back at me.

'Christ!' I put a hand to my chest, leaping backwards.

'What?' Theo looks up, unperturbed.

'Nothing, Lucas and Holly are back, that's all,' I say, though why Holly is standing so close to our window, I don't know.

'Cool,' he says, stretching out on the bed, his long, tanned arms above his head, and I feel a flicker of jealousy – Theo is having the holiday we should all be having – a relaxed, fun trip with his girlfriend and best friends. He has no idea of the cacophony of worry going on inside my head. But that's how it has to be, I remind myself, watching as Holly and Lucas round the corner of the house. I hear the sound of the front door opening, Lucas's voice calling out that they're back, Holly shouting that she didn't mean to scare me like that.

What did you mean, then? I wonder privately. Was she trying to listen in at the window? Does she suspect that there is something wrong?

'Shall we go have a drink together on the beach before we eat, watch the sunset or something?' Theo asks, and I tell him that sounds like a brilliant idea, that I'm just going to shower before we do.

In the bathroom, I stand under the gush of hot water, washing the smell of sex off me. My hands run over the thin white scar on my stomach, the one that Theo thinks I got as a child, a routine operation shortly after I was born. It isn't from that, of course.

It's a scar that came from Andrew.

*

I first met Andrew when I was twenty-three years old. We worked together, at a Wetherspoons pub in south London, near Stockwell tube station. He was hard to miss – he was funny, horribly so, making sarcastic comments about the punters who came in, whispering in my ear as I tried to key in their orders at the till while biting my lip as I tried not to laugh. He had dark brown eyes, black hair, pale skin – he said he had Irish blood in him, and in his mouth, even that sounded exotic.

I was struggling for money at the time; I was working four nights a week in the pub, and applying for admin jobs in law firms during the day, and Andrew offered me something I needed. He showered me with attention – compliments, little gifts, even though I didn't think he had very much money either. But that all changed when he invited me to meet his parents. He wasn't poor at all – he was loaded.

His parents lived in a huge house in East Sussex, in amongst the downs. I remember packing my suitcase to go stay, worrying about what to wear, but they were very welcoming, and I felt like I fitted in for the first time in a long time. I hadn't seen my parents since moving to London, and Andrew's family welcomed me with open arms. I couldn't understand why he was interested in me, but I loved how he made me laugh, how he made me feel like the most special girl in the world whenever we were together.

Looking back, I think he knew exactly how much power he had over me. Those type of men always do.

'Why do you even work in the pub?' I asked him once, when we were lying in bed together. 'You obviously don't need the money.'

'I like it,' he'd said, 'I like the banter.'

Later, he admitted that it was a good way of picking up women.

We got married when I was twenty-four. At that point, he'd never laid a finger on me.

If only I'd known that it wouldn't stay that way for long.

Chapter Forty-Three

Lucas

They're sat on the beach in Koh Samet, just the four of them, another bottle of posh champagne between them, passing it round and drinking from the neck as if they are students again. Lucas has taken his sandals off and is digging his toes right into the sand, trying to force himself to chill out. The day is cooling down a bit, but the sand is still warm, as though it's absorbed all the heat from earlier. In front of them, the sea is so blue that it looks unreal – nothing like the cold, dark English sea you get back home; this is turquoise, sparkling, topped with white foam that looks as though it could belong on a wedding cake.

He's going to ask Theo for a loan. It's the only way out. He'd had another flurry of messages from the bank earlier, which he's deleted in case Holly sees, and he's accumulating interest at an alarming rate now. He just needs to find the right moment to talk to Theo.

It comes as the girls suggest walking the few metres down to the water; Holly says she wants to dip her toes in the ocean.

'We'll stay here,' Lucas says, quickly, glancing at Theo, who nods mildly, happy to go with the flow as he always is. The two girls stand and make their way towards the sea, leaving their shoes with the boys. Lucas swallows and clears his throat, turning to Theo.

'Look, mate,' he says, deciding the best way is just to dive straight in. 'I have a favour to ask. I need to borrow some cash.'

Theo looks up at him. He's sprawled out in the sand, resting on his elbows, propping himself up. Lucas feels the heat rising up his own cheeks – God, it's embarrassing, this, having to ask for a loan like some sort of beggar. But he thinks of the messages from HSBC, the bold capital letters. He doesn't feel like he has any choice.

There is a beat of silence. Lucas realises he's holding his breath.

Then – 'Of course, mate,' Theo says, easily, and Lucas feels a wave of relief hit him, fast and strong. He should have known that Theo would react like this – he's his best mate, after all, they've been firm friends for years.

'How much do you need?' Theo asks, and Lucas tells him a number before he can lose his nerve, a bit more than he'd originally planned to ask for, but it's best to have a cushion, isn't it? Just until he can work out how to earn more himself. He'll start looking for other jobs the second they get back – he's always resisted going into the private sector, believed in the state system, but the recent cuts have been brutal and he has to think about his future, doesn't he? He looks down the beach at Holly, who is ankle-deep in the water, her back to him, her long hair hanging down her back. His future with Holly. That has to come first, before his principles, before his pride. Before everything, really.

'No problem,' Theo says, 'look, I can transfer it now.' He pulls out his phone, thumbs a few buttons. Lucas can't believe the ease and speed with which the immediate problem is sorted.

'Thank you, thank you so much, mate,' he says, feeling simultaneously grateful and ridiculous, that something which has been keeping him awake at night for months has been taken care of with a few swipes from Theo's thumb.

'You're all good,' Theo says, setting his phone down and lying back on the sand, tucking his hands beneath his head, gazing up at the sky. Lucas wonders what it would really be like to be him, to have that kind of money at your fingertips, that level of confidence and freedom. He knows Theo hasn't really worked for it, that it all comes from his father, that it's family money really, but he wishes it didn't make him feel so small.

'I really appreciate it,' he says, lying back down too, joining his friend as they both look up at the sky. Above them, an aeroplane glides across, cutting through the blue like a knife, leaving a trail in its wake. He's expecting Theo to ask more questions, to ask what he needs it for, or how he got into this situation in the first place, but he doesn't, he just stares up at the sky, as if nothing has happened at all. Lucas feels absurdly grateful.

'I'll pay you back, I promise,' he tells Theo, but his friend just half smiles, his gaze still on the plane.

'I know you will, Lucas. I know you will.'

'What you guys chatting about?' A shadow comes over Lucas's vision, blocking out the aeroplane, and Holly's face swims into shot. She flicks a hand and tiny droplets of water sprinkle over his cheeks, salty and cold.

'Oi!' He reaches up, pulls her down towards him.

'We were just talking about how beaut it is here,' Theo says, and only Lucas notices him winking, a flash of an eyelid, when Holly is turned the other way.

Chapter Forty-Four

Holly

I tried to talk to her when we were in the water, our painted toes winking up at us like shells.

'Is everything OK, Saskia?' I asked, and she nodded immediately, as I'd known she would.

'I just want you to know that . . . that I am here for you, if you need me,' I said, a bit awkwardly, I couldn't quite work out how to phrase it. 'You know, if there's anything bothering you . . . you can always come to me.'

I tried to make my voice neutral, light, not put her on the red alert. She didn't answer straight away, just continued swirling her feet in the water, creating mini waves around the two of us.

'Thank you,' she said, eventually, 'but I'm fine, Holly, really. I'd tell you if there was something the matter. Promise.'

I had to leave it after that. We're friends, of course we are, but we're friends because of the boys and I don't feel like we have the kind of relationship where I could push it any further. I didn't want to offend her, of course. So I've resolved to leave it for now, to try to just focus on having a good time. In a few days, we'll be back in London, I'll be back at my desk, wading through my email inbox and dealing with annoying colleagues. I deserve to be able to relax as well, don't I. Whatever secret

Saskia is hiding, it isn't one she wants to share with me, and as far as I'm concerned, I've tried to be a good friend, be there for her. I can't do anything if she doesn't want to be helped.

Back up the beach, Theo says we ought to head back to the villa if we want to get changed for dinner. I suppose I ought to change – I'm just wearing shorts and a T-shirt, and the travelling and walk to the cliffs earlier has left me feeling a bit sticky and dirty. It'll be nice to get a bit dressed up.

The wind feels stronger as we gather up the champagne bottle – now empty – and our shoes, and my hair whips in front of my face as we make our way back to the villa. Behind us, the sea is picking up steam, white-crested waves crashing against the shore, and on top of the cliffs, the trees are swaying more vigorously, their branches moving from left to right in unison.

'I wonder if there's going to be a storm,' Theo says, pulling out his phone and navigating to the weather app. He nods. 'Yep, look, there is one coming.' He shows us the screen and I pull a face at the angry dark cloud icon that's set to approach this evening.

'No midnight swim for us tonight,' he says, and I laugh.

'Was that ever in the plan?'

When we get to the villa, I'm surprised to find the front door wide open, banging against the wall in the breeze. One of the golden flamingos has been knocked over, is lying on its side sadly, and I hesitate before going in the house.

'Who was last out?' I ask the others, and Theo frowns.

'Can't remember. We must have forgotten to close it properly.'

Saskia is hanging back from the group, and I watch her as her eyes dart around the villa – taking in the empty, glistening pool, our discarded champagne glasses, the flamingo on its side.

'Do you think someone might have been in?' she says, her voice a shade too high, and Theo makes a scoffing sound.

'I doubt it. Come on, stop being silly.' He steps over the threshold and I feel a sudden spike of anxiety, as though someone might be about to appear from behind the door. But of course, nothing happens, and gradually, we follow him in, flicking on the lights as we go.

'Can you check the rooms, Theo?' Saskia asks, and he rolls his eyes but dutifully goes from room to room with Lucas, shouting out 'all clear' each time, as if he's in a police drama on the TV.

I feel a bit uneasy too, to be honest, but I wander around the rooms myself and nothing looks out of place, everything is as we left it. I check my bag, abandoned in the room – my passport is still there, so is everything else.

'I think it's fine, Hol,' Lucas says, coming into our bedroom as I'm running a hand over the window latch, checking it's locked. 'We must have just left it open ourselves. No harm done.'

'Yeah,' I say, 'yeah. I guess you're right.'

But I can't shake the feeling of unease that creeps over me as I quickly undress and slide into a red dress and a silver cardigan, as though someone might be watching me, as though Lucas and I are not truly alone.

Chapter Forty-Five

Saskia

When I saw the open door, I thought I was going to be sick. My first thought was Caleb, that he'd followed us here, but there is no sign of him, nothing untoward at all. My eyes scan our room as I get changed and do my hair, looking for one of his tells, a hidden note, an object that shouldn't be there, something missing. Things only I would notice. But I can't see anything; I even open the wardrobe and run my hand along the back, pull out the drawers in the bathroom, searching for something, anything that might prove he'd been here.

I only start to relax when we've been back for ten minutes or so, when Theo's changed into a crisp maroon shirt and I've slicked on a layer of lipstick and foundation, my armour for the evening. My eyes are aching a little bit behind my retinas, a result of the crying fit I had earlier back on the mainland, but I dab brightening liquid underneath them and add lashings of black mascara.

'You look great, babe,' Theo says approvingly, and I feel a bubble of pleasure in my chest.

After years of being with a man who would only tell me how ugly I was, hearing Theo compliment me never gets old.

It was on our honeymoon that it began. Andrew was angry;

the hotel wasn't right, a little place in Paris that he'd booked for us, which I thought was lovely and charming. But he said it was too small – the room didn't have a good enough view, the coffee tasted like shit, the receptionist was looking at us in the wrong way. By then, I'd grown used to the sudden outbursts of temper he had, had told myself they were normal, a sign of a fiery, passionate man – but that night was the first time he ever lashed out. He put his hand through the wall of our hotel room, his fist smashing into the plaster, leaving a dark red smear on the white paint. I'd screamed when he did it, out of shock more than anything, and that was when he'd turned on me.

'Are you trying to get us into trouble?' he'd said, rounding on me – I think he was worried that someone might hear me and get the wrong idea, a woman screaming, a man with blood on his hands.

'Of course not,' I'd said, horrified, and I'd reached up to put my arms around his neck – and that was when he'd slapped me in the face. A sharp sting that left a red outline of his fingers on my cheek, my own skin whitening around them in shock.

It would be the first of many injuries he inflicted on me, but it wouldn't be the last.

*

The restaurant Theo's chosen is right on the beach, only a hundred metres or so from our villa. It looks gorgeous – small and intimate, with about a dozen wooden tables set on the sand, warmed by flame heaters dotted in between them, casting a beautiful shadowy light on the whole scene. The restaurant is shaded by a large, sprawling tree, from which hang brightly coloured, star-shaped lanterns – purples and reds and blues, each fitted with a glowing golden light.

'It's like fairyland,' Holly says, and it does feel like that, especially as the sun dips beneath the horizon and the sky begins to darken, making the space feel cosier, a little haven all of its own.

The waiter greets us immediately, and leads us to a table in the centre, set with a large vase of flowers in the middle, purple petals peeking through green fronds. Two candles sit either side of it, the flames flickering in the wind, and the waiter tuts as one of them blows itself out, then reaches into his apron for a lighter to bring it back to life.

'There's a storm coming tonight,' he says. He smiles at us as he hands out leather-bound menus, one for each of us, plus a wine menu which he puts in the middle of the table.

'We thought so,' Holly says, 'it's quite exciting, in a way.'

The waiter frowns, his brow creasing. 'Must be careful,' he says, 'the storms out here can be quite bad. Heavy rain, lot of wind. You see.' He points towards the trees in the distance that line the cliffs at the far end of the beach. I look up and he is right, they are swaying to and fro quite wildly, now, their long branches silhouetted black against the sky. The sea, too, looks as though it is changing, becoming choppier, more aggressive.

'We're only staying over there,' Theo tells the waiter, pointing in the direction of our villa, and the waiter nods, smiles.

'You will be fine, then. Not too far to go.'

There's music playing softly in the background, drifting out from inside the restaurant, and Theo chooses a bottle of white wine for us all to share, selecting one near the bottom of the list. I see Lucas and Holly give each other a quick look as he does so, and think about gently nudging Theo to choose something cheaper, then decide not to draw attention to it. It probably won't help anyway.

'So, how's the flat hunt going, you two? I've been meaning to ask,' Theo says, looking between the pair of them, and I remember that they've started to look for a place, saving up for somewhere for them to share.

'A bit stop-start at the moment,' Holly replies, moving her menu to one side as the waiter reappears, silently depositing a basket of bread and a little white dish full of oil and balsamic vinegar on the table between us. 'We're just seeing what's out there, trying to work out our options, what we can afford, you know.' She laughs, but it's brittle. 'Not a lot, is the answer.'

I nod, trying to concentrate on what she's saying.

'It's hard, because everywhere is SO expensive,' she continues, 'but we've both been saving hard, and I just can't wait to live together, it's going to be so great.' She smiles at Lucas, who smiles back, but there's something a little weak about it, as though his heart isn't in it, somehow.

'London property is insane these days,' Theo agrees, even though we bought our house eighteen months ago, and have never had any issues at all. I break off a piece of bread with my fingers, dunk it in the oil. I feel as though I haven't eaten properly since we've been out here – I've been too anxious, and when I got changed earlier I felt as though my clothes were a little bit looser already.

'Your wine, sir.' The waiter reappears and offers Theo a splash of the white wine to taste – he does so, swilling it around properly and raising it to his nose. That sort of thing comes second nature to him – always has done, ever since I met him. Some people think he's putting it on, but he isn't.

'Lovely, thanks,' he says, and the waiter fills up all of our glasses. The candles flicker and I raise my hand up to shield one, not wanting it to go out again in the wind. I'm glad I brought a shawl out with me – it's still warm, but the breeze is making it feel colder, and goosebumps are rising on my arms.

We order food, and Theo starts telling a story about a family holiday they went on when he was younger, to Greece, when the clifftops collapsed around them.

'It was fucking terrifying,' he says, tearing off another hunk of bread, 'honestly. Our stuff was buried under the rubble.'

'Did anyone die?' Holly asks, wide-eyed, and it's then that it happens, a shadow falling over our table, blocking the glow from the starry lanterns, the air movement extinguishing one of the candles.

'Who died?' a figure says, and all of us watch in shock as he grabs a chair effortlessly from the next table, pulls it up at the head of ours. He sits on it backwards, his arms resting casually against the back of it, his thighs straddling the seat. Something about the pose is threatening; faux-casual, when I know he is anything but.

'Caleb,' Theo says, eventually, 'what are you doing here?'

'Come to see my favourite people, of course.'

At the sound of his voice, I feel my body freeze, like my knees and hands are locked together, like someone has bound a rope around my wrists. He is looking at us all, grinning from ear to ear, and his gaze meets mine, as if to say: *It's not over yet.*

I stare at him, unable to speak, one thought reverberating round and around my mind. *How did he find us? How the hell did he know where we were?*

Chapter Forty-Six

Lucas

For God's sake. This is the last thing they need!

Lucas can't believe the cheek of the guy, interrupting their dinner like this, coming to sit down, bold as brass, with no warning, no invitation. There's something wrong with him, clearly, some social wiring that's severely out of place. He finds himself shifting in his seat, involuntarily moving his chair away from Caleb's slightly, away from the abrasive energy that the other man is giving off.

Theo being Theo, he asks Caleb whether he can get him a drink, but Lucas feels a flash of anger. He can tell that none of them want him here, that all of them, by now, think his behaviour is weird, that he's crossed a line by appearing unannounced. Theo is just too polite to say anything.

'Actually, Caleb,' Lucas says, holding up a hand in front of him, stopping Theo from passing him a menu. 'Do you mind giving it a rest for this evening, pal? We're trying to have dinner.'

Caleb raises his eyebrows. 'I'm just being friendly.'

'I don't think you are,' Lucas bursts out, unable to stop himself. Beside him, he can feel Holly squirming uncomfortably, and Saskia looks stricken.

'Show of hands,' Lucas says, looking around the table, at his friends' faces, flickering in the light cast by the flame heaters and the one remaining candle. 'Who here wants Caleb to join us for dinner, eh? Who here thinks he ought to stay?'

Nobody raises a hand, and there is a terrible silence that descends over the table, as though the rest of the restaurant doesn't exist, as if it is just the five of them, encased in a deathly little bubble, waiting for the other shoe to drop.

'Sorry, mate, he doesn't mean it like that,' Theo interjects at last, and Lucas glares at him.

'I mean it exactly like that, Caleb. We don't want you here, get it? We've had enough of you sniffing around us like a dog, when we've made it more than clear that you're not wanted. OK? So just take a hint, mate, and piss off.'

He's breathing hard – he never speaks to anyone like that, not really, but there is something about this guy that gets his hackles up. Maybe it's to do with the way he flirted with Holly back on the mainland, maybe it's to do with the fearful expression on Saskia's face, but either way, he knows this guy is bad news, and he's done with being polite. This is his holiday, too – he's paid to come here, using all the money that he doesn't have in the world, and he's sick of it being railroaded by a creepy bloke with too much time on his hands.

Caleb doesn't speak for a minute, he just looks at them all, and the silence seems to stretch out and around them like an elastic band, gripping them all together.

'Have it your way,' he says, eventually, 'I just wanted to say hello, anyway. Let you know I was here. That I'm watching.'

He stands up, his shadow twisting the light again, and knocks back his chair so that it topples over onto the sand, falling down silently on its side. The four of them watch as he wends his way through the other tables and onto the beach, heading away from them in the direction of their villa.

'Christ,' Theo says, 'what the hell was all that about? *Let you know that I'm watching?* It's weird that he's here, isn't it? He's like a sniffer dog or something. Hey, I didn't know you had it in you, Lukey.' He claps him on the shoulder, trying to lighten the mood, but Lucas is stiff with rage, and he's also paying attention to the expression on Saskia's face. They are all shocked at what's just happened, but she looks different. If he didn't know better, he'd say she looked absolutely petrified.

Chapter Forty-Seven

Saskia

A sort of recklessness has come over me, after the initial horror has faded. Caleb is here, on the island, and there is nothing I can do about it – I can't throw him off again, not when he's proved how determined he is to be here. What I don't know is how he found us, when I don't even have my phone. Getting away from him, escaping to Koh Samet – it hasn't worked. I need to think of something else.

We finish the meal after Lucas tells him to leave, though I barely taste anything, going through the motions while my brain is working furiously, trying to think through my options. The others talk for a bit about how weird Caleb is, how great it is that Lucas stood up to him, but only I know that that won't have put him off. It will only have riled him up, encouraged him. He's toying with us, but most of all, he's showing me the extent of what he's prepared to do.

Caleb wants me to kill my husband. And he's not going to stop until I do.

*

At first, with Andrew, I tried to pretend it simply wasn't happening. He cried that night in Paris on our honeymoon, going down onto his knees and kissing my bare feet, promising me that he was sorry, he was so sorry, it would never happen again. He just wanted everything to be perfect, that was all. For our honeymoon. Because he loved me so much.

It was rubbish, of course. Within a fortnight, he'd hit me again. I'd stayed too long at work – I was temping by then, still applying for jobs, but I'd stopped working at the bar, because Andrew didn't like the fact that I met other men there, that they came in and leered at me while I poured them their pints. It was fine for *him* to do that, of course, but it wasn't fine for anyone else to so much as look in my direction, especially once I was his wife.

Saskia Green was my name. I had a ring on my finger, just like I do now, only it was a different coloured band, a smaller, duller stone. Andrew didn't have the level of money that Theo has, but he had enough to keep me quiet, to make everyone think I had it all. Within a few months of our wedding, he'd told me I didn't need to bother temping any more. I could just live off his money, he'd support me. He said I ought to stay home, in the house he'd bought me, like some kind of 1950s housewife. Your textbook stuff, really.

Soon, he began hiding the keys.

I used to think it was lucky that I managed to meet Caleb when I did. I was barely going out at that point, but Andrew had given me permission to go to the birthday party of Emma, one of the only remaining friends I had left. The rest of them had started to drop off, after I kept cancelling on them, telling them I had to spend time with my husband. Emma was the only one who wouldn't stop calling, who seemed to sense that something was up and I only managed to go meet her by telling Andrew that she would suspect something was seriously wrong if I didn't. He never wanted anything to touch him. He didn't want Emma sniffing around.

So he let me go. I got there a bit early; I'd lied to him about the start time, desperately craving an extra hour to myself. He drove me to her house, watched me go to the door, but I pretended to ring the bell and then when I was sure he'd driven off, I ran back down her drive and into the pub a few doors down, just wanting time to think, away from him, time on my own for the first time in months.

It was there that I met Caleb.

He came up to me as I was sitting in the corner, nursing a glass of red wine. It had gone to my head – Andrew didn't let me drink very often, by that stage – but the alcohol was helping numb the pain of the latest set of bruises he'd given me, last night, because of the way I'd made the bed. It was the wrong way, of course. By then, everything I did was wrong. And he always laid into me as a result.

By that point, he rarely even bothered to apologise.

'You look like you could use another one of those,' Caleb had said, gesturing to my glass. 'What's up with you? You look like a wet weekend.'

The phrase had pulled me out of myself – it was old-fashioned, funny somehow, like something my grandmother used to say. I let him buy me another drink – I still had forty minutes or so until I had to be at Emma's – and when I took it from him, my sleeve hitched up, exposing a bruise. I saw him notice it at the exact same time that I did – and though I moved quickly, yanking it back down in the way I'd become accustomed to, he took hold of my arm, gently, asked me to tell him how I got it.

He knew already, of course. I expect it was obvious. A beaten woman, alone with a glass of wine in the corner of a pub. I was a walking cliché. But Caleb was kind to me. He listened. And though I knew I shouldn't tell him, shouldn't tell anyone, I couldn't help myself – the two glasses of wine were more than I'd had in ages – and it all came spilling out, the horror of it, the daily, relentless torture that my life had become.

'And I can't tell anyone, because everyone thinks he's amazing,' I'd cried, the words bubbling out of my mouth before I could stop them, the tears thickening my throat. It was true – Andrew maintained an immaculate image in front of his family, his friends, his colleagues. Nobody who knew him would believe what was happening behind closed doors.

He listened for a while, nodding as I spoke, and then he said he wanted to ask me a question. I wiped my eyes, met his gaze – this stranger who had appeared in my life, who I'd somehow admitted everything to – things I couldn't even tell my best friend, my family. Things I hadn't told anyone.

'If I offered you the chance to escape from him, would you take it?' Caleb had asked me, quietly, in the corner of the pub near Emma's house, our voices hushed, as though already there was something forming between us, something dark and frightening and untouchable, something I couldn't quite look in the eye.

I didn't even have to think about it. I just nodded. And that was all he needed; that was the start. That nod put into place a plan of action, a chain of events that I became powerless to stop, even if I'd tried to.

But I have to be honest, don't I? The truth is, I didn't try. I let them happen. In fact, I took an active part.

Chapter Forty-Eight

Holly

The beach restaurant is almost empty, now – it's a Wednesday night, I suppose, at least I think it is, the days of the holiday are blurring into one – and the weather is visibly worsening. There are just a few couples left, illuminated in the lights hanging from the trees. There's also one party of six, who keep ordering shots from an exhausted waitress.

'Look,' I say, pointing across the beach, above Lucas's head, 'the moon's beautiful tonight.' It is – it hangs like a big white orb in the sky, casting shadows across the undulating sand, illuminating the dips.

'I can't believe he just turned up here like that,' Lucas repeats, again, for maybe the third time this evening, and I squeeze his hand.

'You did a good job getting rid of him, Luke.' I don't know if it's just me, but I feel as though we're all avoiding going back to the villa, as though we're scared that when we leave the restaurant, we might see Caleb again, as if he's waiting for us, lurking in the shadows of the beach. But that's madness, isn't it – he's gone, he went away. I think of him saying he's watching us, and remember the words scrawled on the back of the photograph in our hostel back in Bangkok. *I am watching you*. Could it have been him all along? Some weirdo who likes to play games with travellers? Could there be a more sinister motive behind his behaviour?

'Do you think . . .' I trail off, but the other three are looking at me, and I clear my throat, try again.

'Do you think we ought to report Caleb, to someone?'

Theo snorts. 'What for?'

'Well,' I say, 'I don't know. He's sort of . . . following us, isn't he? Could that be classed as stalking?'

Theo picks up his wine glass, takes a long swig.

'I think you're being a bit dramatic, Holly. He's obviously just some weirdo, a loner type. He hasn't actually done anything wrong. I mean, look,' he spreads his hands out, Mr Reasonable, 'I don't like him hanging around us any more than you do, and I agree his behaviour tonight was odd, but I don't think there's any need to hand him over to the Thai authorities.' He laughs. 'He'd spend the rest of his life in jail if we did that.'

'OK, OK,' I say, feeling a bit foolish. I was expecting Saskia to jump in with me, to be on my side, but she isn't saying anything, she's just playing with her wedding ring, twisting the silver band round and around her finger in silence.

Eventually, it becomes obvious that the restaurant is winding down due to the storm – the wait staff are pulling tablecloths in, stacking up the chairs around us, even though it's not really that late. Theo suggests heading back to the villa and we get to our feet sloppily – we've all drunk way more than I'd thought.

Saskia walks up ahead of us; I can see her striding out along the beach, the sand scuffing up beneath her heels, grains of sand whipping into the air. Theo trails along behind her, and

Lucas and I hang back, slightly, our arms wrapped around each other, the taste of wine on our lips.

'Thanks,' we call out in unison to the waiter, who raises a hand to us and smiles.

The beach is much quieter than it was earlier, now, and the sea that once seemed so inviting has begun to look more sinister. The waves are bigger, and the noise of them crashing against the shore fills my head, building and building until it becomes a wall of white noise.

A group of teenagers pass us, and I catch the strong, sweet scent of marijuana, hear their laughter on the breeze. Lucas sticks his nose in the air like a dog, pretends to sniff, and I laugh.

I stumble, slightly, losing my footing in the sand, but he grabs onto me, hauls me upright and then we both start laughing; silly, giggly laughter, like kids. It's a relief to laugh after the tension of the evening, Caleb's horrible reappearance.

'Shit,' I say, 'we forgot to leave a tip for the waiter.'

Lucas shrugs. 'He'll live. Come on, you,' he says, 'let's get you home.' He pulls me to him and kisses me on the sand, curving a hand around the back of my waist.

'You were quite impressive tonight,' I whisper in his ear, and he smiles at me.

'Race you,' I say, and we run up the beach together, to where the villa is waiting, the light of its windows glowing golden in the darkening light.

Chapter Forty-Nine

Saskia

When I get back to the villa, I'm half expecting to see him waiting for me at the table, sitting by the poolside. But there's nobody there, and the anticipation is almost worse. I know he will be here somewhere, around, waiting for the right moment to strike.

I've gone ahead of the others, in case he says anything – I know he'll be angry. I can't let Holly call the police, because if I do, the first thing he'll do is tell them the truth, about what happened with Andrew, and then – well, then my life as I know it will be over. I imagine Theo's expression if he found out what I did, the way his mouth would fall open, his jaw would slacken, his eyes would widen in shock. He thinks I'm his perfect little wife. And I want to be. I want to be so badly.

But I can't hide from the past any more. I have to face what I did.

*

Caleb had asked me to meet him in the same pub a week later, told me to tell Andrew I was seeing Emma again, that she was going through something with her husband.

'I'll wait for you at this table,' he told me, 'same time. We're going to sort this out, Saskia. We're going to set you free.'

It was difficult getting Andrew to let me go out again, so soon after Emma's birthday, but eventually I managed it. Not before we had a huge argument, though – one which ended in him throwing me across the room, splitting my stomach on the edge of the kitchen counter. It bled a lot, and it left a vivid red scar. Andrew wouldn't take me to hospital, so I bandaged it up in the bathroom, sobbing, the blood staining my fingers. That day, that scar, it also cemented something in me, something that I think I already knew. One day, I thought to myself as I wrapped the bandage around myself, cut the end with a trembling hand, wincing in pain – one day this man, this husband of mine, will kill me. It was only a matter of time.

During the day, while he was at work, I went over and over it all in my mind. I wasn't stupid. I knew all the statistics, the stories about domestic violence. I knew how many women it affected. I knew there were refuges. I knew I had options – or at least, on paper, I did. But I couldn't run. He was locking me inside most of the time by that point, but more than that – if I ran, he'd find me. I knew he would. I'd spend the rest of my life looking over my shoulder, waiting. And he'd spin it all – he'd tell his family some sob story about my leaving him. I'd lose everything. I just couldn't imagine it, a future without him. I needed someone else to help me.

Caleb had been the one to tell me to look up the life insurance claim. In the end, I couldn't believe how simple it was to find out online, because I was a beneficiary – he'd wanted a third to go to me, the rest to his parents. A third was still a significant chunk of money, but all I wanted was to survive; I didn't care about the money.

Caleb did.

He told me he'd give me a cut, enough to start a new life, enough to go somewhere new, far away from East Sussex, enough to get myself my own place, stand on my own two feet.

'That's all I want from you, Saskia,' he kept saying, but I knew he also wanted the money, his fair share. His payment. I may as well be honest about it, call it what it was.

He wanted payment for murdering Andrew. And in the end, I gave it to him.

Of course, I was horrified when he first suggested it. But the more Caleb talked, the more I couldn't see another way out. I knew I wouldn't be able to meet up with him many more times before Andrew grew suspicious, and things at home were getting worse by the day. I was desperate, trapped. Broken. I didn't know what else to do, and Caleb was so convincing. He promised me he'd take care of it discreetly, that he'd done this kind of thing before.

'I think of it as helping people out,' he'd told me, his face half hidden by a pint of Guinness in our usual pub. 'Some men, Saskia, some men don't deserve to walk this earth. And your Andrew is one of them.'

I lay awake at night for weeks, staring up at the ceiling, barely daring to breathe as Andrew slumbered beside me. I wasn't going to lay a hand on him myself, was I? I wasn't a killer. Did it count, if you didn't do it yourself? I knew the answer, deep down – of course it counted. But when I thought of the rage in Andrew's eyes as he threw me across the room, I knew it was becoming a matter of life and death. Of him or me.

And I didn't want to die. I was twenty-five years old.

'The key is for nobody to make the link,' Caleb told me.

'Once we do this, there's no going back. It'll be the last you see of me, you understand.'

I felt a flash of panic at this, even though I'd only known him a short period of time, it felt like he had become my lifeline. He was the only person in my life who knew the truth about my marriage.

'You'll send the money afterwards,' he told me, 'but I'll need something up front.'

'I don't have anything,' I said, 'I can't access any of our money. He doesn't let me.'

He'd looked down at my hand, at my fingers, clasping a wine glass. He'd started buying me mints for afterwards, because one week, Andrew had smelled the wine on my breath, and punished me accordingly.

'What about your wedding ring?'

I'd gasped. 'He'll notice if I don't have it on.'

He'd shrugged. 'You can tell him it was stolen. He can't be angry with you for that.'

He'd taken another sip of his beer; I watched his Adam's apple bob as the liquid slid down his throat, transfixed by him, by how easy he was making the whole thing sound. This was Andrew's life we were talking about, but Caleb made it sound like it was nothing, like we were discussing the price of fish.

'Consider it a down payment,' he'd told me. 'But the rest has got to follow, Saskia. You give me your word, don't you?'

I'd nodded, silently. As if I'd dare not to pay him. He'd be able to tell everybody about my involvement if I didn't.

'I need to hear you say it,' Caleb had pushed, 'I need you to promise that this is what you want. You want him dead, you want him gone. You want to be free.'

'I want to be free,' I said, firmly, clearly, and the words felt like the truest thing I'd ever spoken. 'I want Andrew gone.' A pause. Caleb looked at me. 'I want him dead,' I said, and then I burst into tears. Caleb just nodded.

'Good girl,' he said, 'that's it, let it all out. We're going to set you free, you'll see.'

Andrew was angry about the missing ring, of course, he told me I was careless, stupid, even when I told him someone had ripped it off my finger as I came out of Emma's house and crossed the road to wait for him to pick me up. I couldn't work out if he believed me, but by that point, there were only twenty-four hours to go.

Caleb had told me it would be better for me not to know the details, but he'd promised me it would be quick.

'Not . . . painless, exactly,' he'd smirked, 'but it won't be drawn out. Much as I'd like it to be, after what he's done to you.'

He was tender to me, was Caleb; by the end of our conversations, it felt as though he genuinely cared what happened to me, and when he looked into my eyes, I felt a connection – not a romantic connection, per se, more a sense of electricity, because of what he was offering me. He was offering me a second chance at life.

To me, that was priceless.

Now, of course, I know that everything has a price. Every transaction has a cost. Nobody gets away scot-free.

And certainly not for murder.

*

Inside the villa, the four of us gather in the kitchen. Holly opens the drawers in the big dresser in the hallway and finds a set of candles, sets them out on the table, and Theo goes into our bedroom, comes back with his portable speaker.

'I think there's more booze in one of the cupboards, must be left over from previous guests,' Lucas says, and he fetches a bottle of half-drunk vodka, passes us each a tumblerful.

I feel exhausted; I don't want to stay up drinking, but the others all seem a bit wired after the encounter we had with Caleb and they start playing a drinking game, using a pack of cards Holly pulls out of her suitcase.

'Thought we might need them at some point,' she says, and I watch as she deals them out deftly, gives us each a hand. Theo pulls out a Biro and grabs a piece of paper, says he'll keep note of our scores.

Outside, the rain begins to lash against the windows, and I look out at the dark shimmer of the pool, half lit by little white lights that have come on around it, embedded into the floor. I go to the front door, check that we locked it behind us, then make my way around the house, checking every window and door carefully. It's only when I've finished that the thought occurs to me that Caleb could be inside here with us – I wouldn't put it past him. I might have just locked us inside with him. Quickly, I go back to our bedroom, begin opening cupboards, even get down on my hands and knees and look under the bed. I don't believe he'd just leave it at that. He's planning something, I know he is. I pull back the duvet cover, anger and frustration bubbling up inside me. I have to work out what to do. I can't let this go on any longer.

Chapter Fifty

Lucas

He feels on a bit of a high, now, having been the one to successfully rid the group of Caleb. The vodka slides down easily – too easily – and he feels lighter than he has all holiday; he's sorted out his money issue, for now at least, and he's made himself look like a bit of a hero in front of Holly. Theo turns the music up and Holly squeals that it's her favourite song, and before too long, the night has descended into a bit of chaos, the four of them playing round after round of their drinking game, until everything becomes a blur. Theo does an impression of him telling Caleb to piss off and they laugh raucously; Holly grabs her kitchen chair and spins it around, straddling it the way Caleb did, and the whole thing just feels hilarious now, ridiculous.

There's a pause in the music, silence in the background. Lucas is laughing at something Theo has said, clapping his friend on the back, and Theo is whispering drunkenly that he won't let slip about the loan to Holly. Actually, come to think of it, he's not sure Theo *is* whispering at this stage, but regardless, Holly doesn't seem to have noticed.

She's swiping through her phone, trying to connect to the Wi-Fi so she can get onto Spotify and change the playlist, when suddenly she frowns.

'What the hell . . .' she trails off, then holds out her phone to the others. Lucas squints at it, his vision blurry. The phone looks so small, and he's drunk too much vodka to be able to focus properly.

'What?' he says, hiccupping slightly, and Holly points to the screen, to the small black app that has appeared on the final screen of her phone, hidden within the Entertainment logo.

'That,' she says, her finger touching the screen. Lucas watches as it opens up to a black screen with a little red dot in the middle, the numbers 360 appearing at the top. Holly clicks into it and they stare as the GPS locates. 'It looks like a tracker or something?' Holly says. 'I didn't install it. Jesus, I think someone's been tracking my phone.' She looks up at them all, her expression sombre. 'I didn't notice,' she said, 'I didn't think to look. But I definitely didn't put this there. Look, it's giving away our location.'

There's a silence in the room as they all look at it, and Lucas feels his stomach churning, a combination of too much booze and a rush of adrenaline.

'Could it be Caleb?' he asks. 'Is that how he knew where we were?'

'Fuck, that's creepy,' Theo says, taking Holly's phone and examining the app. 'You definitely didn't put this there yourself?'

'Why would I?' she snaps back, and Lucas lays a hand on her shoulder, trying to reassure her, even though Theo is right – it *is* creepy.

'Maybe you downloaded it ages ago, by accident,' Theo persists, and Holly rolls her eyes.

'Of course I didn't. Jesus, Theo, give me a bit of credit.'

She snatches her phone back, holds her finger over the app

and deletes it, the little icon vanishing under her shiny coral nail.

'I hope that's enough to stop it,' she says, uncertainly. 'God, that must be why my battery has been draining so fast. It must use a lot of charge to be constantly sending someone else updates on our location.'

'Where's Saskia?' Theo says, suddenly, and the three of them look around the kitchen, as if she might appear from behind the fridge, or jump out at them from one of the cupboards. But she's not there – her abandoned glass sits stubbornly on the table in front of them all, her deck of cards discarded.

'Saskia?' Theo calls out, his voice slurring slightly, but there is no response. She is gone.

Chapter Fifty-One

Saskia

I found the note when I was checking our bedroom, looking under the bed, lifting the duvet, then finally picking up the soft white pillow. There it was, a scrap of paper with thick black writing on it. *1am, at the bottom of the cliffs. Don't be late.*

It's twelve forty-five, now, and when I left, the others were still in the kitchen, shrieking with laughter and getting slowly drunker and drunker as they made their way towards the bottom of the vodka bottle. I knew it would hit them hard – none of us are used to drinking spirits any more, I haven't done since I was about twenty. None of them noticed as I slipped away, grabbing my jacket from the bedroom and sneaking out through the doors in our room, the ones that lead straight down onto the beach.

Outside, it's horrible – the wind whips my eyes and the rain slashes against my skin. I haven't drunk nearly as much as the others, have only been pretending to really, but the cold sobers me up completely. I pick my way along the beach towards the cliffs, using a torch I found in a drawer in the villa to light the way, wondering how long I have, how long it will be before one of them realises that I'm not in the villa, that I haven't just fallen asleep in our room.

Twelve fifty. I can see the cliffs rising up ahead of me, hemming me in. I hurry past the restaurant where we had dinner – its shutters are firmly closed, now, the lanterns and candles extinguished. The beach is deserted; nobody would go out in this weather unless they absolutely had to. Adrenaline spikes through my veins as I get closer and closer, stumble slightly on a stone that protrudes from the beach, feel a sharp stab of pain in the sole of my foot.

Then, there's a flash of bright light – a phone light – and Caleb is there, in front of me, a hood over his head, half obscuring his face. He's soaking, too, and he grabs me roughly by the arm, pulls me closer to where he's standing, sheltering under a lip of rock that juts out over the beach.

'You came,' he says, sounding pleased, and I grit my teeth in anger.

'As if I have a choice.'

'Your friends weren't very happy to see me.'

I don't say anything. I don't want to give anything else away.

'Look, Saskia,' he says, 'this whole thing is saddening me, it really is. We used to be friends, you and I. Didn't we?'

He reaches out, touches my chin again like he did in the bathroom back in Bangkok, tips my face up to his as if he's going to kiss me.

'Didn't we?'

I pause, then nod, once, up and down.

'Say it,' he says, and I do.

'Yes,' I say, 'we used to be friends.'

'And friends help each other,' he says, like he's spelling out something blindingly obvious, a schoolteacher coaxing a particularly reluctant pupil.

I nod again. The palm of his hand is rough against my

skin. Around us, the rain continues to fall, and the roar of the ocean keeps on, drowning out his voice so that I have to lean forward to hear what he says next.

'You've got twenty-four hours, Saskia,' he tells me. 'Either you agree to do this, or I go to the cops. Tell them what you did, all those years ago.'

'You can't prove it,' I say, desperately, but he lets go of my face, holds up his phone so that I can see.

'Oh, but I can.'

I peer at the screen. It's hard to see through the rain and the wind but gradually, I realise what I'm looking at, and horror fills my veins. They are photographs, photographs of me in the pub in East Sussex, there is even one where you can see Caleb in the same shot, reflected in the old antique mirror that used to hang behind our corner table. He swipes his finger across the screen, showing me them all – my face is clearly recognisable.

'My mate took these for me. Not bad, are they? We look quite good together. Bit of insurance, I suppose you could call it. You get used to having to do these things, when you've been in the game as long as I have,' Caleb says, almost conversationally. 'I wonder what Andrew Green's family will say when they realise what you did.' At his words, I flash back to them – the people I haven't thought of in years, his kind parents, who only ever welcomed me, who gladly handed over my share of his life insurance without a second thought. They emailed me afterwards, for almost a year, but eventually I told them it was too painful to be in touch, that I needed time to heal. Then I blocked their address and changed my own.

'You owe me, Saskia,' he says, again, like it's a mantra, and as I gaze up at him, into those eyes that have haunted me ever since we got here, I know that he is right, that really, I have no choice. I've done it once, I can do it again. I will reinvent myself, go far away from here, start a new life, a third identity. Caleb will do what Caleb did before. Both of us will walk away, and I'll be free again.

But it comes at a terrible price.

'It's not enough,' I say, 'they're just photos, they just prove we knew each other, that's all. You'd have to implicate yourself too.'

He smirks, taps another button on his phone. I take a step backwards in shock as my own voice plays out into the night. 'I want Andrew gone. I want him dead.' The words ring out, clear as a bell, and I gasp in horror.

'You recorded me, in the pub. You told me to say those things.'

'No one had a knife to your throat, darlin'.' There's a pause, and he plays it again, my words washing over me like the current, loud and succinct and unmistakably me. I close my eyes. I am lost.

'OK,' I say eventually, 'OK. You win. Tell me what you want me to do.'

Chapter Fifty-Two

Holly

It's 1am and Saskia is still missing. We search the villa for her, calling for her in each of the rooms, then flinging open the door and checking the pool, the patio, the area behind the house where the recycling bins are. As I approach the pool I have a horrible feeling, as if I'm about to find her body bobbing in the water, but it's empty, the water level rising due to the rain.

'Saskia!' I call, my voice beginning to sound hoarse. 'Saskia!'

'She can't have gone out in this.' Lucas appears behind me, grabs my hand. 'Come back in, you're getting soaked.'

'We have to find her!' I say. I feel really worried now, thinking of her crying by the pier back on the mainland, her dropping her phone into the water. Maybe I ought to tell the others.

Back inside, Theo is pacing up and down, running his hands through his hair.

'Shit, shit,' he says, 'where the hell is she?'

'She hasn't even got a phone,' I say, and I'm about to tell the boys what I saw on the pier, about her throwing it into the sea, when the door bangs open and she appears, soaking wet, her hair plastered to her skull.

'Saskia!' Theo goes over to her, wraps his arms around her

264

immediately, despite how wet she is. As I watch, she seems to flinch as he touches her, shy away from his touch.

'Jesus, where have you been?'

'I'm sorry,' she says, 'I just went for a walk.'

'A walk?' All three of us stare at her. 'Why would you go for a walk when it's like this outside?' Theo asks, and she shrugs, weakly.

'I just wanted some air. That's all. I'm sorry for worrying you.'

She comes further into the kitchen, goes to the sink and fills a glass of water. Her hand is trembling, but the expression on her face is calm as she says that she's going to bed.

'See you in the morning,' she tells us, and all of us watch, astounded, as she leaves the room, water pooling on the tiled floor behind her.

'I'll go after her,' Theo says, rolling his eyes at Lucas and me. 'God, I don't know what she's playing at.'

'I think she's . . .' I trail off. I'm about to tell them about what I saw at the pier, but something stops me at the last minute. It's something to do with the way she flinched from Theo, just now, as if she couldn't bear to have him touch her. Maybe my instincts have been right all along. Maybe there is something wrong between the two of them.

I run my mind back over the holiday – of the marker pen I found in his room, of the sound of raised voices, the door slamming behind her. I think of Caleb standing too near her by the waterfall. What if she was confiding in him? What if I've got this wrong? Could I have misjudged Theo completely – could Lucas?

'She's what?' Theo is looking at me, waiting for me to speak, but I close my mouth, swallow the words back down.

'Nothing,' I say, 'I'm going to bed too.'

I leave the boys standing in the kitchen and head towards our bedroom. I pass Saskia's on the way and hover outside, wondering if I ought to go in, have it out with her once and for all, ask her what's going on, woman to woman. I press my ear against the door, wondering if I might hear her crying, but there is no sound at all. She must have gone to sleep.

Suddenly, I jump as footsteps come up behind me and I spin around to see Theo, his brow furrowed, his body just inches from mine.

'What are you doing, Holly?' he asks me, and his voice sounds strange. I move backwards, away from him, knowing I've been caught out. My heart is hammering.

'Nothing,' I mutter, 'goodnight.' I turn and walk off down the hallway to our bedroom, close the door behind me and draw the curtains, blocking out the pelting rain outside. I shiver as I get undressed and huddle under the sheets, wondering what's really going on in the other room. Wondering how well I really know the other two at all. And wondering why when Theo came up to me, I felt a dash of pure fear.

The thought nags at me. After a few minutes tossing and turning, I get back up. Lucas still hasn't come to bed. I pad along the hallway to Saskia and Theo's room, press my ear to the door again. I've got to be sure she's all right.

Chapter Fifty-Three

Saskia

He made it look like a car accident. A hit and run.

I only knew when the police arrived at the door, and asked me to sit down. I can still remember it vividly – the outline of their figures against the window in the door, the solemn, sombre way they came into the house, wiping their boots respectfully on our doormat, taking their hats off and holding them awkwardly in their hands. They had to force the door open; he'd locked me inside.

'Mrs Green,' they said. 'Can we ask you to sit down?'

By that point, it had been so long since anyone else had come in the house – Andrew didn't allow me to have any visitors – that I had forgotten what to do, how to be. I made them a cup of tea each, my fingers shaking, and they informed me that my husband, Andrew Green, had been fatally injured in a road collision in the early evening.

'We believe he was on his way home from work,' they told me, and I nodded, like I hadn't given Caleb the exact route that I knew Andrew took, plotted the coordinates out with him on a napkin in the corner of the pub.

I didn't cry, but I don't think they minded – they said I was in shock, asked if anyone could come be with me. I gave them

Emma's name, and she arrived within an hour, held me close to her. It hurt, because of the bruises, but I sobbed on her shoulder, didn't say a word. I think I was crying with relief, only everyone thought it was grief, of course.

'What happened to the other car?' I asked the police, and they shook their heads. 'We're afraid we haven't been able to pick anyone up, as yet, Mrs Green, but it's only a matter of time. The driver sped off, didn't stop. We're so very sorry.'

I nodded, as though absorbing it all, and wondered where Caleb would be by now, what kind of car he'd used to do it in. It had been a blind spot, the place we'd chosen, on a side road just off the A22 between Eastbourne, where Andrew worked, and Polegate, where we lived. He always cut off down a particular road, was convinced it shaved a few minutes off the journey. He'd told me about it when we'd first met, and the detail had stuck in my head, waiting for the time when it would come into use. I knew it was a blind spot because he'd boasted about it, about speeding almost every day, knowing there were no cameras. I'd thought it was funny, at the time – two fingers up to the law. Of course, it wasn't funny now.

The car – stolen – was recovered in a field a few weeks later, burnt to a crisp. Caleb had been thorough. I was still living in the house we'd shared, though of course, now it was changed unalterably – I was free to come and go as I wished, I had my own set of keys, and the various injuries he'd inflicted on me recently were starting to heal up nicely. His parents had offered to come, or for me to come to theirs, but I knew I wouldn't be able to look them in the eye.

The guilt wasn't as bad as I'd thought it might be, to be honest. At night, I stretched out in our bed, let my body relax in a way it hadn't for months, let my coiled muscles unwind, because there was no longer any need to wait for the next blow to fall. I slept deeply, woke up late. The scar on my stomach began to fade, and it only hurt if I pressed my fingers into it, which I did too often, a little reminder.

When the money came through, I followed the instructions to a T. The bank didn't let me take all of it out at once, of course, so I had to do it in chunks, then transfer the rest, to an account he'd written down for me on a pub beermat. I didn't know if it was his or not, I didn't want to ask. The cash, I left in a shoebox in the same blind spot where the accident had taken place, like we had agreed. The same evening as I'd transferred the remainder; that was his alert to come collect the shoebox. We didn't see each other at all – I suspect he sent someone else entirely to pick it up.

After that, it was over. I moved away, cut ties with Andrew's parents, tried to start a new life for myself in London. I reverted to my maiden name, and a few years later, I met Theo. I pushed Andrew, my disastrous marriage, the abuse, all of it, right down deep in the pits of my soul, locked it tight in a box where no one could find it.

Until now, that is. Until Caleb.

*

'We could do it here,' Caleb told me, as we huddled underneath the cliffs in the storm. 'Make it look like an accident. A tragic one, obviously.'

I'd gazed up at them, the dark, grey rocks, the line of trees bent almost sideways in the wind now, like human skeletons twisted down towards the earth.

'I need the money quite rapidly this time, you see, darlin',' he told me, and for the first time, I wondered what he might be caught up in – whether he owed money to someone else, someone bigger, more dangerous than even I could imagine. What he might have got caught up in, in the five years since we'd seen each other. How far a man like him was really prepared to go.

'We do it here, it's a lot easier,' he continued, as if we were back there again, huddled in the pub, plotting and scheming together, Biros in our hands, napkins scattered around us. To outsiders, I always thought it looked like we were playing a game, and that was how he started to greet me, in those few weeks before Andrew's death. 'Saskia,' he'd say, 'do you fancy a game?' It was wicked, when I look back. It really was.

'No British police sniffing around, no one to cause a scene,' he said, wiping rainwater out of his eyes with the back of his sleeve. 'You lure him up there, get him off his guard. I push him, he falls. You leave, go back to the villa. You don't discover him until the morning, along with your little friends.'

I stared at him, my heart thumping. I was freezing by then, my body so wet and cold that my hands were beginning to go numb. I thought of the others, back at the villa – they would have noticed I'd gone by now; they might be coming out to look for me before too long. If they saw us together, it would all be undone.

'Come on, Saskia, don't look so shocked,' he said, and his eyes flashed at me in the darkness, impatient. 'Don't tell me it's a coincidence that you've ended up with another man who has more money than he knows what to do with.' He chuckled. 'I told you, I'm impressed. When all this is over, you ought to come with me, you know. Join forces. I'll teach you the rest of my tricks.' He reached into his pocket, and took something out; it glinted in the darkness, and I felt a sick thud in my stomach as I recognised it.

'Theo's watch,' I said, dully, 'you took it. I knew you had.'

'All in a day's work, darlin',' he said, grinning at me. 'Now, are we agreed, or not?'

I looked at him, those dark eyes, that familiar jawline, the awful magnetism of him. In my head, I played it all out – if I said no, he would pursue me relentlessly, he would tell Theo what I did to Andrew, Theo would divorce me, and worse than that, he would hate me. The world would know the truth. Andrew's family would come after me, there'd be press, headlines, the whole case would be reopened. I'd lose my job – I'd never work again. I'd probably go to prison.

If I said yes, I would lose Theo, beautiful Theo, the love of my life. It would devastate me, it would devastate Lucas. But we would repair. We would go on, living our lives, in the wake of a terrible tragedy, and Caleb would cut me free, set me loose, the debt repaid once and for all.

'This is the last time,' I said, the words sticking in my throat. 'You won't continue to come after me. You won't do this again. You'll destroy the recordings and the photos.'

He laughed, a proper, throaty laugh. 'Saskia,' he said, 'even you couldn't get away with losing three husbands. Two is careless. Three is suspicious.'

I glared at him. 'Nobody knows I lost Andrew, Caleb. That part of my life is over. I'm not Saskia Green any more. And no one in my life now knows that I ever was. I've made sure of it.'

He put his arm around me, pulled me close to his chest, our bodies melding together. 'I'm only winding you up, darlin',' he said, 'this is the last time. Come on. You won't see me after this. I promise. I've got bigger fish to fry.' He winked, and I pulled away from him, hating the sensation of being in his arms. Whatever bond we might have had, five years ago, whatever he did for me, it was gone, it was over. I felt nothing but contempt for him in that moment under the cliffs – contempt, and a cold, pervasive fear. Beneath the chameleon exterior, I knew he was ruthless. And that unless I complied, he would ruin my life forever.

'Tomorrow night,' I said, 'six o'clock. I'll bring him to the top of the cliffs.'

With that, I turned away from him, walked back along the beach to the villa, the tears stinging my eyes, my heart already breaking and my mind filling with numb horror at what I knew I had to do.

Chapter Fifty-Four

Lucas

In the morning, he wakes to find Holly already up, sitting in the bed next to him, a coffee on the side table next to her. He'd been late to bed last night, had sat up alone in the kitchen for a bit, his thoughts whirring. When he'd eventually come up, Holly had been asleep, her breathing steady, her brow slightly furrowed in the moonlight coming through the window where the curtains had fallen slightly apart.

'Any more where that came from?' he asks groggily, meaning the coffee, but she shakes her head. There's a strange expression on her face.

'Last night,' she says, and Lucas pulls himself upright, expecting her to start talking about Saskia, about how weird it was when she went out for a walk. His recollection of the whole thing is a little bit hazy, now, but he knows it was odd behaviour.

But that isn't what she says. 'Am I imagining things, Lucas, or last night, did Theo say something about him loaning you money?'

Oh God. He clears his throat, trying to buy himself a bit more time, but she's frowning at him, and he knows she isn't going to take any bullshit.

'Look,' he says, 'it's not as bad as it sounds. Something happened, at work – I had to take a salary cut.'

'A salary cut?' She looks horrified. 'How much?'

He winces. 'Thirty-five per cent. It was that or lose my job.'

'*Thirty-five per cent?!* Shit, Lucas. When were you going to tell me? Is that even legal? Can schools do that?'

'They can if the employee consents,' Lucas says, 'and I had to consent, or at least, I felt like I did.'

'Jesus,' Holly says, 'that's outrageous. Why did you take it? You could have looked for something else?'

'I know, it is outrageous,' he says, relieved that she appears to be on his side. 'And I did, I tried, I will keep trying. But in teaching, you can't just move partway through the year, you have to start at the beginning of term, and there have hardly been any vacancies. What with the economy as it is, people are clinging to their jobs. It seemed safe to stay. So look, anyway . . .'

'When did this happen?' she says suddenly, her eyes narrowing, and Lucas feels the knot in his stomach beginning to tighten.

'Er,' he says, stalling for time, looking down at the duvet, at the white patterned whorls beneath his hands. 'About . . . well. A few months ago.'

She gasps. 'And what, you didn't think to tell me? You didn't think it was important?' Holly throws back the covers and gets to her feet, clearly furious. 'Here I am, saving every penny I earn, thinking we're going to get a place together, making that *fucking* spreadsheet . . .' She throws her hands in the air. 'I can't believe this Lucas, I really can't. How could you keep something like this from me?'

'I'm sorry,' he says, stammering now, 'I didn't know what to do, I didn't want you to worry.'

'We're supposed to be a team, Lucas,' she says, turning to face him, and her voice is colder now, quieter, yet somehow that is worse than before. 'We're in a relationship. We tell each other things. That's the deal, that's how it works. Christ, if you've kept this from me, what else haven't you told me?'

'God, nothing,' he says, horrified, 'nothing, Hol, I promise.'

'You promise,' she repeats, 'you promise. Oh, well, that's OK then, isn't it.'

'I was going to tell you,' he says, helplessly. 'I was, really. But I thought I could sort it out, on my own, that maybe you'd never need to know.'

He knows it was the wrong thing to say as soon as the words have left his mouth.

'But I don't want you to sort things out on your own, Lucas, don't you see?' Holly says, and she sounds a bit teary now. 'I want us to sort things out together. That's what we're supposed to do. I want you to feel like you can come to me.' She pauses, staring at him. 'But you don't, do you? You went to Theo instead.'

'It isn't like that,' he says, 'Theo is my best mate, Holly, you know that. He was just being a good friend, helping me out.'

'How much has he given you?' she asks, anger streaking across her face again, and when he tells her, she actually stamps her foot on the floor in frustration.

'God, this is humiliating,' she says, 'taking hand-outs from them. Jesus, Lucas. What must they think of us? The whole thing . . . it's so fucking unfair. They haven't worked for their money. They don't even have to try!'

'Theo isn't like that,' he says, again, getting annoyed too now – she's being so harsh on him, for God's sake. He hadn't *meant* to cause this mess. It isn't as if the whole thing was intentional.

'I don't want to be in debt to Theo,' she says, quietly, and there's something else in her expression now, something he cannot quite put his finger on.

'Theo's a good guy,' he says, slowly, 'he doesn't mind, Holly. Really, he doesn't. And you're not in debt to him. I am.'

She throws him a look. 'I don't want *you* to be in debt to him, then.'

Lucas sighs. 'Well, it's a bit late for that now. But look, it's just a loan, OK? When we get back to London I'm going to start looking for other jobs. Maybe in the . . . in the private sector.' He winces, knowing she won't like this either, and true to form, she exclaims in disgust.

'Oh, so we're throwing all our principles out now too, are we? That's great, Lucas, that's great. When we met you told me you'd never go private. Never, not in a million years. I believe that was the phrase you used.' She's staring at him, slightly out of breath, her hands on her hips, and he feels a flash of anger towards her. She's not exactly being understanding, is she. She's got no idea how it's felt to have to carry this worry around for months, to watch the numbers in his bank account dwindling by the day, to grit his teeth on this insanely expensive trip that neither of them can afford.

'I don't want to talk about this any more,' he says, coldly, and she spins on her heel, turns and flings the door to their room open.

'Fine,' she shouts back at him, 'that's fine, Lucas. Consider this conversation over.' She stops at the door for a moment, spins back to face him. Her face is anguished.

'Last night,' she says, 'I overheard something. I . . .'

He looks at her, spreads his hands. 'What?'

But she seems to change her mind the minute he speaks, her face closing down into a tight mask. 'Never mind,' she says. 'Clearly, we don't trust each other enough to tell the truth. Forget it.'

The door slams behind her and Lucas flops back against the pillows. His head is thumping and he feels terrible – guilty, sad and angry all at once. The vodka hangover isn't helping, either. For God's sake. When did this trip start to go so badly wrong?

Chapter Fifty-Five

Holly

I storm outside to the pool, stop short when I find Saskia sat on one of the sunloungers, her back to me. I pause for a second, but she's already heard me; she twists around and smiles at me, tells me to come and sit down.

'You okay?' she asks. 'You look a bit upset.'

Briefly, I consider telling her what Lucas has just told me, but then I decide that she probably already knows through Theo, and that if she doesn't, I don't want the humiliation to go any further, not if I can help it.

'I'm fine,' I say shortly, choosing my words carefully. 'Are *you* OK? That was a bit of a stunt you pulled, last night. We were all really worried about you.'

'I'm fine,' she says quickly, the words coming so fast that I don't know whether she even registered the second part of what I said. 'I'm sorry about last night, I just got a bit overwhelmed, that's all.'

'Right,' I say, nodding. Everything we're not saying seems to hang between us in the air, stifling the silence. I get up, the frustration fizzing through my body, and even though I'm still in my pyjamas, a tank top and shorts, I jump into the swimming pool, feel the water close deftly over my head.

The cold water jolts me, and I surface for air, spluttering slightly. Saskia is sitting still, just as she was, though there are droplets of water on her knees now, on the bottom of her top.

'Sorry,' I say, 'just needed to do something.'

'It's OK,' she says, 'believe me, I understand.'

I tread water for a minute – the pool is much deeper than it looked from above, and I'm enjoying the weightless sensation, enjoying the feeling of the water swirling around me. The sky above is back to blue again, today – though the weather app when I checked this morning said there might be more storms to come this evening.

'Is there anything you want to tell me, Saskia?' I ask her, thinking that I owe it to her to try one more time, and for a second, she pauses, looking down at me from the lounger, her eyes looking directly into mine. It's the closest I've felt to her the whole week, just for a moment, but then the sensation passes and her face seems to close again, like a door that drifted open slamming firmly to a close.

'No,' she says, 'there isn't. Everything is fine.'

She pulls herself up to her feet, then turns her back on me, makes her way to the open doorway of the villa.

'Enjoy your swim,' she calls to me, and I stare at her retreating back, wondering why there's something that sounds so final in her words. Despite the sunshine, I feel a chill run down my spine, and I duck underneath the surface of the water, my thoughts returning to Lucas and the money, and to what I heard in the hallway. For God's sake. Is there nobody on this trip who doesn't have something to hide?

Chapter Fifty-Six

Saskia

I couldn't bear to be around Theo this morning. Looking at him makes me want to cry. I keep trying to think, go over everything desperately in my mind to work out if there is any other way out. But Caleb has me trapped, like a butterfly in a jar.

I don't think I slept at all, and at around six, I got up quietly and went to sit out by the pool. The sun was just coming up and the beach looked beautiful, a million miles away from last night's storm, and just for a moment I almost convinced myself that it was all just a terrible dream, a nightmare of my own creating.

But it wasn't. It was real. I have less than twelve hours until I have to lead my husband to his death.

*

I did love Andrew, at first. Or at least, I thought I did. Over our time together, my definition and understanding of that word became so warped that by the end, it was barely recognisable. He continued telling me he loved me, right up until the day he died.

'I'm working hard for both of us, Saskia, because I love you,' he'd say to me, dropping a kiss on my forehead before he left for work, then shutting the front door behind him and pocketing the only key, leaving me a prisoner in my own home.

'I love you too much, Saskia, so much that sometimes I can't control myself,' he told me, several times over our relationship, usually after a particularly savage beating; usually after he'd drawn blood.

'I love you despite the way you look,' he said to me, back in the earlier days, before we were actually married. He told me I wasn't pretty, that I was lucky to have him, lucky to have someone who found me so attractive. When someone tells you that enough times, you start to believe them. Especially if you're only twenty-three.

After Theo and I got together, I started gaining confidence. I became proud of my appearance, of our life together; I enjoyed posting on social media, seeing my followers like my posts, validate my new lifestyle. It made me feel whole. I never thought about it being dangerous, because as far as I was concerned, Caleb wanted to stay away from me as much as I wanted to stay away from him. We were dangerous to each other. We still are.

As I sat by the pool this morning, I wondered if he'd tracked me down deliberately, followed me out to Thailand. But it doesn't make any sense. Why bother coming all this way? What was it he called it – fate. Perhaps it is. Fate, or a terrible, life-altering coincidence, that he should come across me and see the answer to his problems. That first night in the bar, I wondered what he thought when he glimpsed me through the crowded room, back in Pho Hostel. I wondered if the plan was already forming. I imagined him watching me and

Theo together, him spotting the Rolex on Theo's wrist, the glittering ring on my hand. We flaunted our wealth, and it has been our downfall.

The photograph of Andrew on the locker terrified me. It was a picture from the press, and I can remember the headline that ran above it as if it were yesterday. LOCAL SUSSEX MAN KILLED IN SHOCK HIT AND RUN. He must have saved a copy, or printed one off the internet to get under my skin. His little sign that he was on to me, that he was watching. A reminder of how much power he had, of what he could do.

A warning sign.

I remembered Andrew, this morning, as I sat by the edge of the pool. I remembered the feel of his hands, the rush of adrenaline I used to get when we worked on the same shift in the pub, back when we first met. I remembered those hands tightening around my neck, squeezing my throat until the edges of my vision went blurry. I remembered moving in together, not knowing back then that our house would end up being my jail. I don't ever want to be jailed like that again.

The sky grew lighter and there was the sound of birds singing, high and eerie, as the sun climbed up from the horizon. I checked my watch; it was nearly eight o'clock, and I had been sat out by the water for almost two hours, remembering. In the house, a door opened and closed, and I watched for a moment, wondering who was awake. I felt a prickling sensation on the back of my neck and I wondered if he was here, hiding in the palm trees, watching me, making sure I don't run away.

Holly came out eventually; she looked upset, as if something had happened. Then she jumped abruptly into the pool, the water splashing my legs, but I didn't move from the sunlounger, I just sat there.

'Is there anything you want to tell me, Saskia?' she asked me, and her face looking up at me was so earnest that I wanted to cry, to grab her hands and tell her everything, to ask her to help me, to beg her to take me away from here, away from Caleb, to somewhere safe where he doesn't exist and the past can no longer haunt me. But that place doesn't exist. So I took a deep breath and I told her that everything was fine, and then I went inside to look for my husband, to spend these last few hours with him, the last few hours we have.

Chapter Fifty-Seven

Lucas

They eat breakfast out on the patio by the pool, but the atmosphere between them is tense. They've only got fruit and some juice that was left in the fridge, and Theo says they ought to go to the shop, stock up for the final two days on the island. Holly isn't speaking to him after their argument, and Lucas feels miserable. Nobody seems to want to do much, and so for the rest of the morning they just lie by the pool; Theo's put music on in the background on his speaker, but apart from that and the sound of the crickets, the four of them lie there in silence.

Lucas tries to read the book he brought with him, but he can't concentrate. He keeps darting glances over at Holly, but she has her back to him, is resolutely reading her own novel, her fingers turning the pages every few minutes with a flicking sound that somehow manages to sound angry, too.

He looked at her phone this morning when she was out here by the pool, worrying about the tracker that they'd found last night. Would it have been Caleb? He tries to think if Caleb had the chance to play with her phone, then remembers – of course, the moment at the Buddha, when he found her bag. It feels like a lifetime ago now, even though it's only a few days.

'Holly,' he says, but she ignores him.

'Holly,' he tries again. She reluctantly puts down her book, turns over to face him.

'*What*?'

'The software, on your phone. I've just been thinking about it again. Do you really think it might've been Caleb?'

She frowns. 'Well, yes. How else do you explain him knowing where to find us all the time?'

Lucas thinks of him appearing at their table last night. They'd dismissed it relatively easily in the end, but it is creepy, isn't it, him turning up here, knowing exactly where they'd be. Maybe Holly was right – maybe they should call someone. Report him.

He's about to suggest this to the group when he realises that Theo and Saskia have disappeared, their sunloungers abandoned, the books they were reading lying splayed on the side.

'Where've the others gone?' he asks Holly, but she just shrugs.

'Inside, I guess. How should I know?'

'Do you think we should report Caleb?' he asks her, and she bites her lip, pulls a face.

'I don't know. I mean, what would we say? We think he installed something on my phone? We think he's been following us?' She frowns. 'It just . . . it doesn't sound very substantial, does it? And I'd rather not get the Thai police involved, actually. We'll be home in two days. He can't follow us there, he doesn't know where we live.'

She turns over again, picks up her book. Lucas leans back in his sunlounger, wondering if she's right. Something is nagging at the edge of his conscience, a thought that he can't quite catch. The thought of going home makes him feel immediately miserable, though it's not like this trip has been anything like he'd hoped. Christ, what a disaster.

He picks up his book again and sighs. Above them, the sun beats down.

Chapter Fifty-Eight

Saskia

The day passes in a blur. I want time to slow down and speed up all at once, and I can't take my eyes off the clock, glancing at my watch every two seconds, counting how many hours we have left. I try to run through the order of events in my mind, knowing I need to get my story straight for when I come home later. When the others start to ask questions.

Theo is hungover; he moans at me, says he's never going to drink vodka again, tells me his liver can't take it any more. At about four o'clock, he says he's going for a dip in the sea, before the waves get too intense. There is another storm brewing; you can tell already, by the way the sky is darkening, and the way the clouds are moving across the blue.

'Be careful,' I tell him, and he raises a hand at me as he walks off.

'Always am, babe.'

I watch his retreating back as he begins to run down to the sea, clad only in his red swimming trunks, the ones I bought him two summers ago. He enters the sea straight away, ducking underneath the waves so that for a minute he disappears from sight, and I feel my heartrate accelerate. Part of me doesn't want him to come back.

He does, of course, he comes back dripping like a wet dog, refreshed from his dunk in the ocean. He has always loved swimming. He shakes his head and droplets of water spit all over me, then nuzzles against me affectionately, his skin salty and slick. I place my hand on the top of his head, feel his blond curls beneath my fingers. I love his hair. Always have done.

Holly and Lucas are both in bad moods – they've barely spoken all day, just lain by the pool reading, with the occasional cross words. I don't know what's the matter with them, but I don't have room in my head to care about the answer. Theo tells me he's lent Lucas money, something about Lucas's job, but I'm not really listening. It doesn't matter any more, does it? None of it does.

At five thirty, I tell Theo I want to go for a walk.

'Come on, let's go see the sunset,' I tell him, 'leave these two behind. They're too grumpy to want to come, anyway.' He agrees, pulls on a T-shirt, and is about to push open the little gate that leads down to the beach when I stop him, put a hand on his arm.

'We should say goodbye to them, at least,' I say, 'don't you think?'

'Oh, sure,' he says, looking slightly wrong-footed, and I watch as he goes over to the pool, says something I can't hear to Lucas, then slaps hands with him in a high five. A lump is forming in my throat but I swallow it down. I cannot allow my emotions to get the better of me.

'Bye you guys,' he calls out as we set off for the beach, and I hear their replies on the breeze: 'Bye, Saskia. Bye, Theo. See you in a bit.'

I hang back a little and wave at them, and Theo lopes off

ahead of me, his familiar body a few steps in front, walking along the sand, heading towards the cliffs.

*

'There's meant to be an amazing view from up here,' I tell him as we climb up. It's still warm, and sweat trickles down my neckline, pooling in my clavicle. I'm ahead of Theo, leading the way, taking us up the well-worn path of rocks that leads to the row of trees on the very top. There is nobody around – this part of the island is very private – but I keep watch nonetheless, my eyes darting around to check if anybody else is out walking, if anyone from the other villas might be out over this way. The wind is building, just like it did yesterday, and I have to shout back to Theo so that he can hear me, telling him to follow me, that it isn't much further, now.

I see Caleb first; just a quick movement, over to the left, you'd miss it if you weren't looking for it. He is there and then he is gone, lost in the trees, and I turn back to check Theo is still behind me. He's sweating, too, wiping his forehead with his arm, the tan line where his watch used to be still visible on his wrist. We don't talk on the way up, the only sound the noise of our breathing.

At the top, we stop for a moment, getting our breath back. Theo bends over, his hands on his knees – he isn't as fit as he used to be, back when I first met him, when he was still playing a lot of rugby. He stopped not long after we met, said he wanted to spend his weekends with me, not chasing after a ball with a load of sweaty men. I remember him saying it, how happy it made me.

This part of the clifftop isn't very big – beneath our feet is dusty sand mixed with small rocks, and patches of scrubby grass that might once have been green but has been yellowed in the sun. I look around, carefully, scanning the horizon, the shore below us, checking for anyone who might be able to see us. There is nobody – Theo was right, this beach is one of the most secluded, and we are half hidden by a row of trees to the left. On either side of the cliffs is the beach, but to the front is the sea, a great roaring mass of it, and I walk over to the edge, watch the sun crawling down towards the horizon. The sky is streaked with red and orange, like a crackling fire, and as I turn back towards Theo, I see the colours of it reflected in his eyes.

'Theo,' I say, 'come here.' I put my arms around him, pull him closer to me, our signal. I can hear his heart thundering against mine, the steady, trusting beat of it. The beat I have listened to for the last three years, the beat of our marriage.

And that's when Caleb appears.

He comes from the trees, like a panther, fast and deadly. His body collides with ours and I let out a yelp, losing my footing. We're right on the edge of the cliffs; I look down and see the shards of grey rock beneath us, jutting out of the water like knives. Around them, the sea is swirling, water crashing against the base of the cliffs. I grab onto Theo's collar, reaching my arms up to grip him around the neck.

It all happens very fast. The three of us struggle, but we have the element of surprise. There are two of us against one, even though it fills me with horror to have to do this. Our feet scuffle, the dust and sand kicking up into a cloud around us, and I hear a rip of material, someone's clothing, the fibres giving way. It is awful, the physicality of it, and I pray again that nobody is watching, that we have chosen our spot carefully enough, that our tussle cannot be seen.

Then the balance tips, and I feel the weight lift off me, the sense of release. He makes a noise as he goes over the edge, a high-pitched scream, it could almost be mistaken for the sound of a woman. It could almost have been the sound of my name. One moment he is there, his eyes flashing in surprise and then fear, his hands grabbing and grasping, and the next he is not – he is falling through the air, his arms windmilling desperately, trying to grab onto the surface of the cliff but failing, his hands connecting with nothing but the wind. I don't look as his body hits the first of the sharp, needle-like rocks below; I can't bring myself to see it. I imagine his spine fracturing, the blood rushing to his head and then away again, pumping frantically around his limbs, trying to save his life. I hope he lost consciousness straight away. That he didn't have to suffer.

For a moment after, the two of us stand there on the cliff edge, the wind howling around us, the sea churning below. A bird circles above our heads, a dark spot in the sky, letting out a desperate, cawing keen.

I can't bear to look over the edge, but he does, stepping forward, his neck craning to see the rocks below. To see what we have done.

'I think I can see blood,' he says, 'but the sea will wash it away.'

I pause. 'Can you see the body?'

He shakes his head. 'No. But the blood – he won't have survived that, Saskia.'

We stare at each other. Nausea rises up in my throat, and quickly, I turn away, away from him, away from the cliffs, from the dark stain on the rocks, from the relentless waves that will be wrapping his body up, twisting it and pulling it. I imagine the seaweed sliding down his throat, his lungs filling up with water, the heaviness, the bloating.

'We need to go,' I say, and the two of us move, like puppets on strings, jerky limbs carrying us back down the cliffs. The birds cry above us and the sun dips lower in the sky and there is still nobody around, nobody to witness it, nobody to see the terrible thing that we have done.

I stumble slightly as we reach the bottom, where the rocks give way to sand, and he reaches out, grabs my arm, his fingers cold against my skin. My ankle has twisted underneath me, and I wince in pain.

'You all right?' he says, and I nod at him, my throat thick.

It's not true, of course. I don't know if I'll ever be all right again.

Chapter Fifty-Nine

Holly

'Theo and Saskia have been gone a long time,' Lucas says, appearing beside me, his face creased into a frown. I'm sat outside on one of the chairs by the pool, drinking a glass of white wine with ice in it, trying to read my book. Lucas has been inside for ages, the cold war between us having continued for most of the afternoon.

'Have they?' I say, glancing at my phone to check the time, and then I realise that he's right – they have.

'Maybe they're sick of being around us,' Lucas says. He comes next to me, drops down in the seat beside mine, then nudges me gently. I sigh, look up from my book reluctantly.

'Are you ever going to talk to me again?' he asks, and I roll my eyes, turn the book over, the spine cracking open. The pages are coming a bit unstuck in the heat, the glue that holds them together melting in the Thai humidity.

'I'm not *not* talking to you, Lucas. We're not eleven years old.'

He reaches out, takes a sip of my wine.

'Oi, I was drinking that.'

He pulls a face. 'It's not very nice.'

'I like it.'

He sighs. 'Look, Holly, please. I'm really sorry. I know I should have told you about the money earlier. I fucked up. But it wasn't intentional.'

He looks so hangdog that I can't help smiling, in spite of myself. Perhaps I'm being too harsh on him. I relent.

'No more secrets?' I say, holding out my hand, little finger extended.

'No more secrets.' He links fingers with me. 'Pinky promise.'

'Maybe we *are* eleven years old after all.'

He grins, and the iciness between us breaks.

'So, where do you think the others have got to?'

I frown. 'I don't know. You're right, they've been ages. It's getting stormy again now, too.' Both of us look over to the beach, which is deserted. Then, as we watch, there is a movement on the sand, over by the cliffs. I lift a hand, squint at the beach.

'Oh look, someone's coming.'

Lucas gets to his feet, frowning, his eyes fixed on the figures walking towards us.

'What is it?' I say. 'What's wrong?'

Chapter Sixty

Lucas

'Are you OK?' he says as they reach the gate of the villa. Saskia is hobbling, her face very pale; clearly, she's in pain.

'I twisted my ankle,' she says, 'slipped over on the beach. My own stupid fault.'

'Come and sit down,' Lucas says, opening the gate and taking her by the arm, then giving her his chair by the pool. 'Poor you, what happened?'

'I told you, I just slipped,' she says, and he's slightly taken aback by the snappiness in her tone; it's not like her. She seems brittle, strange, as though she might be about to break.

Saskia sits down, Holly hovering over her in concern.

Lucas meets Theo's eye, but his friend isn't looking at him, he's looking down at the floor, at the splashes of water on the tiles surrounding the swimming pool. He also looks pale, Lucas thinks, his skin has an odd, waxy shine to it. He wonders if they might have had a row.

'Let me get you some ice for your ankle, and you should elevate it,' Holly says, disappearing into the villa for a moment and re-emerging holding a tea towel wrapped around an ice block from the freezer.

'Thanks,' Saskia says, taking it from her, and she winces

as Theo puts it on her ankle, which does look odd – swollen slightly, at a funny angle.

'I've got some ibuprofen somewhere, I think,' Lucas tells her, but she doesn't respond, and he has to say it again before either of them look up and take any notice.

'Good walk apart from that?' he asks them. 'You were gone a long time. Did you head over to the cliffs?'

There's a silence, a moment's pause.

'No,' Saskia says, 'we went the other way, to one of the other beaches.'

'Right,' Lucas says, nodding. He waits for a moment, but she doesn't say anything else, and eventually, the silence among them all becomes awkward, odd. Holly catches his eye, raising her eyebrows.

'Shall we get another drink, Hol?' he says, and she agrees, clearly as keen to get away from the strange situation as he is. They head inside the villa, leaving Saskia and Theo sat outside by the pool, and it's only when they are indoors that Lucas realises that Theo hasn't spoken at all, not a single word, since they returned from the beach.

Chapter Sixty-One

Saskia

We sit in silence. I think both of us are in shock.

Theo's face is as pale as I have ever seen it – paler even than it was last night, when I told him the truth about Caleb, about what I'd done. When we agreed on the new plan.

'How long do you think we have?' he asks eventually. His voice sounds different, odd, a bit hoarse. My ankle is propped up on the chair in front of us, and sharp waves of pain are radiating up my leg. I try to ignore them. They are no more than I deserve.

I shake my head. 'I don't know. It depends on . . .' I look up at the sky, at the dark clouds scudding above us. It depends on the weather, the water, the wind. How far his body is carried by the ocean. Whether it washes up. Whether it's found. I don't feel able to say any of these things aloud, but I know we are both thinking them.

'What do we do?' he whispers, and I glance at the villa. I can see the outlines of Lucas and Holly in the kitchen, moving around, opening and closing the fridge.

'We do nothing,' I say. 'We go home. We stick to the plan. And we forget that any of this ever happened. It's the only thing we can do, Theo.' I pause. 'Theo.'

He doesn't reply; he's just staring at the pool, at the water. There is an absence in his eyes that frightens me, just a little. I need to keep control of the situation.

'Theo,' I say again, and this time he raises his head, looks at me.

'I love you,' I say, but he doesn't respond – there is only silence, and the soft hiss of the wind as it gathers in the air.

*

It's our last night in Thailand, but Theo and I go to bed early, tell the others we're too tired to stay up. Holly and Lucas seem a bit confused, but it's too difficult sitting across from them, pretending nothing has happened, and I know we're both relieved to shut the door and be by ourselves. I keep thinking about how different things could have been, if I'd gone through with it – I imagine myself lying here alone, pretending to the others that Theo had gone missing. Staring down the barrel of a life without the man I love.

This way is better. It has to be.

In bed that night, we lie awake, looking at each other. Theo's eyes stare into mine, but I know that he isn't seeing me, that neither of us is really in the room at all. We're at the top of the cliffs, watching Caleb's body tip over the edge of the rocks, we're imagining it drifting through the ocean, bumping along the seabed, washing up on the beach. We're picturing the dark red blood splashed onto the grey rock, curls of it spiralling into the inky-blue water.

'Do you think it hurt?' Theo asks me, eventually, but I don't reply, I just hold him tighter, press my body tightly against his. There is no point indulging questions like that. I know that from experience. For years, I dreamed about the car hitting Andrew, the bonnet connecting with his body, the thud of his limbs as he hit the tarmac road. I imagined blood-spattered windscreens, a screech of tyres. Then I realised it was pointless. That I was just torturing myself. So I forced myself to stop.

'Go to sleep, Theo,' I tell him now, as though he is a child, and after a while I feel his breathing slow down, and when I touch his eyes gently, the lids are closed.

I don't remember falling asleep, but I must do because in the morning I open my eyes and I am curled up next to him, our bodies curved together. His heart beating against my torso. Alive, alive, alive.

When I told him the truth, when I got back from seeing Caleb under the cliffs, he didn't believe me at first. It took everything I had, every piece of strength, to admit to him what was happening, what Caleb had asked me to do. I risked everything – I risked living with the way he looked at me, when he learned what had happened to Andrew, I risked our marriage, when he realised how long I'd been keeping secrets from him, and I risked both our lives, when we came up with the plan to double-bluff Caleb. To kill him, instead.

'Stop it, Saskia,' he'd said at first, 'stop saying these things, please. They're not true.'

'They are true,' I had said, my fingers curled tightly around my wedding ring, 'they are true, Theo. You have to trust me. I need you.' I'd told him that we must act our parts for the remainder of the day, that Caleb could be watching us, even when we were outside the villa by the pool. I didn't trust that he hadn't tapped one of our phones, that he wasn't lurking in the bushes, that if everything didn't look the way he thought it should he would guess that I wasn't going to go through with it, that I was going to betray him at the last possible moment. I told him that we had to keep it from Lucas and Holly – obviously – that it would need to stay our secret, for the rest of our lives.

I told him that the guilt would go away, after a while. That I loved him, more than anything in the world.

Eventually, he came round to the plan. And together, we took care of Caleb.

I know it will be hard for us, that the road ahead is not going to be easy. That the trust we once had, that the belief in me he had, will take a while to rebuild. But he won't tell Andrew's family. He can't. Not now he's involved. Our secret will tie us together. Along with our love, of course.

Now, as I lie next to him, I know that I did the right thing. I love Theo, with all my heart. I love him enough to kill for him. And he feels the same about me.

He wakes up.

'Was it a dream?' is the first thing that comes out of his mouth, and I shake my head, feel his chest deflate. I can't think of anything else to say in that moment so I swing my legs over the side of the bed, force myself to put my feet on the floor.

It's our final day of holiday. Our flight leaves this evening, at ten minutes past five. We just need to get through the next few hours, make it back to the UK. We'll be safe there. I know we will.

We pack in silence. I have so many things that I want to say, but somehow, my throat feels like it's jammed, and the words die on my tongue. Every time there is a sound outside the room, both of us jump, but it's just Holly and Lucas moving around their bedroom, dragging their suitcases into the hallway, packing up their things. Theo keeps glancing at the windows and the door, as though the police are going to materialise, or the ghost of Caleb is going to rise up from the ocean and appear against the glass.

Caleb.

The full weight of it hits me, and I sink down onto the bed, my knees feeling weak. Knowing he is gone, that he cannot come back this time – it fills me with a sense of relief so deep that my body almost can't cope. But at the same time, I am not a monster – I know what we have done is a crime. That I dragged Theo into it. That I made us both guilty. That we will live with that guilt for the rest of our lives.

I go downstairs, into the kitchen, trying to block out the pounding of my head, the images that swim into my vision.

'Did you and Theo sleep OK?' Lucas asks, brightly, and I nod. He's oblivious, clearly, and I force a smile at him as he pours me a quick cup of coffee, and we drink them standing up in the kitchen.

'Where's Holly?' I ask, and he tells me she's coming, that she's just in the bathroom. Out of the two of them, it's Holly I worry about – she's been suspicious, sending me that WhatsApp on the minibus back from the waterfall, asking me if I'm all right a few times this trip. When we get back to England, it might be time to cool this friendship off a little. Give everyone some space.

'Right, everyone ready? We good to go?' Lucas asks, clapping his hands together as Holly reappears, and Theo and I nod in unison.

As we bring our bags out onto the patio and Theo locks the door of the villa, the little flamingo keyring dangling from his hand, I look around, taking it all in – the beautiful house, the beach, the perfect blue sky, all signs of last night's storm vanished in the break of a new day. Was it worth it, I think to myself, as the four of us huddle together, ready to make our way back to Bangkok for the flight. Was it worth it?

Both of us are avoiding looking at the water as we walk along the beach. Theo strides steadfastly ahead, and I lag behind, my ankle still painful. Lucas carries my case for me, and I know he thinks Theo is being weird by not offering, by not hanging back to help me. Only I know that he can barely stand to look at me, that what we did is hanging between us, like a sword about to drop. He just needs some time, I keep thinking, he just needs some time.

'It's a good job we didn't see that weirdo again,' Lucas says to me, offhand, and my stomach tenses, my breath catching slightly in my throat.

'You mean Caleb?' Holly asks, and Lucas nods.

'Yep. Seems like my telling him to fuck off actually worked this time.' He laughs. 'At least he didn't ruin the *entire* holiday. Just a decent chunk of it.'

I don't say anything. I can't.

'Where do you think he disappeared to, anyway?' Holly asks, and I feel as though she's looking at me, her eyes boring into the side of my cheek, my skull. My whole head feels as though it has a band of tension around it, a band that's getting tighter and tighter, the more questions they ask.

Lucas shrugs. 'Don't know. That whole thing was so weird, wasn't it? Him turning up like that, telling us he was watching. To be honest, I was expecting him to turn up again. I'm surprised we haven't seen him for the last day or two.'

My ankle gives way and I fall, my knees hitting the sand. I cry out, and Holly is there to pick me up, her face wrought with concern. She bends down, and her face is very close to mine, so close that I can see the whites of her eyes.

'Are you OK?' she says. 'You and Theo . . . You don't seem yourselves at all.'

I get up, leaning on her, look ahead to see that Theo hasn't even stopped walking, that he's almost at the end of the beach.

'We're fine,' I say, shortly, 'my ankle's still sore, that's all.'

'You ought to go for a scan when we get back, check it's not broken,' she says, and I nod obediently. Beside us, the waves are unabating. I glance at them, terrified of seeing a flash of white, a swirl of dark hair.

We carry on walking along the beach, towards the pier where the boat will pick us up to take us back to the mainland. Fear claws at my heart.

Chapter Sixty-Two

Lucas

They've just rounded the headland when they see the commotion. Hordes of people are surrounding the pier, and there are two police boats bobbing on the water, grey with white lettering. As they get closer, Lucas can see uniformed officers trying to push back the tourists, who have clearly come to board the boat back to the mainland but who are now crowding forward, camera phones held aloft, filming and taking photos of something that Lucas cannot quite see.

Theo is a few metres ahead of him, and Lucas sees him break into a run. He does the same, eager to see what's going on, then stops short alongside his friend as it becomes clear that something bad has happened, something terrible.

A man is shouting something in Thai, waving his arms angrily, trying to deter the people with camera phones, and above them, there is the whirr of a helicopter, the blades chopping through the sky, the sound roaring in Lucas's ears.

'What's going on?' he says to a woman with a backpack on, who is on the edge of the group of tourists, one of the only ones who isn't trying to film the whole thing on her phone.

'You'll never believe it. They've found a body,' she says,

'a dead body in the sea. It's awful. They've just pulled someone out of the water.'

Lucas blanches, and beside him, he can feel a tremor going through Theo's frame.

'Jesus,' he says, and to his surprise, Theo turns to the left and bends down, vomits straight into the sand. Lucas touches his friend on the back, surprised at the strength of Theo's reaction – it's awful, obviously, but it's not like they've actually seen anything. He grimaces. God, he hopes they don't. He pictures a body dredged up from the water, damaged by the sea. He wonders who it is, thinks automatically of their parents, their family, the impact this person's death will have on countless other lives.

The girls are beside them, now, and he puts an arm around Holly, all of them watching as the police work to restore a sense of order. He wonders where the body is now, assuming it's been lifted onto one of the police boats – he can see figures clad in white suits moving around on deck, their faces covered by masks.

'God, how awful,' Holly says, shivering. 'I can't believe it.'

'Did you see what happened?' a man next to them is asking. He's a young bloke, with hair in dreadlocks, an earring glinting gold in his right ear. Lucas shakes his head.

'It's a man, someone said,' the stranger continues; his own accent is Geordie, Lucas thinks. 'Poor sod. The body bumped up against the pier,' he points to the wooden decking, 'it was spotted by one of the ferry crew. Grim, eh?'

'Terrible,' Lucas murmurs. He wonders who it was, if it was a traveller, or a local. Holly is clearly upset; he can see tears forming in her eyes. She wipes her nose on her sleeve, looks the other way. It's nothing to do with them, after all. It isn't their tragedy.

Chapter Sixty-Three

Holly

It is two hours before we are able to leave the island. The police force us to stand further back, erecting tape up around the end of the pier, and we watch as the boats and the helicopter hover. Everyone around us is talking about it – the body, a man's, what did you see? Someone tells us they saw the corpse, bloated and white, bumping up against the wood of the decking. It was facedown, one guy says, but the story changes, like Chinese whispers, until it's that he was faceup, that there was blood on his temple, that he was missing an eye. Maybe the birds pecked it out, someone says, and I feel sick, nausea rising in my throat. Someone mentions the word 'murder'. Someone says it might not have been an accident. It's all nonsense, rumours: nobody official seems to be confirming anything at all.

Theo is almost completely silent, and Saskia keeps asking him if there is anything she can do, if he needs water, painkillers, food. He shakes her off each time.

'Are you all right, Saskia?' I ask her, as she places her hand on Theo's shoulder yet again, and she jerks her face up at me, her features strangely blank.

'I'm fine. Just tired.'

The news breaks on Twitter. A woman who must be on the

beach with us posts a photo with the words: *Murder on the Island!* and tags a load of true-crime podcasts – she'll have to take it down, I expect, but it starts to be shared immediately, so the damage is already done. Social media becomes awash with it, and we crowd around Lucas's phone, ghouls in the sunshine, watching as the people around us post pictures of the pier, as the news reporters back in the UK get wind of it, start DM'ing people for photos as the gossip begins that it might be a Brit. There's nothing to suggest this was anything other than an accident, someone comments, but it doesn't seem to make any difference. People are hungry: the setting lends itself well to tragedy.

I can hear people on the phone to others, describing the scene, calling it wild, horrible, gross. There is a buzz in the air, though; they are like vultures, excited by the drama of it, safe in the knowledge that it's nothing to do with them, that they were just in the wrong place at the wrong time. Or the right one.

Eventually, we're allowed to board the boat. The crew shepherd us on, their faces grim, and a strange silence falls over the passengers as we pull away from Koh Samet, away from the police presence that is still there, away from the churning blue waves that have thrown up this tragedy.

'What a horrible way to end the trip,' Lucas says, eventually, and I nod, but none of us reply. The air around us feels heavy, leaden. It is a relief to reach the mainland, to immerse ourselves once more in the colour and energy of Bangkok, the city swallowing us back up, as if we never even left.

I wish we hadn't.

Theo has booked a car in advance, and we arrive at the airport two hours before our flight, at ten past three in the afternoon. I picture returning home to my tiny little flat, calling my mum under the grey London sky, and tears prick my eyes. Lucas squeezes my hand.

'I've got the boarding passes,' Theo says, abruptly – he's barely spoken all day. He brings out his phone, and I notice his hand shaking as he scrolls to the right photos, his wedding ring making a small tapping sound as the metal connects with the plastic of his iPhone as a result of the tremor.

'You all right?' I ask him, and for a second, his eyes meet mine, but then he looks away, back down at his phone screen, the light of it making him even paler. He is a shadow of his usual self.

'Shall we get some food?' Lucas says, eventually, and the four of us find a table in a little café near the gate.

'I'm not hungry,' Theo murmurs, and Saskia shakes her head when I proffer her a menu.

'It seems to have really affected them,' Lucas whispers to me when we go up to pay for our food, 'you know, the body. Don't you think? They're so quiet, both of them.'

I turn back to look at them, hunched over the Formica table. They aren't speaking. Saskia's hair dangles down in limp, lank strands.

'It has,' I say, 'it really has.'

And then, when we're all sat around, Lucas and I eating our French fries, the other two watching us mournfully, my phone pings with a news alert, a push notification from social media: *content you might be interested in due to your location.*

It's a photo – not an official one. A picture has surfaced on Twitter. It's blurry, and within seconds, Twitter adds a graphic content warning to it – it will only be moments before it ends up being taken down, but it's already getting a lot of traction, the way these things do. Beneath my thumb, the numbers are ticking up – retweets and likes, comments and emojis. Lucas swears loudly when he sees it, and I see his face change, his expression clouding over.

'It's Caleb, guys. It's Caleb. He's the body they found in the water. Look – someone's put a picture up. Someone who was there.'

And then Saskia and Theo are reaching out, taking the phone off us, examining the screen with trembling fingers, looking at us both across the sauce-stained table. The picture, taken from the pier, shows his face, still recognisable despite the damage done by the waves. It is definitely him.

'Caleb,' I say, 'Caleb is dead.'

'Oh my God,' Saskia says, and Theo swears under his breath, runs a hand through his hair, and for a moment it feels like the hum of the airport slows down and it's just the four of us, trapped together in a little bubble in the busy Bangkok airport, our minds running back over the last few days, remembering our interactions with *him*, the silence among us filling up with all the things we know we shouldn't say.

Chapter Sixty-Four

Saskia

'If anyone asks, we shouldn't admit we had anything to do with him,' I say. My voice is surprisingly calm, now, and I can feel the other three looking at me. I swallow. 'I just think it's easier that way. Don't you?'

Holly frowns. 'But we haven't done anything wrong.'

'I know that,' I say, 'but still, I just . . . I think we should forget all about it. That we knew him at all. He was a – you said it yourself, Lucas – he was a creep. He will have put that tracker on your phone, Holly, he followed us around – he was probably doing it to someone else, too. Or maybe he did this to himself. Maybe he was lonely.' The words hurt to say, they jam in my throat, but I force myself to say them. Theo isn't helping at all – he is almost mute, and I nudge him, hard with my elbow. After what I've done for him, he has to play along. We have to be a united front.

'What if someone comes asking questions?' Lucas says. 'What if they find out we were friends with him? There might be some sort of inquiry. We might have been the last people to see him, depending on when it happened.' He pauses. 'God, do you think it happened that night? After I told him to fuck off? At the restaurant? He walked off along the beach, remember?' His voice breaks slightly. 'They might say we had a row.'

'We weren't *friends* with him!' I snap. 'Jesus, you hated him, Luke!'

'Doesn't mean I wanted him to *die*,' he mutters sullenly, but he goes quiet, stops arguing. Holly is biting her lip anxiously. I take a deep breath.

'This is not our problem,' I tell them. 'We don't need to worry about it. I'm sorry for Caleb, of course I am, but us dragging ourselves into it is unnecessary. He was never our friend. He was a stranger. Something bad happened to him. Some kind of accident. That's it.'

Before any of them can answer, I turn away from them, check the electronic board above our heads again, to see if they've opened the gate. My heart is beating too fast, but I force myself to take calm, slow breaths as I look up, willing it to be open. I follow the lettering with my eyes: *London Heathrow, 17:10. Gate A5.* It's open. The sooner we leave Bangkok, the better.

'Come on,' I say to the other three, 'the gate's open. Let's go home.'

They follow me, the four of us traipsing down Bangkok airport's long, immaculate grey corridors. It takes everything I have not to run – I am terrified of a hand on my shoulder, the angry face of a Thai police officer, the snap of handcuffs on my wrists. But it doesn't happen. We keep walking.

At the gate, I can tell other people are talking about it – some of them must have got the same boat back from the island as we did. I catch glimpses of shocked faces, snatches of hushed conversation. *Awful . . . so sad . . . who was he?*

I try to ignore them, leading us to a couple of seats in the far corner, facing outwards to where the planes are lining up, their huge wings stretching out into the blue sky. I'm gripping my bag so tightly that my fingers are going numb. My ankle throbs with pain.

'Saskia,' Theo says, suddenly, and I look to where he's jerked his head, and my heart stops because there are two Thai policemen, clad in dark blue uniform, striding towards our gate, holding walkie-talkie radios to their ears.

My entire body freezes. I can't look at the others.

'Theo,' I say, my voice a painful whisper, and they're coming nearer and nearer, closer and closer, and then – then they're walking straight past us, their gaze fixed ahead. They're not coming for us at all. My heart is thumping with fear, and my palms are slick with sweat.

'Could be anything,' Theo says, eventually, and I nod, my neck stiff with tension. The two of us have almost forgotten that Lucas and Holly are there, but gradually, my heartrate begins to slow and I see that Holly is staring at us, her eyes narrowed, and I know that there's no way she's missed it, that she's not a fool. I smile at her, weakly, and her mouth twitches, but before she can say anything, there's an announcement over the Tannoy, and our plane is boarding, and it's time.

I don't look at anyone as we are getting on board, finding our seats, storing our luggage in the overhead compartments. I keep my head down, my hair hanging in front of my face. Theo puts on his cap, pulls it low down over his eyes. I remember the way out here, the excitement we all felt, the reverse journey, and it feels already like a lifetime ago. We were different people, I think. We will never be the same.

It's only when the plane begins to move that I feel my body begin to relax slightly, as we taxi along the runway, and

Bangkok begins to disappear, the airport growing smaller and smaller in the window, until I cannot see it at all. Next to me, Theo's hands are clasped tightly together, and I reach out, cover them with my own.

'I love you,' I tell him, but he doesn't seem to hear me. He doesn't reply.

He'll come round, I think to myself, he'll come round, because he has no choice. Behind me, I hear Holly clearing her throat, sense her shift in her seat. Her gaze feels like it is penetrating the plastic seat between us, as though she can see right through the material, right through me, right through to my soul.

Chapter Sixty-Five

Holly

I don't do anything for two whole months. A week passes after we get back from Thailand; then two, and the four of us go back to our lives – I go back to my flat, and Lucas goes back to his. We work, hard. I feel a shiver every time the phone rings with an unknown number, but it's always telemarketing; it's never the police.

Theo and Saskia go back to their house, the four-bedroom house without a mortgage. We don't message much. Someone sends photos to the WhatsApp group, innocuous ones of the city, the beach, the food. I don't send mine – not yet. I always find it's best to bide your time with things like this. Wait until the right moment. Until you're sure.

News of Caleb's death hits the headlines – but fades fairly quickly, when it becomes clear that nobody in particular is missing him much. There are a few photos, some comments from the Thai police, but it doesn't make the front page, probably because it happened so far away. I watch as it gets relegated to page three, page five, but I read every detail just in case. The police think he was in the water for less than forty-eight hours. Possibly less than twenty-four. They trace some thefts, some people coming out of the woodwork to say they recognise the photo, that they think he stole from them – a few claims, dating back over the last few years. It isn't a particularly pretty picture. I think of him, that very first day, running towards me at the temple with my bag in his hands. The hero of the day. I remember him sitting next to me on the bus, asking about my mum, making me laugh. I swallow, hard.

Then one day, there's a smaller piece, online. It's about seven weeks after we get back from Thailand. I'm in the office when I see it, navigating between the document I'm meant to be working on and Rightmove, looking at the dream flat – the flat that somehow still hasn't sold, that flat that, I tell myself often, is waiting for us. Patiently.

I search his name, now, every few days – a habit really, more than anything. Saskia told us all not to, said we had to be careful – but I'm not the one with something to hide. The piece doesn't say much, just that a family member has come out of the woodwork, appealing for witnesses, wanting to speak to anyone who might have been on Koh Samet that week. I minimise the screen, my heart thumping.

I don't tell any of the others. And I don't call the number for information. I can't let Lucas and myself be connected. I have to think of our futures. Our future, combined.

Chapter Sixty-Six

Lucas

For weeks, he feels on edge. The new term starts, and he goes back to school, his wages less and his anxiety more. He keeps thinking back to the moment in the restaurant in Thailand when he told Caleb to leave, snapped at him angrily. At night, he dreams about it, sees Caleb again in his mind's eye, sneering at him from over the table. Sometimes, he wakes up and his heart is pounding, as though he has been running, not sleeping.

His boss, the headmaster of the school, comments that he seems not quite himself. He claps Lucas on the shoulder one afternoon, coming up from behind him, and Lucas's heart jumps into his throat. He keeps expecting something bad to happen, for someone to say something: aren't you the guy who argued with the dead guy? Aren't you the one who told him to fuck off hours before his body washed up on the beach?

But nobody does. His headmaster just tells him that if the pressures get too much, they can have a chat – a sentiment that Lucas isn't sure he actually means. He tries to focus on the job, the students, but the young men remind him of Caleb, somehow, and he finds himself ashen-faced in front of the class, the words he's meant to be saying drying up on his tongue. He thinks some of them, the nicer students, start to feel a bit sorry for him.

'You look stressed, sir,' one of the girls says one morning, and he tries to smile back at her, and fails.

Holly doesn't seem to want to talk about it. He's mentioned it a few times; once, when she'd had a couple of glasses of wine, she got all teary-eyed and admitted that she dreamed about Caleb too, but after that it was as though a wall came down. She keeps saying that they shouldn't dwell on it, that what happened was not their fault, that Caleb wasn't that nice of a guy anyway. That doesn't really help, but eventually, Lucas stops asking her about it. He's WhatsApped Theo a few times, too, asking to go for a drink, but each time, Theo seems to fob him off, or agree and then cancel at the last minute. It feels like they are distancing themselves. Lucas worries that it's about the money, the money he still owes Theo and that he is trying desperately, slowly, to pay back.

He decides to take another job, a part-time one in the evenings, teaching classes at the local college and on Zoom. It's helpful, actually, because it drowns out the thoughts of Thailand and it enables him to start to build up a bit more cash, cash that will have to go straight to Theo. Holly starts getting annoyed with him because the new job takes up his evenings, and they have less time together.

One day, his evening class get talking before the work starts about holidays, and someone mentions Bangkok, a backpacking trip.

'Someone was found dead there a few months ago, be careful!' one of the other students jokes, and Lucas feels his skin go clammy and cold, has to turn his camera off for a few minutes so that they don't see the way he is shaking.

He wishes it had never happened. He's scared that there might still be consequences, somehow, that someone will link him to the dead man, that someone will know he was one of the last people to see him alive.

Chapter Sixty-Seven

Holly

I'm searching again for Caleb's name – it's become such a habit now, a quick check, like brushing my teeth or texting Lucas goodnight. I type in the familiar letters, my hair balled up in a scrunchie on top of my head, my feet up against the radiator because it's March but it's still cold, and this time, there's a new hit. I think it's going to be the family member again, another plea, but it isn't, it's something different.

It's recent, from this morning. It's a piece linking Caleb to a car, found burning in a field in East Sussex, way back at the end of 2018. Someone's come forward, said they think he's the one who stole their vehicle, that the same vehicle turned up days later, blackened – having been involved in a fatal hit and run. They recognised his face from a CCTV still on their street, uncovered by a Neighbourhood Watch group. They said it was reported to the police at the time, but they failed to trace anyone – it happened only a day before a major fire tore through a Sussex street, killing an entire family, and the incident seemed not to have been followed up as efficiently as it should have been. There's a link, too – the words *'fatal hit and run'* highlighted blue and underlined. I click them. My heart is beating a little bit too fast; I don't know why yet, but when the next screen loads, I do.

The photo that appears on the screen isn't a very good one, but it's familiar. It's the photograph that was taped to our locker in Pho Hostel in Bangkok. His face was scoured out, but the background is the same, and the frame of his jaw, his hairline. I look at it for a long time. Andrew Green, killed in 2018, leaving behind his wife. No children. His dark eyes stare back at me.

I save the webpage, but still, I do nothing. I wrestle with it, the decision. I've always prided myself on being a good person. In doing the right thing. I stand up for what I believe in, I make Lucas do the same. But when does doing the right thing cross over into something else? The more I think about it, the more I think about how unjust it is, that people who have money can float through life getting away with things, while people like Lucas slave away over multiple jobs, trying to make a living, trying to build a future. I think a lot about right and wrong, about the differences between them. The subjectivity of it all. The blurred lines.

The moment comes when Lucas cancels on me a third time in a week, saying he has to work, that he's doing overtime to try to pay back the money he owes Theo. He's taken on a second job, as well as the usual teaching. When I do see him, there are dark circles underneath his eyes, so deep they almost look painful.

I sit at my kitchen table, drinking a glass of red wine, looking at the dinner I made for him, the dinner that is now congealing and going cold because he can't make it, because he's working all the hours God sends, trying to earn enough so that we can actually build a life together.

I think about it, rolling the idea around in my head, and the more I think about it, the angrier I feel. At the unfairness of it all.

And it's times like that when my mind drifts back to the trip. To Bangkok. To Thailand. Usually, I push the thoughts away. I'm not that person, I tell myself, over and over again. I'm a good person, or at least I try to be. I *care* about things. I'm not the kind of person who would do something like this.

Not unless I really needed to.

My phone pings, an Instagram notification. Saskia's uploaded new photographs, pictures of the trip she and Theo took to the Maldives a fortnight ago. She's waited longer than usual to post them; I'd wondered whether they actually went. Clearly, they did. She bought a new iPhone when we got back from Thailand, the latest version, so the photos look even brighter and clearer than usual: ultra-high definition. I scroll through them for a while, staring at the hotel room they stayed in, at a photo of champagne in an ice bucket, a plateful of crab. Saskia's nails, painted coral, curled around a cocktail glass. Theo in the background, his face slightly blurry so you can't see his expression.

I take a sip of my wine, look across the table at Lucas's empty seat. And that's when I finally decide.

*

She's home alone when I ring the doorbell. Theo must be out somewhere; to be honest, I doubt they're spending that much time together, despite the Maldives pictures for social media. It must be hard. She blanches a little when she sees me, then tries quickly to cover it up, pasting on that shiny smile, blinking twice, too fast.

'Hi,' I say, 'long time no speak. Can I come in? There's something I want to show you.'

'It's not a great time actually, Holly,' Saskia tells me. Her voice is smooth, but I notice how she puts a foot in the doorway, blocking my entrance, and her hand goes to the latch, her fingers trembling ever so slightly.

'Oh, it won't take long,' I say. 'Theo's not here, is he?' I know he isn't, actually, because I watched him drive away, waited until she was by herself.

'He'll be back soon,' she says, and I smile at her.

'Of course.'

'What is it you want?' she asks me, then, as though giving up on the pretence of normality, the mask slipping, as I knew it would.

'I just wanted to show you something, like I said,' I tell her, 'but first, I wanted to ask you something, too.'

When I name the sum, she goes white. It's enough for the flat Lucas and I have been looking at, the one I dreamed of throughout our holiday – and it's a bit extra, too, because look, I'm not a saint. I never said I was. And what I want more than anything is for Lucas and me to have a future together. A proper one. If that means I'm not as good a person as I used to be, well, then, I'm not as good a person as I used to be.

But I'm not a murderer, either. I show her the photograph I took of her and Caleb, the zoomed in one, his arms around her waist at the base of the waterfalls; it would be quite a beautiful picture, actually, if it wasn't so damning. It's framed nicely, from above, the water tumbling down, their figures clearly recognisable at the bottom. For a few seconds, she just stares at it. She doesn't say anything.

'I overheard you, you see, in the villa, the night before he

322

died,' I tell her, standing there on the doorstep, my phone with the photo on stretched out between us. The sun is breaking through the clouds a little, filtering yellow light onto us; it's a cold, crisp day, a million miles away from the crushing heat of Koh Samet. I think back to the night it happened, the night before we left – when I'd got back out of bed and listened at the door of their room, worried that Theo might be hurting her. Wanting to be there for her, as a friend, as a woman. Needing to be sure that I wasn't right about my suspicions.

How wrong I was.

What I heard took my breath away. I heard her telling Theo what they had to do, that they had to kill him to save Theo's life. I heard his shock, his disbelief. I heard her tell him about Andrew. She might think that that kind of situation allows her to play God, but I don't agree. Not when the stakes are so high. I know I should have intervened, should have said something to her at the time. But I didn't really believe they'd go through with it, not until I saw the photograph of him with my own eyes. And then I was frightened. I had to keep quiet, to think about what to do with the information I had. That doesn't make me guilty. I'm not the one who pushed him.

Saskia stands there, staring at the photograph of her with the man she killed. The moment stretches between us, and I wait, knowing that she has no choice, knowing that for once in my life, I am the one with the power.

Then she stands back, takes her hand off the latch, and opens the door to let me inside. I smile at her, a real one this time. She doesn't smile back, but she will, in time. She'll appreciate the fact that I haven't gone to the police, haven't called Caleb's family. I've just gone directly to her, given her the chance to set things right.

We're good friends, after all. And fair is fair.

This way, we all get what we deserve.

Besides, I never said I was a saint.

Acknowledgements

Thank you so much to everyone at HQ and at Darley Anderson, particularly my agent, Camilla Bolton. Thank you to all of my readers – it's a privilege to write for you and I always love it whenever you get in touch – so please continue to do so! And finally, thank you to the people I love who have supported me as I wrote this book during a pretty difficult few years; you know who you are.

Get in touch on Instagram @phoebeannmorgan, Facebook @PhoebeMorganAuthor, Twitter @Phoebe_A_Morgan or visit my website (where you will find lots of tips for getting published): www.phoebemorganauthor.com.

Hungry for more from Phoebe Morgan? Try one of her other gripping psychological thrillers. . .

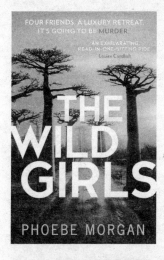

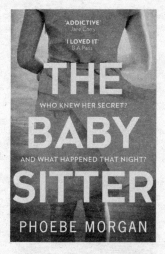

All available now!

ONE PLACE. MANY STORIES

Bold, innovative and
empowering publishing.

FOLLOW US ON:

@HQStories